DISCARD

Also by Will Thomas

Some Danger Involved

To Kingdom Come

Will Thomas

A Touchstone Book
Published by Simon & Schuster
New York   London   Toronto   Sydney

TOUCHSTONE
Rockefeller Center
1230 Avenue of the Americas
New York, NY 10020

TOUCHSTONE and colophon are registered trademarks
of Simon & Schuster, Inc.

For information regarding special discounts for bulk purchases,
please contact Simon & Schuster Special Sales:
1-800-456-6798 or business@simonandschuster.com

Designed by Melissa Isriprashad

Manufactured in the United States of America

10 9 8 7 6 5 4 3 2 1

Library of Congress Cataloging-in-Publication Data
Thomas, Will.
To kingdom come : a novel / Will Thomas.
New York : Touchstone, 2005.
p. cm.
1. Private investigators—England—London—Fiction. 2. Great Britain—History—
Victoria, 1837–1901—Fiction. 3. Irish Republican Army—Fiction. 4. London
(England)—Fiction. 5. Bombings—Fiction. I. Title.
PS3620.H644T6 2005
813'.6—dc22   2005041740

ISBN 0-7432-5622-0

All changed, changed utterly:
A terrible beauty is born.

—William Butler Yeats,
"Easter, 1916"

To Kingdom Come

Prologue

———◆———

I WAS FALLING THROUGH AN INDIGO SKY. I REMEMber the wind whistling in my ears and my coat flapping about my knees as I plummeted. My head hurt, and as I gazed up into the remote, star-studded vault of the heavens, I was having a little trouble piecing together exactly how I had gotten there. I felt as if I'd suddenly fallen off the edge of the earth and would hurtle forever, but the logical portion of my mind told me that all this falling must ultimately end. Unless Parliament had suddenly repealed Newton's law of gravity, I was eventually going to strike something, and it wasn't going to be pleasant.

Raising my head just a little, I saw the large edifice of a bridge passing swiftly by, black against the cobalt night. Vaguely, I remembered thoughts I'd had once of jumping from a bridge and shuffling off this mortal coil, but that had been a few months ago. Had I finally done it? I wondered. To be truthful, I wasn't sure I had the nerve. If this was an attempt, I could congratulate myself that it was successful, which was a novelty, since I'd rarely been successful at anything in my twenty-two years. If that actually was a bridge above me, then presumably I would strike water shortly, which was far preferable to pavement, being less messy. I had another thought, or the beginning of one, but then I struck the water, and it was gone forever.

Water is something I've always considered soft, yielding, and changeable. One drinks it, pours it into vessels; it soaks into the ground. This water was about as yielding as cement. I struck the water with a loud slap, limbs splayed, flat upon my back. It actually might have killed me were it not for the coat that my employer, Cyrus Barker, had given me and insisted I wear. It was of Barker's own design, with built-in pistol holders and a lead lining, near impervious to bullets. I account that it saved my life. It was also very heavy, unfortunately, which explains why I did not dawdle on the surface of the Thames but continued my descent.

The Thames is not the most pristine of rivers, despite the paintings one sees in Grosvenor Gallery of idyllic country scenes, men punting along the river, poles in hand, while their best girls lie in the stern in immaculate white dresses, shaded from the sun by parasols. It's not like that at all. I would think twice about offering a glass of it to even the most hateful of aunts, even if I were her sole legatee. It was certainly not a place to go swimming in July. But then, the choice had rather been taken out of my hands.

Eventually, I came to rest on the bed of silt at the bottom, among the rubbish and detritus of London civilization. I lay for a moment, blinking up into the total blackness. *Perhaps I should just give up*, I thought. It would certainly be easier. But, no, something within me refused to surrender life without a fight. I had to get out of that coat, but it clung to me like a paramour. I struggled and flailed until reluctantly it started to give me up. I was tugging desperately on the second sleeve when I realized I was clutching something that was too big to get through it. It was my pistol. I'd forgotten that I'd been holding it before the fall. No matter. I let it go and pulled my limb through, finally free of the coat.

All I had to do was to swim to the surface and to breathe sweet air again. But in which direction was it? I was in stygian darkness, and my convulsions had even lost me the bottom I had just rested upon. I began to panic, and some of my precious air escaped. I reached frantically after the bubbles: they went down or, rather, up. I was on my head. I turned and swam after them.

I had no idea how far I'd fallen through the water, but the air I'd let escape needed to be replenished. I thrashed upward as my lungs began to insist, to scream for air. I became convinced I wasn't going to make it. In two seconds, I was about to breathe in that fatal gulp of water. Thomas Llewelyn was going to fulfill his destiny and become another anonymous floater on the river.

Give up, my limbs cried, going slack. *It's dozens of feet to the surface. You'll never make it.* Just then, my mind seemed to split in two. One part began to make peace with its Maker, preparing to be ushered into His presence—*The Lord is my shepherd; I shall not want*—while the other, less pious, more skeptical side wanted to unravel one last puzzle before going into the beyond. I needed to disregard the pain of my splitting head and aching body and try to remember the events that had brought me here. In effect, before I died, I wanted to solve my own murder.

1

BOOM.

It was a sublime sound, seeming to come from everywhere and nowhere at once. It wasn't loud—not much more than a thunderclap, really—but it was profound. I felt it echo from the outbuildings in our garden before reaching my ears. My employer, London enquiry agent Cyrus Barker, looked at me through his opaque spectacles, as if to ask *What the deuce has happened now?*

Barker and I had been in the garden behind his house, performing what he called "internal exercises." It had been two and a half months since he'd hired me as his assistant, and I was still recovering from the effects of our first case in which I'd been injured severely, not to mention nearly killed. It was in the back of his mind, I believe, to take advantage of my convalescence and turn me into a wiry bantamweight through the physical training he taught at Scotland Yard. He had me at the dumbbells and Indian clubs constantly. I didn't object, because, first of all, he paid my salary and, second, I felt the training was to my benefit. The internal exercises were another matter.

There we were in our shirtsleeves, moving placidly across the lawn, waving our arms in slow, precise movements resembling postures of self-defense, save that one would have been struck long before completing any of the motions. Barker, who had learned the art while growing up in China, took it all very seriously, but to me, the exercises were no more useful than playing hopscotch. I did them all the same, of course. Aside from paying my salary, he also provided room and board.

The sky had been clear that day, and we had been treated to a shimmering sunset, blood red at first, as if a volcano were spewing forth west of us, then giving way to salmon and violet and finally deepest blue. The ornate garden behind Barker's house in Newington was a pleasant place to be on a warm evening in late May. When I had first seen it in mid-March, I thought it austere and exotic with its large rocks, pebbles, and dwarf evergreens. Now the garden had erupted in a riot of color, resembling one of Mr. Whistler's mad canvases, and Barker and his crew of Chinese gardeners were hard-pressed, clipping and pruning, to return it to its more stoic appearance.

Harm, self-appointed guardian of the property, reigned over his domain from a flat rock in the stone garden. Barker had informed me he was one of less than a dozen Chinese temple dogs, or Pekingese, in Europe. The dowager empress of China had given the dog to him "for services rendered," but what those services were, he had not revealed. The Guv'nor could be exasperatingly reticent when it suited him. Our motions might have interested the little dog had he not seen us do them a thousand times. From where I stood in the bed of thyme, slowly waving my arms about like an inmate from Bethlehem Asylum just down the street, I could hear the dog snoring on the rock. I rather envied the little fellow.

It didn't help my concentration that we faced the back of the house. On the other side of the door, there was a well-appointed kitchen with a pantry, which at that moment contained an apple pie with cognac and caramelized sugar, prepared by one of London's premier chefs, Etienne Dummolard. Etienne came in most mornings from his Soho restaurant, *Le Toison d'Or*, with enough freshly prepared food to last us through the day, like so much manna from heaven.

After the pie, I promised myself, I would sit down with a book in the library. Barker was an inveterate book collector, and being a Scot, he had a complete set of the Waverly novels. I had been working my way through them and was now up to *The Heart of Midlothian*.

"One more time, lad, and we're through for the night," Barker said.

I sighed and raised my protesting arms again. It was then that we heard the boom. We both knew instantly that something had happened. If we hadn't, Harm had. He began barking hysterically. It was his clarion cry, his alarm for us mortals too dull to appreciate that something significant had occurred. In answer, we heard dozens of responses from other canine sentinels across London.

We needed no other warning. Barker and I sprinted across the lawn toward the back door. Once inside, we skidded across the polished floor and climbed the first staircase. Running past my room, we mounted the stairs to Barker's aerie. My employer seized a small box I'd never noticed before from one of the tables and tripped its latch. Inside was a brass telescope, a relic of his sailing days, I presumed. He flicked open the telescope and scanned the horizon to the west from one of the dormer windows.

"Anything?" I asked. "Anything?"

"Nothing appears to be on fire, but there is a haze on the far side of the river," Barker responded.

I took the telescope eagerly and looked myself but saw only what my employer had said, a whitish haze over the river where our offices stood.

"What should we do?" I asked.

"I suppose we should go and see if anything is amiss."

The latter seemed as sensible a decision as any. I left him and went down to the first floor for my jacket. When I came downstairs a few minutes later, knotting my tie, Barker's butler, Jacob Maccabee, was waiting in the hall with a look of concern on his face.

"It could have been a factory accident, I suppose," he said, straightening my knot. "Could you hear which direction it came from?"

"You know the garden," I answered. "It's like sitting in a soup bowl, with those high brick walls. The Guv looked toward the west."

I hoped Mac was right, and our going out would be for naught. A factory accident would be preferable to the other possibility, a bomb. Since the previous year, a radical group calling itself the Irish Republican Brotherhood had been leading a dynamiting campaign against the city in an attempt to force a bill for Home Rule. Several bombs had been located safely by the authorities, and one had exploded harmlessly in the baggage room of Victoria Station, but the fact that the attempts had been unsuccessful was not a comfort to most Londoners. The Criminal Investigation Department at Scotland Yard hastily formed a new section, the Special Irish Branch, to safeguard the public and the Royal Family. Despite their efforts, neither Mac nor I was surprised at the thought that the I.R.B. might strike again.

Finally, Barker came down the stairs. He was soberly dressed in a black cutaway coat, his maroon tie thrust up under a wing collar and held with a pearl stickpin. He stepped between us and reached for a stick from the hall stand before opening the door. I naturally followed. The pie and *Midlothian* would have to wait.

Our hansom cab, which Barker had acquired during our last investigation two months before, was quartered just a half mile away to the east. I assumed my employer would send me to rouse the stable boy, something I'd prefer not to do after a full day's work and those dratted exercises. As it turned out, that would have been preferable to what Barker had in mind.

"Right, then," he stated. "Let's hop it, lad."

"Hop it, sir?"

"Aye. We'll walk. You can use the exercise."

He didn't waste breath on conversation, but set off northwest along London Road, his stick swinging dangerously back and forth. At an inch or two over six feet in height, he was a head taller than I. Consequently, I had to double his footsteps in order to keep up.

Most of the streets on the south side of London were empty, the shops locked and dark. The residents, enjoying their well-deserved evening of rest, seemed unconcerned by the noise that had brought us out on this quiet evening. A chorus of crickets chirped in the vestiges of Lambeth Marsh south of us, accompanied by the low croak of the frogs that fed on them. If I closed my eyes, I could almost feel as if I were back in the country at my childhood home in Wales.

Barker suddenly dodged off Waterloo Road, and had I not been trying to stay close, I would have shot past the lane he ducked into. For the next several minutes I felt as if I were in a maze, following my employer from street to passage to alleyway. Before I knew it, we'd come up along some railroad sleepers, and then we were on a bridge. Not Waterloo, nor Westminster, but a smaller bridge between the two.

"What bridge is this?" I asked, peering over the side at the Thames, which looked as thin and black as India ink.

"The Charing Cross Railway and Footbridge," he called back, over his shoulder.

"Where does it fetch up?"

"On the Embankment behind Scotland Yard."

"Wait," I said, trying to catch my breath. "You mean there's been a *footbridge* right by our offices all this time, and you didn't tell me?"

"If I told you everything, Llewelyn, how ever would you learn anything for yourself?"

I noticed an immediate difference on the west side of the river. There was a chalky grit in the air. The gaslights were balls of light on stalks, as if a globe of frosted glass had been fitted over each one. The haze grew thicker as we approached, and as I watched, wraithlike figures began to come forward out of the gloom. I'd have taken them for ghosts, if I believed in such things, but as we passed among them, they seemed tangible enough; normal citizens, covered in brick dust from head to toe, all staring with dazed expressions out of red-rimmed eyes. Barker and I reached for our pocket handkerchiefs and pushed ourselves through the foglike haze and the crowd of shocked and bedraggled residents. In Whitehall Place, we had to pick our way around piles of fallen bricks. It was only when we crossed Whitehall Street and looked back that we could see the full devastation.

"My word," I murmured. It was the thirtieth of May 1884, and someone had just blown up Scotland Yard.

2

THE ENTIRE NORTHEASTERN CORNER OF THE Criminal Investigation Department had been blown out, revealing a jumbled interior and carpeting the area in brick and rubble. In the gaping hole that exposed several floors, the denizens moved about like ants, already beginning to repair their hill. From where I stood, I could see the splintered wooden floor of the gymnasium in which Barker trained constables in physical culture. Our minds registered the fact that we would not be practicing there for some time to come.

"We must lend a hand, Thomas," Barker said in my ear.

He joined a ring of men around a dying cab horse whose cries were setting my nerves on edge. I stepped back, and found myself standing outside the Rising Sun, a public house in which Barker and I had just eaten lunch a few hours before. The pub looked desolate and open without its glass, but there was activity inside. *Surely, they could not be open for business, as if nothing had happened,* I thought, as I stepped through the open door.

The building had been turned into a makeshift hospital. Everywhere, people were injured and bleeding, their wounds wrapped in tea towels or handkerchiefs. I noticed some of the less badly wounded were trying to tend those with more severe lacerations. I started when I heard a gruff voice addressing me.

"You! Boy! Come here."

An older fellow was gesturing to me. He was kneeling by a supine figure, a medical bag at his feet. Unwittingly, I'd stepped into an operating theater. Barker's last words were still in my ears, and I stepped forward.

"How can I help?" I asked, crouching beside him.

"Get on the other side of this fellow and hold the wound closed, so I can stitch it. Are your hands clean?"

"I think so," I said, holding them out. The doctor raised an open bottle of brandy from the floor and dashed some of it over my hands. Shaking them, I stepped over the body and got a good look at the victim for the first time. His face was soaked in blood. Between the horse, the patrons, and this patient, I'd seen more blood in the last three minutes than in my entire life.

"It looks bad, sir," I couldn't help commenting.

"Oh, he'll live," the old surgeon said. "Head wounds always bleed like this. Hold it just there. Pinch the wound closed."

I did, and the doctor poured another jigger over the open wound. The patient jumped and let out a curse. I'd thought him senseless. Instead, he took a healthy swallow from the brandy bottle before the doctor leaned forward with the needle and thread.

Just then, there was a loud report outside and all cries from the horse ceased. I thought I had recognized the sound of Barker's American Navy Colt revolver. A minute or two later, after the patient was finished being stitched, I looked up and saw that my employer was standing behind me, the reek of gunpowder still on his clothes.

"Good lad," he said, after I'd mopped the patient's bloody face with a rag and lifted his head enough for the physician to bind the wound with gauze. I stopped and wiped the gore from my hands with a towel. A half hour before, I'd been waving my arms in the garden, and now I was assisting at an operation.

"Come, gentlemen," the doctor admonished. "This is not our only patient."

Barker and I responded by removing our jackets and rolling up our sleeves. What happened over the next half hour was more of the same: a number of nasty-looking surface injuries but, thankfully, no fatal ones. Just when my energy was flagging, a brace of capable matrons from nearby Charing Cross Hospital bustled in and immediately set to work. We were able to don our coats and steal away. Barker was anxious to see after his own chambers in the next street.

Debris had been blown over the buildings onto the roofs and cobblestones of Craig's Court. Our offices looked solid as ever, but without benefit of glass, save a few shards. Broken bricks and slates had fallen upon the steps. Barker unlocked the door, though it was obvious that anyone could have vaulted the sill and climbed in.

In our waiting room, glass was strewn across the floor and furniture, and dust coated everything; but nothing appeared damaged. Barker moved on to his chambers quickly. There was more destruction there. A few bricks had come through the window. Fortuitously, I had closed and locked my desk, a maple roll-top that Barker had acquired for my predecessor. There was a large chip out of the top where a brick had struck it. A pedestal lay on its side farther into the room, with shards of what had been an antique Chinese vase, whose worth I couldn't begin to calculate. Glass was scattered over the Persian rugs here, and a thick layer of dust coated the rows of bookcases that lined the room. Even Barker's spartanly neat desk had not been spared. The few papers he'd allowed to remain were scattered and the inkwell had been knocked over, its contents dribbling down the side of the desk. Barker set the inkwell upright, then bent down and picked up some of the shards of porcelain from the floor.

"Blast," he muttered. Barker was a gentleman by decision, if not by birth. It was the most he would allow himself to say about the loss. I assumed the vase had some sentimental meaning to him, aside from its obvious intrinsic worth.

"It is in whole pieces," I pointed out. "It can be mended. I saw an advertisement in *The Times* for an agency that promised they could make them look as good as new."

Barker gently collected the pieces and set them on his desk, then befouled his handkerchief with the ink, wiping down the corner and sides of the desk. He had better luck here; the desk was kept so highly polished with beeswax that the ink could not penetrate to the wood. It had seeped into the floor, however, and those few spatters of ink would forever remind me of this night's occurrence. Barker stepped by me and pitched the sodden handkerchief out the window into the dustbin.

"Unlock your desk and get out your pad, lad," he ordered. "Let us make a list."

I took the key from my waistcoat pocket and unlocked the drawer, removing my stenographic pad and a pencil, while Barker surveyed the room.

"We'll need to get the glaziers in, first of all, of course," he said. "I suggest we try someone from Lambeth. All the local tradesmen shall be besieged in the morning. Next, we must send this rug to be cleaned. Your desk shall have to be repaired and refinished. It was a good suggestion about the vase, though we both know it shall never be the same again. Perhaps you can track down that advertisement for me. Of course, we have hours of work ahead of us. Dusting these books will take days in itself. I wouldn't want to be continually pulling bits of glass out of my fingertips from now on, whenever I needed a reference."

"Certainly not," I agreed. "Anything else?"

"I wonder . . ." he said. I knew the look in his eye, or at least what he was thinking. The next thing he would do was unlock his smoking cabinet and take out one of his meerschaum pipes. It was a smooth finished pipe this time, instead of one of his more elaborately carved ones. The rim of the pipe was blackened, giving way to yellow and finally to purest white on the bowl. Barker pulled out his chair, reached for his handkerchief, and realized he'd thrown it out. He accepted mine, dusted the chair, and was soon seated, smoking his pipe and looking out through the bare window frames at the darkened offices across the street. I knew better than to interrupt him while he was thinking.

After five minutes or so, we heard the crunch of glass out front. Someone was in the waiting room. Barker pulled the pipe from his mouth and looked over. My hand went into the drawer of my desk, where I kept my Webley revolver. The door opened slowly, and a head peered around it, its face dominated by a huge, sandy mustache and side-whiskers.

"Poole!" Barker said. It was Terence Poole, an inspector from Scotland Yard, and one of my employer's closest friends.

"Hello, Barker. Quite a to-do, isn't it? I've been keeping an eye out. Plenty of thieves and pickpockets about already, looking for spoils. I didn't want to see your digs picked clean."

"Sneak thieves, eh?"

"Sneak thieves, pickpockets, the lot. Scotland Yard's blown up, and the criminal element won't let the grass grow under its feet. There was a second bomb that went off at the same time in Pall Mall at the Junior Carlton Club, but the damage there is not as bad as at the Yard. The gymnasium is gone, I'm afraid. Changing room as well. Of course, we'll rebuild. Your classes will have to wait, unless we find another place to meet."

Barker nodded his head, registering that several parts of his life had been altered by the explosion. We could be back in business in a day or two, but it would be weeks before the Rising Sun was open again, and Scotland Yard would be inconvenienced by masons, plasterers, and painters for months.

"What have you discovered so far?"

"An infernal device went off in a public lavatory inside the Criminal Investigation Department. We found part of a clockwork mechanism. Nothing complicated—parts salvaged from a mantel clock or the like—but effective for all that."

"Has anyone claimed responsibility?"

Poole looked grim. "Not yet, but they don't need to. The explosion was set right under the offices of the newly formed Special Irish Branch. It can't be coincidence."

"What are the higher-ups saying?"

"Williamson's livid and Munro has vowed he'll track them down." Superintendent Williamson was head of the Criminal Investigation Department and James Munro the chief inspector of the Special Irish Branch. I wouldn't care to trade positions with either of them at the moment.

"And the Home Office?"

"No word yet. A few of their johnnies strolled up the street for a look, cool as you please. There's no love lost between them and the S.I.B. I suppose it's a small matter to them if their police force is blown out from under them."

Barker dumped the contents of his pipe into an ashtray already half full of dust from the explosion. He heaved one of his sighs.

"It's no good starting to clean up now. We shall start in the morning. Are you heading home, Poole?"

"Yes, I'm done here. If I'm lucky, I'll get three hours kip."

"Ta-ta, then. We shall speak in a few days."

The two friends shook hands, and the inspector shook mine as well before he left. Perhaps it was the dust from the explosion, but there were lines about his eyes I hadn't noticed before and gray in his hair.

When he was gone, I stood and yawned. It had been a long night already.

"When are we going home, sir?" I asked, trying not to sound as if I were complaining.

"We aren't," my employer responded. "We will sleep rough tonight. There is a cot in one of the back rooms, which we will carry to the waiting room. Follow me."

I did so with as much ill grace as I could get away with. Still, I was curious. The rooms in the back were a mystery to me. Barker kept most of them locked. None of them had windows, so presumably they hadn't sustained any damage. Barker set his key in a lock and opened one of the doors on the right. If I was hoping for pirate costumes or the lost treasures of the Incas, I'd have been disappointed. There was a simple cot, a small table and chair, and some anonymous cupboards. Did the Guv'nor take an occasional nap while I was running errands? We carried the cot into the waiting room. Barker went back into the room and returned with a pillow and blankets.

"You shall bed down here for the night," he said.

"Where shall you sleep, sir?" I asked.

"In the office, of course," he responded. "I have expensive furnishings and books here, not to mention files some would pay large sums to obtain."

"You'll sleep in a chair?"

"No, on the floor."

I followed him back into the office. He went to a shelf and took down a thick book, *The Complete Works of Shakespeare*, I believe. Pulling the chair away from his desk, he set the book on the floor, then removed his shoes and jacket, collar and cuffs. Then, as I watched, puzzling over his next move, he lay down on the Bakhtiari rug behind his desk where no glass had fallen and pulled one end over him, his head resting on Shakespeare for a pillow.

"Sir!" I said, appalled. "Sir, no. You take the cot! I can't let you sleep like this."

"Thomas, there have been nights in my life when I would have given a kingdom for a soft rug and a book to rest my head upon. You get some sleep. I want you fresh in the morning. Be a good lad and turn down the gas on your way out."

The last thing he did after rolling away was to reach up and put his spectacles on the desk above his head. It was the first time I'd ever seen him remove the black lenses, and they looked strange and empty on the blotter without his face behind them. If only he would turn my way. I idled about a moment, hoping he'd do just that, hoping just once to see how he looked without them.

"Thomas."

"Yes, sir. Good night." I turned down the gas and left the room.

3

———◆———

I WAS HAVING THE MOST WONDERFUL DREAM. I was in an outdoor café slathering gooseberry preserves on a fresh croissant. I felt the boulevard breezes on my face and smelled the heavenly aroma of fresh coffee. My attentive waiter refilled my porcelain cup with coffee and cream from matching silver pots before I could ask.

I was just beginning a second roll when a beautiful woman began wending her way toward me among the tables. She had lips the color of poppies, and a vibrant cobalt blue dress hugged her every curve. I leaned forward, longing to know what intimate secret she wished to reveal to me.

She came closer and bent toward me as I looked up into her pellucid blue eyes, drinking in her beauty. She took my chin lightly in her gloved hand and brought her impossibly red lips to my ear.

"Eh, Thomas! Wake up, you idiot! Your coffee ees getting cold!"

Someone's boot was on my hip, shaking me awake, and none too gently, either. Reluctantly, I opened my eyes, my dream in tatters. Etienne Dummolard's face is difficult to take on any morning, let alone in comparison to the beauty in my dream. He is built along the lines of a bear. His purple nose resembles a turnip freshly pulled from a field, and his hair looks as if a miniature haystack had been set down upon his head.

"What are you doing here?" I mumbled, sitting up.

"Nobody was at home for breakfast, so I brought it here. Coffee and fresh croissants and jam. Monsieur Mac has sent along a fresh suit of clothes for each of you."

Losing the girl was a disappointment, but I sat at the clerk's desk and contented myself with the coffee and rolls. It was better fare than I had anticipated under the circumstances. The boulevard breezes of my dream, I reasoned, had been due to the missing glass in our waiting room windows.

"While you are enjoying your meal," Etienne said, "I shall step around and see this amazing sight, this Scotland Yard all *en déshabillé*."

"I'll go with you," I said, rising.

"If you insult my croissants by standing, I shall kick the legs from under you. Sit and digest," he ordered.

I nodded and poured a second cup of coffee from the pot he had brought. It's not a bad thing to be forced to eat fresh pastry prepared by a master chef. After he left, however, I committed the sacrilege of chewing the last of my roll while crossing to the office.

Inside, Barker was seated at his desk, for all the world like any other day were it not that the office was in shambles. He was engrossed in conversation with a workman over the telephone set at his desk. *The Times* was spread out under his elbows.

I was standing in the doorway, remarking to myself that it was seven o'clock by the extremely loud tolling of Big Ben just down the street, when I was struck a glancing blow on the shoulder. I almost thought it was another explosion, and it was. It was Jenkins.

Our clerk leapt into the room, taking in the windows, the overturned pedestal, the dust-covered books. His eyes were the size of billiard balls. It was the first time I'd ever seen him fully awake. Neither Barker nor I had thought to send word to him that we'd been bombed. He'd known for less than a minute.

"Wha'—what's happened here?" he demanded. "And what are you two gents doing here at this hour on a Saturday?"

"A small matter of an explosion at Scotland Yard last evening," Barker explained. "We thought it necessary to spend the night."

"Cor! It'll take days to clean this place up. Look at all this winder glass. It's everywhere!"

"It gets worse," I told him. "The Sun was also damaged, I'm afraid."

Our clerk looked stricken. The Rising Sun was Jenkins's port of call, when not at work. I can only compare it to telling a man from the Exchange that the Market has plunged. He went white.

"Oh, s'truth, not the Sun!" He rushed past me and out the door. I heard his footsteps echoing down the court.

"The news is worse this morning," Barker said, handing me *The Times*. "Aside from the dozens hurt in Whitehall, fourteen men were injured at the Junior Carlton Club. Also, two servants were blown off their feet at the private residence of Sir Watkin Williams Wynn, across the street in St. James's."

"Sir Watkin!"

Barker's brow sunk between the twin disks of his spectacles.

"You know Sir Watkin?"

"I don't know him personally, but he has always been revered in Wales. He's a landowner who has given back much in charity to the Welsh people. Was he injured?"

"I don't know anything beyond the published account. Have you finished your coffee?"

"Er . . . yes, sir."

"Good. We have an appointment at the Home Office at eight

o'clock. The ministries are awake early this morning, thanks to the bombing that occurred there last evening. Do try to get cleaned up, Thomas. Your appearance might be suitable for the public houses but not for visiting one of Her Majesty's government agencies."

Barker led me to the back room where the cot had been and removed a black leather bag containing toiletries from one of the cupboards. There were brushes for hair and teeth, a mirror, a razor, and a small ceramic bowl. I took it outside to fill from the pump in the yard. In twenty minutes I was changed and clean-shaven again, and my medusa head of curls beaten back into submission.

Jenkins looked unwell when he returned just then, leaning on the arm of Dummolard like an old man. We sat him in his chair while the Frenchman poured him coffee. I thought our clerk might faint.

"I can't believe it," he said. "This is a nightmare."

It took some time to calm him and then to get him started cleaning up the glass about the place. Dummolard left for his restaurant, and soon it was a quarter to the hour.

"Are you ready, lad? Capital. Let's be off, then."

Skirting the debris from the explosion, we reached the corner of Downing and Parliament Streets and looked up at the tall, nondescript exterior of the Home Office. The building projected an aura of wisdom and competency, but at the same time, I almost felt it willing us to go away. I saw it for what it was: a vault of secrets. From here, the eyes of the British government were watching. If my few months in Oxford Prison caused me to distrust policemen, my natural antipathy toward spies and spying was stronger still.

Understandably, the guard at the Home Office was reluctant to let anyone as formidable looking as my employer into the building. He let us cool our heels in the lobby and sent a clerk along to deliver our cards to Mr. Robert Anderson. After a wait of a quarter hour, the man himself came out to meet us. He was a mild but capable-looking fellow in his mid-forties with a salt-and-pepper beard, which belied his official title of Spymaster General.

"Mr. Barker," he said, giving us a brisk bow. Barker stood, and they shook hands.

"Mr. Anderson," my employer answered in his foggy voice. "Thank you for responding to my note. May I present my assistant, Thomas Llewelyn?"

"How do you do. Will the two of you care to step down the hallway with me? There is someone I wish you to meet and something I very much want you to see."

Anderson led us down a carpeted hall, lined with offices containing government employees, all intent upon the latest outrage. I wondered how those men felt this morning when they arrived at work. I don't believe any violent results of their policies had ever occurred so close to their offices before.

We reached a room dominated by a long table. It seated twenty, by the number of chairs that were around it, and was built of dark mahogany, several inches thick, with heavy legs carved like the limbs of a lion. There were two things I noticed as I stepped into the room: the gentleman seated at one end and the large carpetbag at the other.

"Sir Watkin," Anderson said, "may I introduce you to Mr. Cyrus Barker and his assistant, Thomas Llewelyn." Anderson turned to us. "Sir Watkin is here at Her Majesty's request as a liaison between the Crown and the Home Office."

Sir Watkin Williams Wynn shook Barker's hand, then turned to me. I wondered what my father would have said if he could have seen me shaking hands with the great man now.

"*Pnawn da,*" I said, as the old gentleman grasped my hand.

"Good morning to you," he replied in Welsh. "It's good to

hear the old tongue so far from home, especially on a day such as this."

Instinctively, Cyrus Barker gravitated toward the bag at the other end of the table. "Is that what I believe it to be?"

"Yes. It was found this morning at the base of Nelson's Column. So far, we have not notified the gentlemen of the press." Anderson's lips curled as he spoke, but whether it was due to the bomb, the press, or the bag's garish colors, I couldn't say.

"May I?"

"You may. It failed to go off, and we have had the wires cut by one of our experts."

Barker opened the satchel and motioned me over to look inside. The first thing I saw was a small clock, the kind one keeps on one's night table. The back plate had been removed and a pistol wired to it, the muzzle almost facing a small detonator. It had missed by a hairsbreadth and there was a scorched hole in the bag. Beneath the clock were several claylike cakes wrapped in paper with warning labels on them. Dynamite. I had heard of it, seen it in political cartoons of anarchists and Fenians, but this was my first time to see it in person. If this bag were like the one that had been left at Scotland Yard, it contained enough explosives to blow us and everything in this room to kingdom come.

"Atlas Powder Company. American made, like the carpetbag. Probably American funded, as well. Very basic," my employer commented. "But they didn't get it right. We can be thankful that the Irish are still tyros at bomb making and that, so far, they have been unwilling to take human life."

"Not for lack of trying," Sir Watkin spoke up. "My butler and footman were thrown into the hall by the force of the explosion across the street, and are both in hospital. These bombers are serious. London is shaking in her boots this morning."

"Nevertheless," Barker stated, "this satchel proves that their knowledge of making explosives is still rudimentary at best. No doubt you are aware of the failed attempt last month to blow up the English police barracks in Dublin. That is three unsuccessful efforts in half a year, hardly a distinguished record."

"Now, Mr. Barker," Anderson said, "perhaps you will explain to us why you felt the need to offer your services to us today. Surely, a man of your experience would know we have our own resources."

"I am aware of the reach of the Home Office and the abilities of the Special Irish Branch, who no doubt are stinging under the effects of last night's humiliation. I merely thought it would be remiss of me not to make myself available, as I am something of an expert on secret societies. I assume you've read my dossier from the Foreign Office."

"I have, and, I must say, it made for interesting reading. The consensus seems to be that your methods are irregular, but you generally succeed in what you set out to accomplish." Anderson paused a moment, to let Barker comment, but my employer merely sat there—blinking, if, in fact, he ever blinked behind those spectacles. He may not have realized he had been given a compliment and merely thought it his due. As for me, I would have liked to read that dossier. I had at least a thousand questions about my employer I'd like answered.

"Hmm, yes," Anderson continued, glossing over the small breach in etiquette. "Patriotism aside, I fail to see what you hope to gain. You are a private detective, not a spy. Did you wish to add a line to your advertisements in *The Times* as 'The Man Who Brought Down the Fenians'? What is your motive?"

"It is not to seek advertisement for my agency, Mr. Anderson. I assure you, I do not need the custom. This is my city. I live and work here. Llewelyn and I helped some of the people injured by the explosion last night. Wherever one stands on the Irish Question, all but the most extreme will agree that bombing is not the way to achieve sovereignty. There is a fatal streak of nihilism in this action, like a child losing at chess who upsets the board. I'm thinking not merely of the English citizens in hospital today but also the shocked Irish readers of *The Times* this morning, who see their chances for independence pushed even farther from their grasp because of a few embittered and overzealous individuals. I am for healthy debate in the House of Commons, at the proper time, not for innocent civilians being bombed. It is a Pandora's box, and it has been opened. If we don't nail it down immediately, we may never get the lid secured again."

Anderson tapped his finger on the table a few times in thought. "Granted, for the moment then, that you are offering your services for altruistic reasons. I'm wondering what you, with your limited resources, can do that the combined services of Her Majesty's government cannot? Can you really believe you will succeed where we will not?"

Barker gave one of his cold smiles. "An acrobat, for all his skills, employs a net to catch him if he falls. I merely suggest that you hire me to be that net. My sources are not as limited as you might believe. I shall meet with no one but you, and if I fail—or if Inspector Munro and your own agents get in ahead of me—I shall not tender a bill for my services."

"Munro will not appreciate your interference," Sir Watkin put in. "How do you propose to catch the rascals?"

"By locating and infiltrating the responsible faction."

Both gentlemen smiled. It seemed a rather impetuous plan, even to me.

"I've done it before," he continued, "as my dossier no doubt attests."

"Impossible," Anderson said. "You are Scottish, and your assistant is Welsh. Even some of our best Irish-born agents have tried it, only to come home in a pine box. The faction cells are very close-knit. Many of the members have known one another since their school days. Sometimes they are even members of one family. What makes you so bold as to think you can succeed when all others have failed?"

"Oh, come, sir. Not all have failed. What of Lieutenant Le Caron?"

Robert Anderson jumped from his chair, as if he'd sat on a hornet. "How the devil do you know about Le Caron?"

"Henri is a friend of mine, aside from being your best spy among the Irish for the last ten years. I trained him in hand combat for a month. He's a good man. More important, he is an example of a non-Irishman who appears devoted to their cause; in this case, a Frenchman. Or rather, an Englishman impersonating a Frenchman, since we both know that Le Caron is not his real name."

I pricked up my ears. I hadn't heard Le Caron's name before. When had he known the Guv?

"It seems you know an awful lot, sir, about something that is not your affair," Sir Watkin blustered.

"As far as I am concerned, gentlemen, it became my affair when they injured innocent London citizens and damaged public buildings. Something must be done, and I'd rather be working with the official enquiry than on my own. How long shall it be before the Irish radicals throw off their gloves and go after the Crown itself?"

Anderson gave Sir Watkin a significant glance, which Barker noticed immediately. "They have communicated."

"They have," Anderson said, removing a folded slip of paper from his pocket. "This was delivered to the Prime Minister in his office this morning. I must ask that you not mention this to anyone. It shall dampen your enthusiasm, I must warn you."

Barker took the typewritten note and I read over his shoulder.

" 'Dear Mr. Gladstone, This is just a taste of what we can do. You have thirty days to propose a bill for Home Rule, or your government and the Royal Family shall fall. You have been warned.' "

"Thirty days," my employer rumbled.

"Do you withdraw your offer, Mr. Barker?" Sir Watkin asked. "Thirty days does not give you much time to become an Irishman, join a faction, and convince them to trust you."

Barker sat and pondered a moment, absently rubbing his finger under his chin. He did not seem to mind letting two of the most important men in England wait upon his reply. Finally, he let his hand drop to the table.

"My offer still stands, if you'll accept it. I believe I can deliver whoever set those bombs and sent this note to you. I shall require Scotland Yard to take them into custody at the proper time. During the month, I would like both Llewelyn and me to be working for the standard fee you pay Le Caron, contingent upon whether we succeed."

"Upon my soul, I wish we were as confident as you seem to be, Mr. Barker," Anderson continued. "How do you propose to convince the faction cell to trust you?"

"By offering them someone they very much need: Johannes van Rhyn, the reclusive inventor of infernal devices. I understand they have attempted to recruit his aid for some time, but he will not see them. I intend to impersonate him."

"Van Rhyn has turned down all requests to help the Home Office. We've sequestered him at the military base in Aldershot. How will you . . ." Anderson asked. "Do not tell me. You are acquainted with the German, as well as Le Caron?"

My employer said nothing but gave the spymaster a thin smile.

"You have interesting friends, Mr. Barker," Anderson continued. "We were not aware of that. One final thing. Her Majesty's government does not bargain with terrorists. If the two of you are captured, we will be unable to step in and come to your rescue."

"Understood," Barker said. "I would not wish to endanger your other agents."

"What think you, Anderson?" Sir Watkin asked. "Shall we trust Mr. Barker and his mad scheme to hoodwink the Irish?"

"It is a slender thread, I'll admit," Anderson said. "But I believe the peril we are in warrants a secondary plan. Very well, gentlemen. I shall take your proposal to the Prime Minister. I cannot speak for him, but for now, it would be to your advantage to set your pawns in play."

"What about you, young fellow? Are you up for all this?" Sir Watkin asked, as he shook my hand before we left.

"I trust my employer implicitly, sir," I stated, but to tell the truth, just then I was wondering the same thing myself.

4

AFTER WE STEPPED OUTSIDE INTO KING CHARLES Street, Barker stuffed a finger and thumb under his mustache and emitted a shrill whistle, loud enough to make an old pensioner on the pavement flinch in astonishment and mutter about the Empire going to ruin. A cab drew up to the curb, and we clambered aboard.

"Claridge's," Barker called over my head, and we bowled off.

"Why Claridge's?" I asked. What business did we have in one of London's most prestigious hotels?

"It is the hotel of kings, and Parnell is the uncrowned king of Ireland. I must speak to him."

Perhaps there was some savage living in the Sudan who had never heard of Charles Parnell, but the rest of the world most certainly had. He was the closest the Irish had to a real leader since St. Patrick. A Protestant, he had courted the Vatican in the hope of gaining support for Irish Home Rule. A onetime Land League radical who had spent time in Kilmainham Gaol, he was now creating a union that included everyone from the most pacifist groups to the most militant in Ireland. Though there were still many in Parliament who saw him as no better than an anarchist, he was the darling of many a soirée in London, and it was rumored that Prime Minister Gladstone himself had offered him a sympathetic ear on more than one occasion. I had heard that his framed image hung on the wall of thousands of homes across the Irish Sea.

"I understand why the bombers would attack Trafalgar Square and Scotland Yard," I said, "but why the Junior Carlton Club, sir?"

"You must study English politics a little more thoroughly, lad," Barker replied. "The main opposition to Home Rule will be the old dogs sitting around the fire at the Carlton making decisions, but it will be the young pups at the Junior that will dictate policy over the next twenty years. The Irish are sending them a very clear message."

There is a right way to do things and a wrong way, and then there is the Barker way, which is a third choice no one had thought of yet, because they were not clever enough. Had we gone in the front entrance of Claridge's, we would have been stopped at the desk, but the Guv walked in the service entrance as bold as you please. We worked our way through the kitchens and the dining room, facing nothing more challenging than a few questioning stares. In the hallway, he went so far as to buttonhole a steward.

"Tell me, my man, in what room is Mr. Parnell staying? We are from the Home Office."

I was debating whether we could accurately be described as "from the Home Office," but it was not precisely a lie. It is one of Barker's axioms that one must make use of whatever leverage one can muster.

"Room three eleven, sir," the man responded.

"Have the reporters all gone?"

"They have already left, sir. Mr. Parnell had them in for a statement."

"Thank you." I saw him discreetly press some silver into the steward's hand. The two of us climbed the servants' staircase and soon found ourselves in sole possession of an elegant corridor. Barker knocked on the door marked 311. Perhaps it would be more accurate to say that he thumped. With that ham-sized fist of his, it was just short of beating down the door.

A moment later the door opened, and a man looked out at us in minor annoyance. I was more accustomed to seeing his face in engravings in *The Illustrated London News*. He was a tall, well-built man in a frock coat of light gray, with a long but well-groomed beard.

"Yes?" he demanded. "What do you want?"

"Mr. Parnell, my name is Mr. Cyrus Barker. This is my assistant, Mr. Thomas Llewelyn. I believe I am in possession of information you shall find useful." He offered his card. Barker has a way of snapping the pasteboard in his thick fingers as he presents it that has so far eluded me, no matter how often I try.

"I doubt that sincerely," Parnell replied drily, looking at the card. "Barker. I've heard of you, but I assure you I don't need to hire an enquiry agent."

Barker would not be put off so easily. "I have a matter of great importance to discuss with you, sir, but I would not care to do so in this hall."

Parnell shrugged and stepped back, opening the door wide. "Very well, come in. Half of London has been in here today already. I don't recall your name being mentioned by Scotland Yard this morning."

"You won't," Barker said, as we stepped into the room. "We are working *sub rosa* for one of Her Majesty's agencies. I am taking you into our confidence, because I am convinced you had nothing to do with the atrocities that occurred last night. I am going to risk revealing what I have learned because I believe you can be trusted, even if Her Majesty's government does not."

"It's nice to know someone trusts me. I spent most of the

night being questioned by Scotland Yard. The newspapers today are wild over this new outrage. I won't be surprised if I'm burned in effigy at a rally tonight. Everyone seems to think I can wave my wand like Merlin and every faction will fall into line like so many ducks. I wish it were that easy."

"I'm afraid the situation is worse than you've been led to believe. According to my sources, if a bill for Home Rule is not rushed through Parliament within the month, there will be a second series of outrages much larger than the first."

"Good lord," Parnell said, falling into an overstuffed leather chair and running a hand through his scant hair.

"Precisely. Should that occur, it will not be an effigy they shall hang. All your attempts at forming a legitimate coalition for Home Rule will have been set to naught. It is vital that you help me, you see. I am your only hope of containing the more militant factions of the Brotherhood."

"If another series of bombings occurs, it could throw back the chances for Irish democracy thirty years or more," Parnell agreed. "Believe me, gentlemen, I want to help you, but I know nothing about the bombings. I assure you, none of my associates had anything to do with them."

"Somehow, a group of factionists from the more radical fringe were able to smuggle in dynamite from America. They prepared and delivered their bombs and got away without being detected. Obviously, that requires a high level of organization. Who has such an ability to command men and use strategy among your compatriots? Who is both ruthless and radical enough to threaten the government and the Royal Family?"

"I scarce can say," Parnell said vaguely.

"You need assurances," Barker said patiently. "I know there are dozens of factions out there, with a like number of ideologies. Some are militant, others philosophical, and some are merely formed to take in money. I have one mission and one mission alone: to find the faction that blew up Scotland Yard last night. I must find them, shut down their operation, and turn them over to the authorities, and I shall do so privately. This is not for the newspapers. You cannot use this as proof of your sincerity, not publicly, anyway. Give me names, Mr. Parnell, the names of the more militant leaders among the I.R.B., or Clan Na Gael, or whatever they are calling themselves this morning."

"How do I know," Parnell asked, "that what you uncover won't go to the Special Irish Branch who've been kicking in doors and harassing innocent Irishmen?"

"I've trusted you just now with privileged information that could be passed on to the press or to other factions because I believe your efforts to help the Irish people are sincere." Barker moved over to the window and looked out into the street, his arms crossed. "Now you shall have to trust me. I cannot put it any plainer than that. The names, sir. In your heart of hearts, who do you think it might have been?"

The Irishman picked up a silver case and lit a cigarette. His hand, I noticed, was not steady. Surreptitiously, I pulled my notebook out of my pocket.

"You do realize what the punishment among the factions is for informing, do you not, Mr. Barker?" Parnell asked.

"If you are referring to Peter Carey, who was assassinated for informing on the Invincibles last year, I do. They tracked him all the way to South Africa. But he had definite information and was one of the conspirators. I merely wish to be pointed in a direction."

"Very well. I cannot give you a definite name, but I can give you a list of a half dozen capable enough. There is Peter Davitt, O'Donovan Rossa, Michael Cusack, Alfred Dunleavy, Henri Le Caron, and Seamus O'Muircheartaigh. Most have spent time in prison, and Dunleavy and Le Caron have commanded armies. If he isn't among one of them, he is unknown to me, and I'd like to think that such a fellow would have been brought to my attention before now."

"Have you got all that down, Llewelyn?" Barker asked.

"Almost, sir. I didn't get the last fellow's name."

"I know him," Barker said. "I shall spell his name for you later. That is all I need of you, Mr. Parnell. We won't take up any more of your time. Come along, lad."

Barker led me down the grand staircase to the lobby, where we evoked the scrutiny of the hotel manager. One cannot be faulted for leaving an establishment, however, and we left unhindered. Two thirds of detective work, I believe, is sheer brass.

Outside, my employer led me to the curb and stood for a moment, his walking stick on the pavement. I assumed he was awaiting a cab, but when one jingled up, he stepped back and offered it to a woman and her daughter leaving the hotel. He then led me down Brook Street a block or two. As we were passing a quiet tea shop, his strong fingers gripped my elbow in that way of his, and we entered. Without a pause on our way to the farthest booth in the room, he called for a pot of tea and three cups. Three cups? I wondered. It wasn't until we arrived at the booth, and he sat on the same side as I, that the light dawned. We had a second assignation.

I took a sip of the tea, and as I set the cup down, a man slid silently into the booth across from us. He was a thin fellow, whose long coat and pants were so tight he appeared even thinner. His head was bulbous, the scanty black hair plastered across it, and his thin mustache was waxed into points.

"Barker," he said, bowing his head respectfully, then took a delicate sip from his cup.

"Henri, may I present my assistant, Thomas Llewelyn? Thomas, Mr. Henri Le Caron. He was spying on us earlier from the second-floor rooms across the street from Claridge's with the aid of a telescope."

"Was I that obvious?"

"Not at all, but, then, I was looking. I suppose you could just as easily have been the Special Irish Branch."

"They were in the attic above me, watching Parnell until last night, but they shut down their operation this morning. I do not believe they consider Parnell a suspect."

"Do you?"

Le Caron took another sip of his tea to sum up his thoughts. "Probably not, as far as the bombings are concerned, but I'm throwing my net a bit wider. Anderson wants to know how capable he is, and whether he has any weaknesses that can be exploited, if necessary. I believe Parnell quite capable of persuading Gladstone to sponsor a bill for Home Rule, but he is not without flaws. He's living above his means and has an English mistress, a married one, at that. If the Irish intend to throw all their eggs in his basket, I believe they shall find them dashed to the floor."

"Have you spoken to Mr. Anderson since last night?"

"Yes, by telephone. He's apprised me of the situation. I must say, I don't envy you or the Special Irish Branch your deadline. It has taken me years to earn the trust of the Irish Brotherhood, and that is merely in a general way. The factions themselves are very close-knit."

"How many groups would you estimate are functioning at the moment in Ireland and England?"

"I'd say two dozen or more, but some are merely Irish youths looking for a reputation. Less than half that are true terrorists, radical enough to bomb and kill, or to die in the attempt."

"Parnell has given me a few names of possible candidates for leadership of the faction who planted last night's bombs. One of them is a dangerous Frenchman named Le Caron."

Le Caron laughed, revealing a space between his teeth. He seemed the total opposite of a successful spy, but then, I suppose, a ruddy-cheeked, solid fellow looking like an Eton and Cambridge graduate would have raised the Irish hackles in a heartbeat.

"Yes," Le Caron said. "Watch out for the Frenchman. He's a dangerous fellow. Who were the others?"

"Davitt, Cusack, Dunleavy, and Rossa. Oh, and O'Muircheartaigh."

Le Caron emptied his cup and set it down. "For a politician, Parnell has more acumen than I would credit. Unless the faction leader is a new fellow we haven't heard of, it will be one of the five. I've worked with the rest before, but I only know of O'Muircheartaigh by hearsay. He contributes heavily to the Irish cause, but his organization is mostly composed of Irish criminals. His base is here in London."

"I'm familiar with Seamus," Barker stated. I noticed Le Caron gave him a shrewd glance, flicked a second one my way briefly, and went on.

"That leaves Davitt, Dunleavy, Rossa, and Cusack," Le Caron continued. "All of them are green with envy over Parnell's hopes, though between you and me I don't think the Crown will ever countenance state visits from a former prisoner."

"Rossa has schemes of his own. He's being funded by groups such as the Ancient Order of Hibernians, but he's got them so confounded, they don't even realize they are funding a terrorist. Davitt's more a politician, a great orator, but not the sort for this kind of mission. As for Cusack, he's attempting single-handedly to bring back the Irish language and sports. I think his plate is full already, and he rarely leaves Dublin.

"Dunleavy's an old Irish-American warhorse, who fought as a colonel on the secessionist side during the American War Between the States. He saw action at Antietam and Vicksburg. I was on the opposing side, but after the war, we worked together on an Irish raid into Canada, in an attempt to trade Toronto for Irish freedom. Of course, I sent word ahead and the attack was scuttled. I think Dunleavy still seethes over the losses of the Southern states but having a role in the new Irish government would more than make up for it. He's ruthless and wily enough for a campaign like last night, when he's not on the bottle. He's got his share of the Irish melancholy and occasionally goes on bouts of drinking."

"Thank you for the information," Barker said. "You don't think Parnell capable of subterfuge?"

"It is possible," Le Caron acknowledged, "but I'd sooner suspect one of the others. Parnell is already in a good position politically, not that we couldn't bring him down, if we needed to. The mistress alone is enough to discredit him. For one thing, she's married to an English officer."

I got a glimpse then of the kind of politics that went on in the rarefied circles the Home Office worked in. I had to say, I didn't care for it and hoped that working for the government was not something my employer would do often. I felt as if we, as pawns, could be too easily sacrificed.

"I must get back, as boring as it is to watch him read newspapers and wring his hands," Le Caron said, preparing to leave. "I wish you both *bonne chance* in your search for the faction. I hope you get to them before Munro and his boys do. The Home Office has no love for the Special Irish Branch and their tactics. They may be new, but they have already stolen several of our informants and scared off or worried others. Strong-arm bullyboys is what they are. Is this little fellow going with you? Is he being trained in faction fighting?"

"I am having Vigny give him lessons this week."

"Close enough. Good day, and good hunting." Le Caron rapped his knuckles on the table and was off.

Outside, Barker whistled again for a cab, while I pondered the last exchange. Who was Vigny, and what was faction fighting?

"Why do I feel as if you're not telling me everything?" I asked.

Barker gave that short cough that passes for his chuckle. "Lad, you don't know the half of it."

5

W E RETURNED TO OUR OFFICES AND HELPED
Jenkins with the cleaning for an hour or two, and then went to
lunch at Ho's, an Oriental restaurant and Barker's base of operations in the East End. I speculated he was part owner of the place,
as he was of Dummolard's *Le Toison d'Or*. The cab let us out in
front of what I've come to call Ho's alley. It is one of the most desolate spots in London. Old stone arches, like the bare ribs of an
antediluvian dinosaur, vaulted overhead. Bills, placards, and
advertisements had been plastered to the walls and tattered by
wind and rain. We stepped over rubble that was good for nothing—that could not be sold or burnt for fuel—until we arrived at
the nondescript door at the far end. There is no sign over Ho's
entrance. He caters to a specific clientele. If one did not know
where it was, one was not welcome.

We plunged through the door and down the steps. Ho's
restaurant is reached by means of a walkway under the Thames.
Beside the entrance there are lamps to light your way, but regu-
lars go through to the restaurant at the far end blind. So far, I had
not broken my neck, but it only needs to happen once. Several

minutes later, we were seated at a table over our first course.

"There's a chicken head in my soup, sir," I said, nudging it with a dubious finger.

"It is just garnish, Thomas. You do not have to eat it."

"What is that in yours?"

"This is bird's nest soup. What do you suppose is in it?"

There is always a moment before I begin to eat when I think Ho is trying to poison me. Then I taste my food, and realize what a master chef he is. Ho is a true Chinaman. He'll serve anything that lives, from seaweed to elephant. In the West End there are restaurants that will take a breast of fowl, cut it from the bone, stuff it, bread it, cook it, cover it in sauce, and garnish it until one is not sure what kind of animal it was to begin with. With Ho, like as not, there will be eyes regarding you from your bowl.

I was still dipping my spoon away from the head when the bowl was wrenched from my hands and the next course served. Ho's is famous for its service, or lack thereof. The Chinese waiters are notoriously surly, and none more so than the owner himself. He came out in a stained singlet and apron and stood, eyeing us unpleasantly. I suspected he and Barker were close friends, but they certainly were discreet about their friendship.

"We shall be away for a few weeks," Barker stated, between selecting morsels of Chinese sweetbread with his chopsticks.

"You could use time away," Ho said. "You are getting sleek and fat."

I nearly swallowed my tongue. I trembled at the thought of anyone daring to make such a suggestion. True, Barker was a good fourteen stone, but I knew from personal experience in the boxing ring that none of it was fat. Barker only smiled, however. He allowed Ho liberties denied to us mere mortals.

Ho stepped away and disappeared into the gloom. The low room was lit by small penny candles and was full of tobacco smoke. After we finished our main entrée—a large, unidentifiable fish, its body cavities filled with some kind of stuffing—Barker contributed his pipe smoke to the general effluvia.

Just then, a man stepped in the door and stood, allowing his eyes to adjust to the meager light. He seemed out of place in this den of anarchists, criminals, and enquiry agents. He looked more like a government accountant or a banker, a thin ascetic-looking fellow, balding at the temples, with a sharp nose, a pointed chin, and very deep-set eyes. He could have played Mephistopheles at the Lyceum.

Having caught my employer's glance, the man raised an eyebrow, then crossed the room to our table.

"Barker," the fellow acknowledged coolly, seating himself across from us. "I hear you had some excitement in Whitehall last night."

"Yes, thanks to your countrymen. Three bombs in one night."

"That many? I only heard two."

"Oh, come now, Seamus. It's not like you to get your facts wrong."

A waiter appeared out of the gloom and bowed to our companion.

"The usual." He turned back to us. "We are all fallible, Cyrus. Even you and me."

"I know I'm fallible," my employer rumbled, "but it's nice to hear you admit the same. Still speculating?"

"A flutter here and there," the fellow admitted. "The pound is strong at the moment."

"And the business enterprises, are they going well?"

"I'd be lying if I said they weren't."

"Is there anything I should know about?"

"Nothing of interest. Is the agency up and running again?"

"Not fully," Barker admitted. "I'll need to have some repairs made. I'm thinking of taking a trip for the duration. Vienna is doing some marvelous improvements in criminalistics."

"Still continuing your oriental studies?" the man asked, stifling a yawn. He seemed like the sort who is interested only in his own pet subjects.

"There is always more to learn."

"And more to acquire."

"Word on the street says you've been buying some paintings lately."

"Word on the street should mind its own bloody business," the fellow snapped. He shrugged his shoulders. "A Bouguereau or two came on the market unexpectedly. I like Bouguereau's little shepherdesses. Innocence interests me."

"You have expensive tastes, Seamus."

"Not at all," he said silkily. "My tastes are simple. I only like the best."

The waiter arrived and then did something rather amazing. He set the man's frugal meal of rice in tea in front of him gently. Where was the rudeness for which Ho's waiters were famous?

"Stay for lunch?"

Barker shook his head. "We have already eaten, and I've got a lot to do before our journey. We'll leave you to your solitary repast. Come, Llewelyn."

The Irishman and I bowed to each other, and wordlessly I followed my employer through the door, down the steps, and across the echoing corridor. It wasn't until we were back on the street looking for a hansom or an omnibus that I broke the silence.

"Was that the fellow on Parnell's list?"

"It was. He often eats lunch at Ho's at this time. His name is Seamus O'Muircheartaigh. He's got his fingers in more pies than a baker: land speculation, stock exchange, high-interest loans, blackmail, extortion."

"My word!"

"Do you remember Nightwine?"

"Sebastian Nightwine?" I did indeed. I'd met him during my

first case with Barker. The fellow was a big-game hunter by trade, but it was rumored he was also attempting to organize London's underworld.

"He has moved on. Africa, I believe. It's his one saving grace: he doesn't stay in one place for long. He sold off his holdings in the East End to O'Muircheartaigh recently, or so I've heard. He always turns a profit."

"So he's little more than a criminal, then."

"Yes, but of the first water. A criminal's criminal. He trained himself by reading Machiavelli's *The Prince*. Some of the money he brings in is funneled through to the Irish Republican Brotherhood. I can't be certain whether he is a true patriot to the cause, or if it is just a good business tactic."

"But you ate with him!" I protested.

"I did not. You saw me leave the moment his food arrived. I refuse to break bread with the man, and he knows it."

"You acted very civil toward him. You called him over. You called him by his Christian name."

"Make no mistake, Thomas. If I could toss him in Wormwood Scrubs today, I would. And if he could splatter my brains across the London cobblestones, he would. We respect each other for our talents and professionalism. We shall treat each other with courtesy until one of us eventually does the other in."

We returned to our office, and for a moment I felt that everything was as it had been. Jenkins was seated at his desk with the *Police Gazette* in his hand, the glaziers had completed their work and gone, and all vestiges of dust and debris had been removed from the waiting room by our clerk's broom and duster. Barker stopped for a moment to discuss with Jenkins a potential client who had appeared in our absence, while I continued into the inner office.

All was not the same here. The carpets were gone, and the

vase was still a stack of shards on the corner of Barker's desk. More obvious was the street urchin who sat in my employer's chair, with his feet on the blotter and a lit cigar from the box the Guv reserved for guests in his hand.

"How'd you get in here?" I demanded. "Get out of Mr. Barker's chair before I drag you out."

"You and the Coldstream Guards," he jeered. "Go soak your head."

I made for him, but he was up and on his feet in a trice, keeping the desk between us and taunting me all the while. As a Classics scholar, I had to admit he had an imaginative way with words. In half a minute, he made my blood boil. I wanted to see just how far my fingers would reach around his throat.

"Ah, Vic," my employer said, suddenly behind me. "Good to see you. I'll take it from here, Llewelyn."

" 'Lo, Push," the tattered boy said. I'd heard Barker called "Push Comes to Shove" in our previous case. " 'Oo's the shirt?"

"Thomas Llewelyn, my assistant. Thomas, this is Soho Vic."

Vic wiped his none-too-clean nose with his hand, then offered it to me to shake. When I refused, he stuck his tongue out and returned to sucking on his cigar, which he was puffing in quick drafts like an engine about to leave a station.

"Found the Sponge for you," he said cryptically.

"Excellent. Where is he?"

" 'Round the corner, paying 'is respects to the Sun. Said 'e'd be 'long directly."

The Guv pulled out a half-sovereign from his waistcoat pocket and proffered it. The boy snatched the shining coin from Barker's fingertips and thrust it between his dirty teeth. It passed inspection there, so he tossed it in the air a few times, as if admiring its weight, before thrusting it into his waistcoat pocket.

"Pleasure doin' business wiff yer, Push. Got other errands to run. Cheerio!"

"You may use the front entrance," Barker said, pointing toward the door.

"No fanks, Guv," came the reply. "Got to 'ave me exercise. Not gettin' any younger, am I? Fanks for the smoke and the beneficence." Then he was gone out the back door, and presumably over the back wall as well.

"Soho Vic," I said to myself. "What names these street arabs have. I assume he was born in Soho?"

"Kraków, Poland," Cyrus Barker informed me. "His real name is Stanislieu Sohovic. It's amazing how foreign names get anglicized, isn't it? Came here with his father when he was still in nappies, then the old man was killed in a boatyard accident. Vic's been fending for himself ever since."

"You trust him to do business, then?"

"As well as any other merchant in London. Any enquiry agent worth his salt uses Vic and his kind to deliver messages and track down people. He's got a number of mouths to feed, and despite his flippant exterior, takes his work very seriously."

"And this . . . this Sponge person will help us find the Irish faction?"

"We can but cast our nets, lad," Barker said, and with that bit of philosophy, nothing more was mentioned of the matter.

The Sponge, if I may call him that, arrived shortly after four, when Jenkins came into our chambers with a calling card in his hand for Barker. It was none too clean, I noticed, and a corner had been creased and straightened. It bore the legend: HENRY CATHCART, ESQ.

"Show him in, Jenkins," Barker said, after a glance at the card.

"Very good, sir," Jenkins replied, but as he passed me he raised his eyebrows as if to say *Wait until you see this one.*

In a moment, our visitor came in, slowly, gravely, as if he were a headmaster at vespers. I saw what had caused Jenkins's brows to flutter. First of all, the fellow had the purple ears, veined cheeks, and swollen nose of the inveterate drinker. His pale eyes did not seem to focus on anything in particular but floated about like poached eggs in water. His clothes were patched, the bottoms of his trousers frayed, and his collar had been worn on both sides, and yet there was something in his well-cut, gray-shot beard and the careful knot of his tie that told me he still cared about his appearance. It had been I who had undergone such a scrutiny of dress when I was hired a little over two months earlier, and now I was doing the scrutinizing. Mr. Cathcart did not come out well. I began to think the Sponge soaked up nothing more than liquor.

Barker rose. "How do you do, Mr. Cathcart?"

"As well as to be expected in this hard world of ours, Your Honor, I thank you. And you?"

"I am well. May I present my assistant, Mr. Thomas Llewelyn?"

The old fellow, if indeed he was old, bowed gravely to me.

"Good afternoon, young man," he said. "I hope you appreciate your position here. There are many who covet it."

"Yes, sir, thank you," I said, wondering if he had been one of the applicants for the position.

"Would you care for a cigar, Mr. Cathcart?" Barker continued, raising the lid of the box on his desk. He was treating the old sot well, I thought.

"I thank you, sir," Cathcart said, taking one from the box and pocketing it. "I shall enjoy it later, with your permission."

"But of course. I would like to avail myself of your services for the week, if you are available."

"As it happens, I am between engagements," the fellow said with a slight air of pomposity, as if he were a master craftsman. "Where might I be working, if I may ask?"

"The Crook and Harp in Seven Dials."

"Ah! The old Crooked Harp. I know it well. The main room

seats over seventy, and the Guinness is always fresh, since they go through it so quickly. A word of warning, however: they water down the whiskey after nine of a Friday night." He tapped the side of his nose with his finger.

"Er, we shall remember that, thank you. Are your terms still the same?"

"Well, sir, I've been much in demand of late among your brethren. I still charge a pound a night, but some have been good enough to add a small remuneration at the end of a case." Cathcart stroked his beard daintily. I had to stop myself from laughing.

"I would expect nothing less. Thomas, give Mr. Cathcart a five-pound note." I took out the note from the wallet I carried for my employer, and then subtracted the amount from the ledger on my desk. Henry the Sponge pulled a change purse from his pocket and folded the bill until it finally fit.

"When shall I report?"

"Friday, before five."

"Is there anything specific I should listen for?"

"Fenian activity involving the bombing of Scotland Yard."

The old man nodded sagely. "Presumed as much. Friday it is, gentlemen." He raised a disreputable bowler an inch off his head, then solemnly made his way out of the room. Something about his stately manner made us go to the bow window and watch as he passed down Craig's Court and into Whitehall Street.

"So, he's an informant. One of your watchers," I said.

"Henry Cathcart has a unique gift. He can slip into a public house unnoticed and drink himself into oblivion."

I smiled. "I gathered that, but so could anyone."

"True, but who else could wake the next morning and be able to repeat word for word every conversation that went on around him all night? They don't call him the Sponge for his intake of alcohol. He's got a horror of the regular police, but he's worked for me on a case or two. He works for whom he wishes and can pick and choose."

We took a cab home and changed for dinner. Though it was just the two of us, Cyrus Barker insisted upon formal attire when we dined together. There were to be no dressing gowns and no lounge suits or smoking jackets. The Guv had stated on several occasions that it is all too easy for standards to slip, and when that happened, it would be easier to glue an eggshell back together than to return things to how they had once been. For my part, I appreciated observing the formal rituals of a genteel life. The moldy garret of three months ago was still recent enough for me to remember how hard the world can be.

We were halfway through dinner, and Barker was making some point about the Irish view of English imperialism, when the telephone rang. My employer frowned. Modern contrivances are all well and good but not when they interrupt dinner.

Mac came in from the hall.

"Sir, there is a telephone call for you."

Barker wiped his mustache with a serviette and muttered, "Confound it," before going into the hall. I assumed it was Anderson, calling to confirm the acceptance from the Home Office of his terms. Mac watched him go and for a moment, everything was quiet, until my eyes registered a sudden movement. Our butler was standing quite still, but one of his hands was gesturing wildly behind his back.

"What is it?" I asked, *sotto voce.*

"The Prime Minister, sir," he said out of the side of his mouth, "on the wire now!"

Jacob Maccabee might have been able to stand still, but I could not. I bolted from my seat and leaned into the hall with my hand on the door frame. The Guv was standing in front of the little alcove in the hall, speaking into the new Ericsson telephone he'd had installed there.

"Yes, sir," he said. "As you say . . . No, I will not do anything to hinder Scotland Yard's investigation. I do not wish credit for the case . . . Thank you, sir. Good evening to you."

Barker hung up the receiver. I backed up, stumbling into Mac, who had been leaning over my shoulder. We almost fell over, but if Barker noticed, he didn't show it.

"Mac."

"Yes, sir," Maccabee said, all dignity and poise again.

"Bring a pot of green tea up to the garret. I shall be up much of the night planning. Thomas, come with me."

I followed him into the library. I believe Barker could tell me the books on every shelf in order, though there didn't seem to be any system to their arrangement. He pulled one book from a lower shelf, then used the ladder on a rail to reach another one on the highest shelf on the opposite wall. He dropped them into my hands, then scooped up the little dog from one of the green leather chairs, and tucked him under his arm as if he were another book.

"Study those. Good night, lad."

The volumes were *Traits and Stories of the Irish Peasantry*, by William Carleton, and an American book called *The Molly Maguires, the Origin, Growth and Character of the Organization*, by F. P. Dewees. I'd never heard of either one.

That was it. Barker went to his room without a word about the Prime Minister. I thought I deserved at least some information. After all, he was risking my neck, too.

6

IT WAS SUNDAY MORNING, AND I HAD GONE UP TO
Barker's room. With its red sloping ceiling lined with weapons, it
is rather bloodthirsty in appearance. On a Sunday, the attention is
drawn to the strong, mote-filled light from the two large sky-
lights, and the room's resemblance to a Mongol leader's campaign
tent rather recedes into the gloom. I was all for talking about the
case, but Barker would have none of it. His Sabbath day mornings
were sacred, literally. He was reading his Bible and slowly emptying his pot of gunpowder green tea into his handleless cup.

"What are our plans for the day?" I asked.

My employer held up a finger, then used it to turn a page in
Deuteronomy, and promptly was engrossed in his reading again. I
was getting nowhere. Barker is like a bad water pipe. I could
spend half the day trying to get something out of him, then he
would gush out in a torrent of words, and promptly clog up
again.

Barker poured me a cup of tea, and I emptied it in one swallow, then grimaced. Green tea is a misnomer, I think. It's more
gold than green, and it tastes more like dishwater than anything

else. I know many people go through a lot of trouble so that the tea grown in Fukien ends up on our Newington breakfast table, but if it were all for my benefit, they needn't have bothered.

I sighed and went downstairs. Sunday is the only morning when Dummolard does not dominate our kitchen. He makes up for his absence with a bakery's worth of sweets. Privileged to be the only other person allowed to touch Etienne's coffeepot, I made myself coffee and looked over the assortment of pastries. Though I was sad to see the apple and caramel pie was gone, I chose a currant scone instead and put a dollop of clotted cream from the larder on top.

After I'd eaten, Barker came down in what I've come to call his Sunday suit, a frock coat less ostentatious than his normal wear, with a black tie. Mac had set out Barker's Bible on the entry table by the door, a book so well thumbed all the lettering on the cover had worn away. We walked the short block to the Baptist Metropolitan Tabernacle and when we got there and were just about to go inside, he made a telling gesture. He reached out and his hand lightly touched one of the marble columns. I knew what he was thinking, for I was thinking the same: How long would it be before we would be enjoying another quiet Sunday here again?

The Reverend Charles Haddon Spurgeon had one or two words to say about peace in his sermon that morning. While many pastors across London were no doubt calling for peace after the recent bombing, Barker's pastor warned us of false peace-makers and assured us that there would be no peace in the world until the Lord's return. It was a pessimistic attitude, perhaps, but I didn't doubt it was true. There is always some deviltry afoot in the world, and not a little of it here in our corner itself.

Afterward, I was looking forward to a nice lunch before whatever my employer had planned for the day, but apparently he thought otherwise. He raised a cane for a cab, rather than shatter the Sabbath peace with one of his whistles, and we bundled in.

"The City!" he called out. "I suppose you can make do with a roll and coffee in the East End until we can eat properly, lad?"

"Certainly, sir," I said. After all, who has need of a nice Sunday dinner when one can eat a tooth-breaking bun topped with stale onions and poppy seeds?

"It is time to visit the Lane, Thomas."

There was no need to ask which lane he was talking about. Our first case had begun when a poor Jewish scholar had been found crucified on a telegraph pole in Petticoat Lane, the City's Sunday market. It is a farrago in the middle of the Jewish quarter, where one can buy everything from Chinese silk to Scottish tweed. Most of the clothing was used, and the Jews were old hands at repairing and reselling items "good as new." Now we were in need of clothing for our disguises as van Rhyn and his assistant, and it would be suspicious if we presented ourselves in a completely new wardrobe. What better place could we have come to than the Lane?

On a normal Sunday, Middlesex Street, to give its more prosaic name, resembles a football scrum, with enough people knotted together to fill half of London. It functions, somehow, and everyone eventually reaches his own destination. Barker, at least, knew where he was going; he stepped up to one of the more established tailor shops, with its hoardings overhead in Hebrew and Roman letters, and spoke to the proprietor. The latter pulled his measuring tape from his pocket and invited us into the shop's interior.

My employer had spent a great deal of money on our wardrobes, most recently equipping me with hats, coats, and shoes, but I was not surprised to see him lift the sleeve of a disreputable-looking garment and ask to try it on. He selected four suits for himself and three for me. We were fitted by the proprietor, who was doing his best to keep his thoughts to himself, if not for his raised eyebrows. I knew what Barker was thinking, however. In our ordinary clothes, we would never be able to fit into a group of Irish misfits and radicals.

"I'll take them all," Barker eventually said, producing a card. "Have them sent to this address."

"Very good, sir," the tailor replied between tight lips. I would have thought he'd have been glad to rid his shop of these items. He took the card and nodded to us as we left.

Passing into Aldgate Street, we hailed a hansom cab. No sooner had we settled in than Cyrus Barker said, "You need a name to use among the Irish."

"I'm not certain whether I could do the accent, sir," I admitted. "Not convincingly, anyway."

"Very well, we'll keep you a Welshman. Easiest is best. Do you have any family names other than Llewelyn?"

"I have an uncle whose surname is Penrith."

"Penrith. That's a good Welsh name. What is his first name?"

"Odweg."

My employer scratched his chin for a moment in thought. "Perhaps we'll just call you Thomas. Thomas Penrith. That's easy for me to remember. Your name is Thomas Penrith. You are from Cardiff and are van Rhyn's assistant, a disaffected student with anarchist beliefs and a grudge against England. You have been trained at Nobel's factory near Glasgow and have worked with your new employer for six months. You have a certain natural ability with explosives, and you show great promise. Have you got that, lad?"

"Yes, sir."

"Excellent. The reason Le Caron has succeeded, and all the others have failed, is that he did not try to pretend to be Irish."

"I say, sir, have we anything else to do this afternoon? I thought I might stop and see Ira Moskowitz and Israel Zangwill. If I may, I'd like to tell them I was leaving town."

"Certainly, lad. See your friends. I'm going out myself. I'll see you back at home for dinner."

I didn't ask where he was going, and I don't think he would have told me had I asked, but I had my suspicions. My employer kept company with a certain woman whose identity one would almost suppose was a state secret. Mac referred to her only as the Widow and she was never to be spoken of. I didn't intend to do so now.

I jumped out and was soon walking down Commercial Street, that great aorta of London trade. Three months before, this area on the east side of the City was unknown to me, but now I knew it as well as the Elephant & Castle. If I had taken anything away with me from our last case, other than several torn ligaments and injured joints, it was my friendship with Israel and Ira. A quick cut up Bell Lane, and a few odd turnings, and I was in Spitalfields. The two of them lived in a boardinghouse for Jewish teachers and scholars. I'd visited enough times that I had become a nuisance to open the door to, and so had been given leave to enter as if I were a boarder. I slipped in, climbed the stairwell to the first floor, and rapped loudly on a door. A voice bade me enter, and I stepped inside.

Israel looked up from his studies. If someone had told me a year before that my two closest friends would be Jews, I would have laughed, having never even met one before, but so they had become. Israel is all head on a stalk of a body, with more nose and less chin than he knows what to do with. At the moment, his nose was propping up a pair of half-moon spectacles, for he had been preparing lessons for his third-form class.

"Thomas!" he cried. "What brings you to Whitechapel?"

"I was wondering if you were interested in sponsoring Ira Moskowitz in the club."

Israel gave me a shrewd look. "You deem him worthy?"

"I deem him unlikely to ever be asked to join any other club," I said.

"You are right there. But I'm just a humble teacher, not a

famous detective's assistant. The fourpence nomination fee might break me. Besides, I sponsored you. It's your turn now."

"Very well, I'll pay. In fact, I'll pay for everything."

"You've ended a case?"

"No. Begun one. I'll explain when we're there."

We quickly liberated Ira from his studies at the yeshiva, and spirited him away to our little club. Ira was mystified at his abduction, and more so when we turned in to St. Michael's Alley, off Cornhill Street, unchanged for two hundred and fifty years. We opened the door of the Barbados, not a private club at all, really, but the most ancient coffeehouse on the street, and bowled him into the dark interior.

The proprietor came forward and bowed. "Good afternoon, Mr. Zangwill, Mr. Llewelyn. Have you brought a guest?"

"We'd like to sponsor this fellow for membership," I said.

The owner looked Ira over doubtfully from head to toe. He does not have a prepossessing exterior. He is stout and pale with wiry hair that flies in every direction, and he wears spectacles. The proprietor bowed again and went to get the membership book, but he shot me a look, which said I was no longer in his good graces.

We sat down in a booth in the common room and caught up on recent history. When the proprietor returned, I plunked down the membership dues, fourpence, the cost of two cups of coffee when the street was built. St. Michael's Alley was the heart of the West Indies trade, bringing coffee, tobacco, cane sugar, cotton, and cocoa back to Europe, hence the club's name, Barbados. Ira was presented with a clay pipe, which he signed with a quill pen, and added his name at the tail of the subscription book. The owner brought Israel and me our own pipes, and we all lit up.

"Three black apollos," I ordered. "Some beef chops from the grill at your convenience and a barrister's torte for our friend."

"Hear, hear," Zangwill agreed.

"This is marvelous," Ira said. "And you say they'll keep this pipe forever?"

"Yes. Upon your death, which we all know shall be a hundred years from now, they shall break it in twain and hang it in a place of honor."

Our coffee arrived, and soon the proprietor set down our freshly grilled chops. Ira's eyes lit up at the sight of food. The poor scholar rarely got enough to eat, and his landlady's inedible cooking was legendary in Whitechapel. A chop and a nice dessert would suit Ira to the ground.

"Gentlemen," I said, looking at my friends, "there's a reason I convened this meeting today, beyond initiating Ira in the mysteries of the Barbados. I'll be gone for a while, close to a month, I think. It's a case, of course. It is dangerous, but Barker sounds confident that we'll succeed. That's about all I'm allowed to say."

"We understand, Thomas. We'll say a prayer for you," Zangwill said.

"Thank you," I said.

After our meal and a final pipe, we surrendered our clay churchwardens to the proprietor and watched him settle them in racks overhead. We hesitated to leave, or at least I did. I didn't know when I'd be back here again, enjoying a pipe and cup and the company of my best friends. In fact, the odds were in favor of my not returning at all. Out in Cornhill Street, I hailed a cab, and solemnly shook hands with each of them.

"We'll see you in a month, then," Zangwill said.

Ira reached for my hand, then stopped. "Wait! Thomas, lend me a shilling!"

I shrugged my shoulders, and pulled the coin from my trouser pocket. "Here you are. What's this all about?"

"Now you're sure to come back alive," he said. "People don't die when someone owes them money. I would never be so lucky as to have someone to whom I owed money pass away!"

"Listen to him, Thomas," Israel said. "There is wisdom there."

Twenty minutes later, when I was reaching the step of Barker's domicile, there was a clatter behind me, and his cab pulled up to the curb. He nodded and we went in together. Mac appeared from his little sanctum sanctorum off the lobby and took our hats and sticks.

"Mac," our employer said, "Thomas and I shall be away for about a month, and I want the house to remain open while we're gone."

"Very good, sir," Jacob Maccabee responded. He took our leaving in stride, though I knew it would alter his schedule even more than our own. There was packing to be done and arrangements to be made. Mac is a very capable fellow and an excellent servant. I have nothing against him beyond the fact that he despises me. I think he is jealous that I get to go out and have desperate adventures with Barker, while he stays home and polishes the silver.

"The garden must still be tended, and there is no need to shut the house up for just a few weeks. Besides, it would upset Harm's schedule."

I saw Mac's lip curl slightly. The dog was the bane of his existence. Harm shed a pound of hair daily, chewed up the cushions, and spent half the afternoon by the back door, deciding whether he wanted in or out. The thought that he would be forced to stay alone in the house merely to look after this little oriental demon must have made Mac's blood boil.

"Couldn't he stay with *her*, sir?"

Had I been a dog myself, my ears would have perked up. I knew whom Mac was speaking of. Harm had received a savage kick during a little contretemps in our garden during our first case together, and had been taken away and nursed by a heavily veiled woman all in black. I had handed the dog into her lap in a mysterious black brougham. It turned out that she came and tended Harm regularly once a week, at six in the morning, before I got up. I was very curious about her. What did she look like behind the veil? Was she young or old? What was her position? I had tried to question Mac about her, and got nothing out of him.

"No," Barker said with finality. "Were it November, I might have considered it, but it is June. I cannot deprive Harm of his afternoons sunning in the garden. It would put him quite out of sorts."

I had to cough to smother a laugh. Barker doted on Harm, or Bodhidharma, to use his full name. He fancied the dog something between an English gentleman and a Chinese prince. Mac, on the other hand, generally used the term "mangy cur" when describing the dog, though not in our employer's presence, of course. I looked over at Harm, who wagged his plumed tail. I could swear the little rascal knew we were talking about him.

"You sound as if you've got this all planned out," I said to my employer, after Mac had slithered away in abject misery. "Would you mind telling me a bit more about our itinerary?"

"First thing tomorrow, you're going to Aldershot to study bomb making under Johannes van Rhyn for a week," Barker informed me. "And then, in the evening—"

There was a sudden sharp rat-a-tat of someone beating his stick on the front door. Despite the fact that we have a perfectly good knocker—a brass affair in the shape of a thistle—the fellow smote the wood. It set the dog off immediately, shrieking until Mac tossed him into the library and closed the door before answering the summons. Not knowing what to expect, I removed a stout cane from the stand, just in case.

"Yes, sir?" Mac asked our visitor upon opening the door.

"I wish to speak to Mr. Barker," an angry voice answered.

"Who shall I say is calling, sir?"

—

"Chief Inspector James Munro of the Special Irish Branch, my man."

Barker came up beside his butler.

"Thank you, Mac, that will be all. Good evening, Chief Inspector. Won't you and your colleagues step in?"

Three sturdy men entered our hallway. The inspector was the smallest but also the most commanding. He was a bullet-headed little fellow, with a thick mustache and a beetling brow. His assistants could not be taken individually. They were oversize bookends to the inspector's single compact volume.

"Barker, I need to know what was discussed at the Home Office yesterday morning."

"Mr. Anderson is in charge," my employer stated. "You must take it up with him."

"Don't cut up clever with me, Barker, or we can discuss this at Scotland Yard."

"Certainly not in your office," the Guv retorted, "unless it is to be an outside meeting."

Munro turned red, trying to control his temper. "This is a Special Irish Branch case. We don't need an outsider coming in and gumming up the works."

"The Home Office seems to think otherwise. Robert Anderson hired me to work for them and I intend to do so. I suppose you could say Llewelyn and I have joined the secret police."

"You can't expect to investigate a case from inside Newgate Prison," Munro blustered.

"On what charge, may I ask?"

"On suspicion. You'd be surprised at how long I can hold someone on suspicion."

My stomach seemed to drop away from me. One cannot understand how a former prisoner feels when confronted by incarceration again.

"Should you attempt to detain me, Munro," Barker said as easily as if they were discussing a game of whist, "I will see that my solicitor calls on Mr. Anderson. He in turn shall call upon Prime Minister Gladstone and the Prime Minister shall summon Commissioner Henderson and Superintendent Williamson. The superintendent shall then summon you and ask you what you are about, locking up hired agents of the Home Office. Have you been apprised that Scotland Yard will get the credit should we succeed?"

"I am highly suspicious of your little arrangements, Barker."

"I certainly don't want credit for capturing and imprisoning Irish terrorists," Barker said. "It would be like putting a price upon my own head. I have nothing like your resources, and still your offices were blown up."

Munro stepped forward, toe to toe with Barker, though my employer was a good head taller. "Why are you getting involved?" he demanded. "You've lost a little glass. You can afford it."

Barker shrugged his beefy shoulders. "I don't need to give my reasons to you, Chief Inspector. Anderson offered a price and I accepted it. That is hardly your concern."

"We shall take the blame if you foul things up."

"Foul things up?" Barker rumbled. I could see his own temper rising. "Foul things up! You haven't successfully protected your own offices, let alone London. Didn't the danger of having public lavatories so close to Scotland Yard occur to you? A child could see it!"

Munro stepped back and glowered as menacingly as he could. "When the corner of Scotland Yard is rebuilt, I shall see to it that the former gymnasium is turned into offices. Your precious physical training classes shall be a thing of the past."

"Very well, but you can't blame me the next time one of your constables snaps the neck of a fellow while trying to subdue him, when his only crime was a few too many pints of a Saturday evening."

"You'd best watch your step," the chief inspector threatened.

"That will be impossible, since my assistant and I shall be out of town for a month or so. Would you like an itinerary, or shall I just send you a *carte postale* along the way? I promise to send word when we return, in plenty of time for you to claim all the credit and glory."

Munro opened his mouth to reply, could think of nothing more to say, and stormed out, leaving his satellites standing like maids at the gas-fitters' ball awaiting a dance. They nodded to each other and left. Barker closed the door with his foot, then slammed the bolt home with an angry fist.

" 'But whosoever shall say, Thou fool, shall be in danger of hell fire.' Matthew five: twenty-two," he growled, still trying to control his temper. "Some verses are harder to keep than others."

7

BARKER SAW ME OFF AT WATERLOO STATION THE next morning. I had to admit I was going with some trepidation, though I tried not to show it. I'd never been at a military barracks before, and van Rhyn was a complete cipher to me. The thought occurred to me as well that if I mixed two parts A with one part B, instead of the other way 'round, I might not be coming back at all.

"You'll get on, lad," my employer assured me, as if reading my thoughts.

"Yes, thank you, sir," I said, but my mind couldn't help but go back to something he'd said to me during our first adventure: *You'll get on. Or you won't.*

I boarded the Great Western express, and by the time I found my seat, Barker had slipped off. I sat, let out a sigh, and suddenly wished I'd brought one of my books to study. I spied a bookstall among the other shops in the station and jumped out, knowing I had but a moment or two. The stall specialized in mystery thrillers and women's publications. I'd been hoping for something more classical. Just when I was about to give up and jump back on the train empty-handed, I spied a book on old Irish legends. I handed over a few shillings and hopped on the footboard just as the final command to board was shouted out. I settled in my seat and began to read.

Since childhood, my brain had been steeped in the old Welsh legends, of Prince Pwyll and the underworld of Annwn, not to mention Arthur and his Round Table. The book in my hand was full of tales new to me, featuring the Irish heroes, Cú Chulainn and Finn MacCool, as they faced giants and Grendel-like monsters in the misty land of old Hibernia, and all this just a short boat journey from Pwyll's kingdom. Times were certainly exciting in those ancient days, though they were not exactly a stroll through Hyde Park now, considering where I was headed at the moment.

I received the first sign that I was nearing my destination half an hour later when we passed a brigade of soldiers in their scarlet tunics and chalky helmets, marching in full kit. I was accustomed to seeing the Horse Guards rattling through Whitehall on their chargers, gold helmets gleaming, but the lads marching on this road in the drowsy June sun would soon be fighting the Mahdi's fanatical hordes in the blistering heat of North Africa.

Ought I to join them? The thought of going for a soldier had never really occurred to me before. I'm certain that several of the lads I'd gone to school with were even now in the Sudan, and some had already given their lives while I'd been at university, wrestling with nothing more dangerous than *Paradise Lost*. Now I was employed by Barker. Were the words on the placards at the station correct? Was it my duty to go and fight for my country? As I sat in the railway carriage, I realized that I was already a soldier, a mercenary one, newly hired by Her Majesty's government to safeguard the English way of life, and the Irish were a good deal closer than the Mahdi's Muslims in the Sudan that the papers were thundering about. Suddenly, I missed my Milton.

The train stopped at Aldershot, and I was able to cadge a ride to the barracks aboard the supply vehicle, once I supplied an abbreviated version of my purpose in coming. We followed the canal and soon found ourselves riding down a wide thoroughfare, a parade ground in which a dozen men could walk abreast. Off in the distance, I saw a long line of buildings, clusters of huts and barracks which collectively were known as North Camp. I began to wonder if we'd actually sent anyone to the Sudan at all. The whole English army appeared to be here. As I stepped out into a beehive of activity, I felt as if I were the only man in civilian dress within one hundred miles.

Everyone but me appeared to be moving with a purpose. My attempts at stopping someone to ask for directions were rebuffed several times. I thought I might spend the day searching in vain for the address Barker had given me on a slip of paper, when I finally found a chaplain who was willing to show me the way. It was a good thing, too. My next plan would have been to announce in a loud voice that I was a Russian spy, there to steal the plans to the Northern Frontier.

I was led to an outbuilding set far back from the others, whose doors and windows were open. As I stepped inside, and my eyes adjusted to the relative gloom, a voice spoke up.

"You are late!" the fellow protested grumpily, but I had passed a clock tower on the parade road, and had noted the time.

"No, actually, I'm still a quarter hour early."

The speaker, a squat, slovenly-looking fellow in a white lab coat, consulted his timepiece, held it to his ear, and shrugged.

"No matter. I am van Rhyn."

So, I thought to myself, *this is the fellow Barker is to impersonate.* They didn't look much alike. Johannes van Rhyn was a much shorter, rounder fellow, for one thing. His thick, graying hair was in wiry strands combed back severely behind his ears, and his short beard looked as if it were made of steel wool. His face, like my employer's, was dominated by a pair of black spectacles, but van Rhyn's had brownish glass pieces covering the sides. They are commonly worn by the blind, but he appeared to see perfectly. He had a ferocious nose which curled over his mustache, and his tie and linen were stained and in need of pressing.

"You are Llewelyn?"

"Yes, sir. Thomas Llewelyn."

"As you say. Bombs, sir. You are here to learn bombs."

The word came out *bompss* in van Rhyn's German accent.

"Yes, sir."

"Good! Now, a bomb by definition is a device exploded by means of a fuse or by impact or otherwise. By a chemical process, energy is released very quickly, often with devastating results. Bombs are often made of common materials one can pick up anywhere. Look at this here. What is this?"

"It is a bottle of whiskey, sir."

"*Ja.* Now you see, I take a strip of cotton and insert it in the bottle, and push it in tightly with a bit of cork. Now we have a bomb. It is inert, of course, and could sit on a shelf for years, completely harmless. But, if I light the cotton from this Bunsen burner, like so, we begin the reaction that results in a chemical change."

He handed me the bottle with a look of mild interest, as if I were one of his experiments. The cotton hanging out next to the cork was already emitting a large flame. I knew enough from my chemistry classes in school to say what would happen next. If I didn't get rid of it immediately, the cotton would burn past the cork, ignite the liquid inside, and the entire bottle would explode. A glance about the room told me I was surrounded on all sides by beakers and bottles of various compounds and chemicals. Even if we did survive the initial blast, the explosion might ignite the chemicals around us and kill us for certain. I did the only sane thing: I turned and tossed the bottle out of the door. There was a sudden loud report, and the walls and windows outside were showered with fragments of glass.

"Lesson one," van Rhyn said. "After you set a bomb, get rid of it. Very good reflexes, by the way."

"My word!" I said. "You nearly got us killed!"

"There is little chance of that," van Rhyn assured me. "The urge for self-preservation takes over, you see. It is a powerful force."

"I'm glad of that," I said, my heart still racing.

"Come. Look here. Each of these materials can be turned into an infernal device. Here is ammonia, isopropyl alcohol, glycerin soap, common manure. A trained bomb maker would find an average home a treasure trove of materials. A few ingredients from a local chemist are also helpful. In these bottles are sulfur, magnesium, and sulfuric acid. Of course, we need not start from scratch every time. Here are primers, timers, fuses, blasting caps, a plunger. This cylinder is an artillery shell."

"I must say, it seems strange to see a notorious bomber with his own explosives hut, in the middle of an army base," I said.

"*Ja,* well, there was a time when I would have blown myself to bits before working for a government agency, but since then, I have learned to listen to the demands of the stomach. That, perhaps, and the fact that I have been deported from most of the countries in Europe. I have no desire to leave this one. Luckily for me, Britannia is a sentimental old girl, and she has hugged many a socialist, nihilist, and anarchist to her bosom while her sisters have shown us the door."

"Yes," I countered, "but they seem to have you under lock and key here."

"She is sentimental but not stupid. Have no worries for me, young man. I've blown my way out of worse situations than this, when it suited me. I am comfortable here. For one thing, I am not being pestered by factions such as the amateurs who tried to blow up Scotland Yard."

"What do they have you working on, may I ask?"

"A new and improved form of dynamite at their request, a malleable form that can be pressed under a bridge or against a building. To tell you the truth, I am tinkering with it but not very hard. I have reached the twilight of my life, and this is the best an old bomb maker like me can expect. Believe me when I say I have no intention of giving anyone yet another and more dangerous type of bomb with which to inflict more carnage on the world."

"How did you meet Mr. Barker?" I asked.

"He scooped me up in the street. I had only been in London a few days, and he hailed me from a passing cab. He said he recognized me from a photograph in an obscure Yiddish newspaper, the only one I have allowed to be taken of me. He took me to the most unusual restaurant."

"Chinese?" I asked.

"*Ja!* They served rice and watery tea and animal parts that even a witch would refuse. Your master is a very unusual fellow, but—what is the Scottish word? Very *canny.*"

"I'm sure he'd say the same about you," I commented.

"I? I am merely an old tinkerer. One day some Serbian anarchists came into my laboratory in Bonn to ask if a bomb could be fitted into a coronation crown. The would-be king was deposed, it turned out, before he could be crowned, but I'd made the device and my career was born. My most difficult assignment was to build a bomb into the revolver belonging to a Russian general. I hollowed out the cylinder and handle, and filed the barrel down to the final inch. When it blew up, it took him and several of his closest subordinates with him."

"Amazing," I said, trying not to picture the carnage. "And what, if I may ask, are your politics?"

"I thought that would be obvious, young man. Like all makers of wholesale destruction, I am a pacifist. The bad thing about war is that it makes more evil people than it can take away, as Kant said. But come. We have work to do."

I spent the morning assembling a picric bomb, the small metal sphere one sees in political cartoons, then we took it out and exploded it in a small bunker that had been dug for the purpose. Van Rhyn pointed out the pieces of shrapnel on all sides of the dirt walls and described in too-vivid terms the results if my sphere had been thrown under the carriage of the Czar or Emperor Franz Josef. At least he stopped at mentioning the Queen.

We ate in a small mess, a term which in every way describes the lunch I had there, then returned to the eccentric bomb maker's little potting shed laboratory. Van Rhyn seemed no more particular about food than Barker, and he came away wearing much of it on his beard and shirtfront. He had another similarity to my employer, I thought, which was a detached air, as if while speaking to you, he was also thinking other, deeper thoughts. With van Rhyn it was abstruse chemical formulas and shrapnel trajectory, while with Barker . . . well, one never knew with Barker. He was either contemplating the universe or figuring out the most expedient way to get someone in a headlock.

In the afternoon, we made our own version of Mr. Nobel's dynamite. We started out with a bowlful of crystalline silica, which van Rhyn insisted was known as kieselguhr, and a test tube that contained a yellowish liquid that he informed me was nitro-glycerin.

"This is very unstable. The least thing could cause it to blow up—sudden jarring, a change in temperature. I would swear that sometimes it explodes out of sheer bad temper. I am very vain, Mr. Llewelyn, about the fact that I have all ten of my fingers, and each one is intact. You don't know how many of my associates are missing digits. It is the badge of our profession. We are not a long-lived group, you see, and so far, there has been no need for pensions."

One would think pouring some crystals into a cardboard tube, saturating them with liquid, and attaching a fuse and primer would be a matter of a few minutes, but producing dynamite is a slow and dangerous process. The kieselguhr is supposed to stabilize the nitroglycerin, so it can be transported and handled safely, but the old bomb maker handled the harmless-looking length of tubing far more gingerly than the lethal-looking sphere of the picric bomb. He also made sure the length of the fuse was long enough for us to get far away. Van Rhyn lit a little German cheroot that looked like a sausage, and used it to light the dynamite. He tossed it into the bunker and we didn't need an invitation to run as fast as our legs would carry us. The second explosion was much louder than the first. I momentarily lost my hearing, and there was a high-pitched ringing in my ears when we came back to explore the bunker. Actually, "hole" would be a better word now. The shape had been altered from a rough rectangle to a circle, and there was a concentric ring of dirt clods around it. Van Rhyn was going on about the purity and simplicity of explosives, but I was catching only every fifth or sixth word.

That was my introduction to the world of bomb making. Johannes van Rhyn promised that the next day we would explore low-impact bomb making, followed by high-impact explosions on the next; and near the end, the course would conclude with me actually making my own nitroglycerin from scratch in van Rhyn's little lab. I wasn't looking forward to that. For one thing, I'm awfully fond of my fingers, every last one of them.

"Allow me, sir," the German said, taking a heavily carved walking stick from a corner, and locking the windows and doors, "to walk you partway to the station."

"That is almost two miles," I said. "There is really no need."

"I am a great walker, young man," van Rhyn told me. "It shall give us a chance to talk further. How long have you been working for Mr. Barker?"

"About two months, sir."

"This is quite a plan Barker has concocted," he said. "Your employer will have to keep his wits about him, but he is essentially correct. The Irish have laid hands upon a supply of old industrial-use dynamite from America, but it had degraded. Some of it will no longer explode, and some will at the slightest provocation. They need an explosives expert, and I am the only recognized authority. I have been wooed by the Irish before. Some of them tried to recruit me half a year ago."

"Really?" I asked. I was curious about the old German. "Why didn't you join their organization, if I may ask?"

"I thought it unlikely that they would win, and I had just arrived in England and did not relish the idea of being thrown out."

Van Rhyn and I walked along the side of the wide road talking, while uniformed soldiers marched and drilled at our elbows.

"So how did you get tossed out of your own country?" I asked.

"There was a little misunderstanding. Filling a statue of Bismarck with explosives did not necessarily mean that I wished it to be delivered to the Iron Chancellor himself."

"Of course not," I said, wondering what the English authorities would think of a hollow statue of Her Majesty, filled with explosives. "But, tell me, what do you get out of this?"

"Well, Mr. Llewelyn, I have been promised a small remuneration from your boss, but, principally, I am paying off a debt. It was he who helped to secure me this work. He spoke to the army, and told them who I was. They are not pushing me here, and, for once, I have room and board and a place to work in peace. They let me alone most of the time, and they are never so happy as when I blow something up. We shall make them very happy this week."

"Do you really think you can train me in a week?"

"Well enough," van Rhyn said. "If you can show them a few simple tricks, they will take you for a genius. My impression is that the slightest thing will impress them. Here we are."

We were at the gate near the entrance to the drive. I had driven through in the cart before.

"Is this where you stop?" I asked.

"*Ja*. They do not use the word 'prisoner' around me, Mr. Llewelyn, but I cannot exactly walk about freely. The English are not so stupid as to let a German bomber go anywhere he wishes. Tomorrow morning, then. Be early. And bring some schnapps, if you can find some. All I can find here is English beer and Scotch whiskey."

"Schnapps, then. Good day, sir. Thank you for the lesson."

As the train steamed out of the station back toward London, I wondered to myself what would happen if I couldn't remember all the instructions that were to be given to me during this all too brief week of training. Could I carry out such complex instructions, in the midst of trying times? Then, a worse thought gripped me. What would happen if I could?

8

————◆————

I CAME HOME TIRED FROM MY DAY AT ALDERSHOT. The work itself hadn't been strenuous, but emotionally I'd been conscious the entire afternoon that any moment I might be atomized. It did not make for a relaxing day, and I still had four more to go.

Having the cab drop me in the alleyway, I lifted the small ornamental latch and opened the moon gate. I always liked going from the rather ugly and prosaic alleyway into a miniature Eden. The latch clicks home and one is in another world entirely: a stream mutters, a small windmill turns. Birds come from miles around to congregate in our garden.

Using one of the little tricks Barker taught me, I inhaled slowly through my nose, then exhaled through my mouth, mentally sloughing off all the details and distractions that had mounted since breakfast. I'm not as good at it as Barker, of course. It took me a couple of times before I got it all out. I passed by an archipelago of black basalt rocks in a sea of white stones. One of the rocks stirred and looked at me. It was Harm, of course. He had a way of blending in among the elements of the

————◆————

garden, as he had the first day I'd seen him, when he'd imperson-
ated a bush. I wondered if it was accidental, or if Barker had
trained him—if in fact the little creature was able to be trained at
all.

I came into the dining room just as Barker was finishing his
meal, a feast consisting of roasted capon, potatoes with chives, an
asparagus salad, rolls and butter, and lemon curd tarts. Barker's
little teapot sat on the end of the table, and my own silver coffeepot had been swathed in a linen towel, to keep it hot.

"Ah, Thomas," my employer said. "Tuck in, lad. How was
your training?"

"Good, I think, sir," I said, helping myself to a slice of breast
from the platter. "You knew what you were about when you said
van Rhyn was eccentric. He realizes the need to stick to the schedule, however. I believe I can bear it for a week."

"Good. A week is all we'll get, I'm afraid. You shall be interested to learn that I have eliminated one suspect today. It is Rossa.
He is on a liner bound for New York at the moment. He's booked
for a lecture tour. Davitt is doing much the same thing in
Scotland, but with the railways as fast and efficient as they are, he
could be here in a matter of hours."

Barker charged one of his little handleless cups with green gunpowder tea, and sipped while I ate. Just then, there was a knock at
our door. Barker got up, as if he'd been expecting a visitor.

Maccabee answered it, but the Guv was no more than a few
steps behind him. I thought it might be Inspector Poole, but when
Barker raised his voice, I distinctly heard him say "Pierre." I put
down my fork and turned around, expecting our visitor to be
shown into the sitting room behind me. Instead, they all seemed
to vanish. I wiped my mouth and put my head out into the hallway. It was empty. My ear told me they hadn't gone upstairs. I
walked to the end of the hall, but the back door was bolted and
the kitchen and library empty. That left only one place where

they could be. I opened the narrow door that led to the basement and crept downstairs.

Barker was waiting impatiently in our basement room, skirting the mat where we often practiced our physical culture throws. He was alone. I was about to make some comment when the door to our lumber room opened and a man stepped out. He was about my own size but a great deal more muscular. His hair was brilliantined to a high gloss, and his black mustache waxed to points, as Le Caron's had been. There was nothing absurd about this fellow, however, and he wore a leather coat much like a fencing master's tunic.

"Pierre, Thomas Llewelyn, my assistant," Barker said. "Thomas, Pierre Vigny, of the Swiss Army, attached to the military college at Aldershot."

"At your service, sir," the Swiss said with a sharp bow and a click of his heels.

"At yours," I responded.

He looked me over speculatively, as if I were a horse he was considering buying. I cast an enquiring glance toward my employer.

"All the faction cells are trained in stick fighting, lad, and I thought it possible we might have to defend ourselves. I couldn't find an Irishman willing to teach his art to us, but Pierre here is the leading expert in the next best thing, *la canne.*"

"Cyrus," Vigny chided with a wounded air. "You make it sound as if what I teach is inferior. Besides, you know I have made many improvements in the art of *la canne.*"

"My apologies, *maître,*" Barker said, bowing.

"Accepted. Leave this little fellow to me."

"I do have something to attend to," Barker said. "Thomas, I shall see you in the morning."

"Go, go," Vigny said impatiently, waving him away.

To think I should live to see the day when Barker was dismissed in his own home like a schoolboy. Whoever this little fellow was, he was big enough to have my employer defer to him. I watched the man I'd seen order half London about bow almost meekly and climb the stairs, leaving us alone. He didn't even issue the grumble he generally did when he felt put upon.

"Mr. Llewelyn." Vigny called me out of my reverie. "I do not think you realize how fortunate you are to have been chosen to learn my art. I have reserved it solely for the officers of the Swiss and the British armies. Only a friend of your employer's caliber could have prevailed upon me to give you private instruction. It is unfortunate that we have less than a week for something which should logically take a lifetime to learn, but as I have trained your employer, I hope the two of you will continue to practice together. He tells me you have had some experience in fencing and singlestick."

"Just a little in school, sir," I told him. "I never progressed beyond foil."

"That is good. I do not want you to bring bad fencing habits into our *La Canne* training. Take this," he said, placing a slender walking stick in my hand. "What do you suppose this wood is?"

I turned the stick over in my hands and examined it. It was made of some sort of light-colored wood with a silver knob at one end. When I held it in both hands, it flexed. "Willow, perhaps?"

"Very close, sir. It is actually malacca from Malaysia. Very strong and flexible, as you can see. One can lean upon it and it remains rigid, but one flick with the ball and it curves around a sword or another stick enough to deliver a sound thrashing. Like so." He took up a second, identical one, and began to swing it by the bare tip back and forth; it hummed like an angry bee. I thought I wouldn't want to be on the receiving end of that silver head, which was just what happened next.

"Ow!" I cried, holding a hand over my waistcoat pocket, where it felt as if he'd just broken one of my ribs.

"My apologies," the little Swiss said. "It is necessary to feel the effects of the stick firsthand before one can learn. It stings, no? Rub your hand across the wound several times, swiftly. It will pass. From the day the earliest man picked up a fallen branch to defend himself, it has been his boon companion. A pity that it is only now, with the advent of the pistol, that Pierre Vigny was born, to turn stick fighting into an art."

I let the last remark pass without comment, though inwardly I smiled at the conceit.

"But come, sir," he continued. "Time is precious, and we have much to do. Take the position on the floor, as I do, with your feet at a ninety-degree angle. Step forward with your right foot, but keep most of your weight on the back one."

By the end of the lesson two hours later, I had shed my jacket and was perspiring freely, unlike my leather-clad companion, who looked fresh enough to go on for several more hours. I'd had a long day at Aldershot and had been looking forward to a tranquil night, studying the books Barker had given me. Instead, I was remarking to myself that while I was well paid, as far as my employer was concerned, my time belonged to him. I would sleep well that night, provided he didn't have yet another instructor waiting somewhere in the wings. What was left to teach me, Irish Gaelic?

Gradually, as my blocks got lower and weaker, Vigny saw that my arms were growing tired, not to mention sore. One of my hands was swollen from a sound whack, an ear was stinging, and I lost count of the number of blows he'd administered to my ribs or the top of my head, which would now interest a phrenologist.

"That is all for tonight." Maître Vigny stood in the formal stance, holding his stick vertically in front of his face. I did the same. He swished it forcefully down and away, and bowed.

"Your arms will be a trifle tired in the morning, Mr. Llewelyn. I suggest you do not coddle them. A few choice strokes with the cane in the air to improve the circulation will be beneficial. I give you the malacca stick from my personal collection as a present."

"Thank you, sir," I said, surprised he'd give away such a beauty.

"Now, go take a hot bath in Cyrus's bathhouse and go to bed. . . . Well, go! Don't take all night."

"Yes, sir."

I awoke the next morning feeling like one of those bodies that had been unearthed from Pompeii: calcified, hard as stone. "A trifle tired" were not the words I would have used myself. I felt my exercises since becoming injured two months before had all been for naught. I was back to where I had started, unable to wave my arms.

Lying there immobile for the rest of the day seemed an excellent plan, but Mac had other ideas. He was throwing open curtains and welcoming the day in a rather loud voice.

"I've brought you some liniment, sir. I made it myself. It should do the trick for those sore muscles."

I pushed myself into an upright position. There was a fresh cup of coffee next to an unlabeled blue bottle. I pulled the cup and saucer off the desk. They felt as heavy as a bucket of water, and I nearly dropped them.

"It will be warm today, I think. Your train leaves the station in about ninety minutes."

"Thank you, Mac," I said, hobbling to the window. It was nearly six. I watched the activity in the garden in my nightshirt while drinking the coffee. There were over half a dozen Chinese men toiling with rakes and hoes and clippers.

"Shall I set out your clothes?" Mac asked solicitously. Ordinarily I thought him as solicitous as a landlord on rent day. He was enjoying seeing me in pain.

"I'll get my own clothes, thank you," I said.

In the four days since the bombing, the only success I could see in this case was the progress of Barker's beard. With the thick stubble on his chin, he looked less the successful London detective and more the convict or pirate.

"That you, lad?" Barker called from his rooftop aerie as soon as I closed the door to my room behind me. He may have had no ear for music, but his hearing was keen enough. I climbed the stairs and found him, as usual, sitting in front of his fireplace, though the grate was empty and all the dormer windows open to the warm June sun.

"How did your training go last night?" he asked. He was feeding a saucer full of tea to Harm. Barker doted on that dog, who was living a life of idle leisure, while I was being sent hither and yon and being trained in lethal arts by foreign masters.

"Good, sir, but I strained my arms a little. They are sore this morning."

"Shake them out," he said. "Lift the Indian clubs for five minutes before you leave."

Harm had finished the tea and was panting a little in the warm room, but for a moment, I swore that the dog was laughing at me.

"Yes, sir. How was your errand yesterday?"

"Er . . . it was fine, lad," Barker said, looking a little uncomfortable.

"Learn anything new?"

"My errand did not involve the case," he answered a trifle frostily. "Dummolard had just put on coffee, when I was downstairs a few minutes ago. You mustn't forget your breakfast and your Indian clubs before you leave."

Dummolard had taken over his kitchen again. He was smoking one of his short French cigarettes and transferring the contents of a pan into a waiting piecrust.

"What are you making?" I asked, pouring myself a cup of coffee. "It smells wonderful."

"Quiche Lorraine. I shudder to think what refuse the two of you shall live on while you are gone."

I looked over to the counter, where there were three more pie shells waiting for fillings.

"You are cooking for the restaurant here?" I asked.

"*Non,*" Etienne replied. "*Mon capitaine* has given me orders. I am to fatten him up. He wishes to gain at least half a stone by the end of the week. Meat pies, quiches, venison stews. You may be blown to bits next week, but for now, you shall eat like kings."

I couldn't help but feel there was a more tactful way of putting that.

9

THE DAYS RAN TOGETHER AFTER THAT. TUESDAY through Friday were all of a pattern: exercise in the morning, to counteract the soreness of my arms; the short trip to Aldershot during which time I read the books Barker had given me; training with van Rhyn in the making of explosives; the journey home; a heavy meal, watching my employer stuff food into his mouth as if his life depended on it while I wondered if it did; combative training with Maître Vigny, during which I was thumped so often I began to feel like a drum; my much anticipated bath, accompanied by Epsom salts for the pain; then, blessed slumber.

The books were instructive. Carleton's treatise on the Irish poor was about the rise of the factions and how stick fighting came to be the natural defense of Ireland. At its heyday in the early part of the century, whole villages used to go at each other with sticks and rocks, the way one parish will challenge another now to a cricket match. Apparently, they'd match blow for blow until sundown, when one town was declared the victor. The women pitched into the fight along with the men; and in fact, in Irish culture, they were considered equal to men.

The other book was even worse. It was the story of a group of Irish coal miners in the United States during the 1870s, who had banded together to form a union against the mine owners. The Molly Maguires had carried out assassinations, bullied its own members to keep them in line, and dynamited mine shafts and buildings. The mine owners had hired a Pinkerton agent to infiltrate the gang, and he had barely escaped with his life. Perhaps Barker thought the volume informative, but just then, it was a little too close to what we were about to do for my comfort. It was a relief to get back to the Irish legends when I was done. Cú Chulainn fighting a hideous monster was far more remote than a secret society of Irish miners beating a man to death for turning traitor.

I had brought Herr van Rhyn his schnapps, and he had trained me in several types of bomb making as well as how to acquire materials, both legally and illegally. The German showed me some of the latest work he was doing—whether for the English army or not—and on the final day, we made nitroglycerin from scratch, which process gives the bomb maker a terrible headache. I wasn't expecting a diploma or certificate when I was done, but van Rhyn seemed satisfied with what I had learned. At the Home Office's request, he would be under double guard and his walks curtailed until our assignment was done in case the Irish should catch on that Barker was not who he said he was and try to see if van Rhyn was still sequestered here. Before I left, he extracted a promise that I would return someday with another bottle of schnapps and a detailed account of our adventure.

As for Pierre Vigny, I have never seen a man so obsessed. To him, the world began and ended with a stick. He had gathered every reference ever written about the use of the stick, from Aaron's rod to Napoleon's sword cane. He'd studied primitive cultures for their use of cudgels and tried to reconstruct their techniques. The fiercer the battle between us, the more his eyes lit up and a smile grew on his face. I don't know how good I was, but I loved the feel of the wood and felt an affinity for it that I would never feel for a dagger or my revolver. On the final day, he finished up the lesson by informing me that I had gone from the beginning to the apprentice stage. Barker was present, and I think he looked on with some degree of satisfaction.

I was the one that was dissatisfied. With all these train rides and nightly instruction, I had been removed from the actual investigation. What of Davitt and Dunleavy, and that cool fellow from Ho's, O'Muircheartaigh? Had anything turned up on Parnell, and how close were the Special Irish Branch to finding the secret faction? Just how much had Henry the Sponge soaked up, besides five pounds' worth of alcohol? These were the questions I put to Barker when I returned to the office a little early from my final lesson with van Rhyn, my head thumping from the chemicals I'd inhaled during the nitroglycerin-making process.

"One at a time, lad. All your questions shall be answered," Barker said, from the recesses of his leather chair, as placid as a Tibetan lama. He didn't have the demeanor of a man about to set out on a dangerous mission. I still didn't know where we were going. It could be Dublin or Manchester or Paris. The faction could even be concealed in London, for all I knew.

"Are we closer to finding out the leader of the faction?" I asked casually.

Barker looked over his tented fingers. "We've already ruled out Rossa, Davitt, and Cusack. I'll admit I'm not certain about O'Muircheartaigh. He is a master strategist, and he plays a subtle game, but how much Irish freedom means to him is anyone's guess."

"Wasn't there another one, though?" I asked. "Another name beginning with 'D'?"

"Very good, lad. There was. Dunleavy, the American. He's

American by birth, Irish by descent. He's dropped from sight. Very possibly, he is our man. I'm hoping Mr. Cathcart will have turned up some information."

Just then, Jenkins came into the room. He had very definitely begun to show signs of strain. The building was still standing, figuratively speaking, but there were cracks in the foundation. I am all for temperance, and I must admit that our clerk's nightly self-pickling had concerned me in the past, since he had become something of a fixture in my life, but watching him in the throes of sobriety was almost more than I could take. I wished he would break his vow and frequent another public house until the Rising Sun reopened, for all our sakes.

He entered with the afternoon post as usual, but the orbit he made by my desk was slightly elliptical and the letters in his hand flapped like pigeons in Trafalgar Square. They came in contact with the edge, but only partially, and when he let them go, they all slid into the dustbin. Jenkins tottered off like a clockwork toy while I retrieved the post. A few minutes later he returned, bearing the same tattered business card we had seen at the beginning of the week.

"Mr. Cathcart," Jenkins announced. The inebriate came slowly into the room, step by step, as if gravity were a tricky business and not to be taken for granted. Eventually, he came to a halt in front of Barker's desk.

"Your Honor."

"Good afternoon, Mr. Cathcart," Barker said. "Have you anything to report?"

"I have. I've become such a fixture at the Crooked Harp that they've given me the run of the place. I was fortunate enough to even get a glance into the register. Several rooms were hired collectively for three days leading up to the night of the thirty-first. No names were written down, and for once the Irish were rather close lipped, but I overheard a sobriquet that might have some meaning for you. Someone said, " 'Flashing Alfred's boys shall be back in town soon.' "

"Flashing Alfred, eh?" Barker asked. "I see. Anything else?"

"Well, sir, another fellow said, 'That's a mercy,' and everyone laughed. Might that be of use to you?"

"It most certainly would. I wonder if you might be interested in prolonging this assignment a few weeks longer, if you have not been otherwise engaged. You would not be reporting to me directly, but Mr. Jenkins here shall take down any words you over-hear for my benefit."

"That would depend," the Sponge stated. "Are you working upon a case involving the explosion at Scotland Yard, if I may ask?"

"I am, and you may."

"One of the best public houses in London was damaged in that explosion. I do not take kindly to people thinking they can blow up institutions like the Rising Sun merely because they happen to be standing adjacent to something as inconsequential as Scotland Yard."

"Hear, hear," Jenkins put in. Henry Cathcart gave him a grave bow.

"I thought I recognized one of the gentleman patrons of that establishment. How was it you yourself were not injured in the explosion?"

"My old man was taken poorly that night with pleurisy," our clerk responded. "I had to cut my evening short."

"And the Sun was the worse for your absence, I am sure. Still, it was fortunate that you left when you did. Yes, Mr. Barker, I shall continue our agreement for the rest of the month or until such time as you dispense with my services and settle our account. I shall, of course, require lubrication, to grease the wheels of commerce, as it were."

"Certainly," Barker stated. "Would you like it all up front now?"

"I fear not, sir. I often find my pockets gone through in the mornings. It is a drawback of my profession. Perhaps if I were to drop by a couple of days a week and could speak with your esteemed clerk."

"I would consider it an honor," Jenkins piped up. *Really,* I thought. *These two tosspots are forming a mutual admiration society right here in our office.*

"Very well. Thank you for your services, Mr. Cathcart," Barker said. "So far, they have been most insightful."

Summoning his dignity, Cathcart turned and walked ponderously out of our chambers.

"Could you make heads or tails out of that?" I asked, when the Sponge had gone.

"Of course. Flashing Alfred is Colonel Dunleavy. He earned the nickname in the battle of Antietam, when he led his troops into battle, both pistols blazing and the reins of his horse between his teeth. According to Le Caron, he has a wonderful set of teeth, of which he is quite vain, and it was said he blinded the Union side with their brightness. Obviously, he is leading a faction that was already here during the bombing and shall return again. I think these could be the lads we're searching for."

"And the reply. What's that about?" I asked.

"It was meant as a joke or pun, Thomas. *Mercy.* The faction is hiding in Merseyside, Liverpool, which has the largest Irish population in England."

"So that's where they are," I said. "It's just a ferry's ride due west to Dublin."

"Precisely. With the London and North Western Railway's express, they could be out of the area entirely within a couple of hours and even out of the country, if they wished. I would imagine, however, that they would have found the last step to be unnecessary. There are plenty in Liverpool who are sympathetic to Irish Home Rule, enough to hide them away."

"So, what do we do with the information, sir?"

"We're going to Liverpool, and we're going to track down Dunleavy and his faction. We'll offer our services as bomb makers," Barker said, leaning back in his chair and folding his hands over his expanding waistline. He had already put on several pounds.

"Making real bombs, sir?"

"Real enough, though I hope they will be disarmed by the time we hand them over."

"As simple as that?"

"Simple enough. Not easy, mind you, but simple."

"How shall we convince them of who we are?"

"We shall answer that question a little closer to the time. For now, it is vital that we move on to Liverpool. Before we leave, I'd like to speak to the cabman whose horse I shot the day of the bombing. I believe he may have caught a glimpse of the bomber."

Later that afternoon, we found ourselves at Charing Cross Hospital, to see the one witness to the bombing of Scotland Yard. He wasn't a young fellow, and his head and arm were encased in plaster. His face was a mess of lacerations and abrasions, and the plaster skullcap occluded one eye and covered his ear. The arm and head, I hazarded a guess, had been broken when he'd fallen backward off his perch.

"How are you feeling, sir?" Barker asked, after the porter had returned to his station.

"Take more'n this to do in John Farris," the cabman said.

"Mr. Farris, I am an enquiry agent and have come here to ask you a few questions. Did you bring a fare to Whitehall?"

"Yes, sir, I did."

"Where did you pick him up, and where did he ask to be dropped?"

"I picked him up in Seven Dials, and he asked to be dropped off in Whitehall. Didn't say his exact destination, just told me to stop when we was near the Yard. He paid me off, including a tip. I was in the process of turning my cab around when the explosion happened about a minute later."

"Could you describe the fellow?"

"Not real well, sir. The problem with hansoms is a fellow can come out of nowhere and hop into your cab before you get a good peep at him, and the only glance you'll get is a bird's-eye view down the trap, which is to say you'll see his hat and shoulders and not much else. He were rather like this fellow here," he said, addressing me, "only pale complected, like. He was young, and had an accent but was trying to hide it, I think. Didn't sound real natural, if you ken my meaning, but he didn't talk between 'Take me to Whitehall, my good man,' and 'Thank you. You may stop here.' Could have been Irish, but could have been almost anything."

"How was he dressed, this youth?"

"Long coat, tannish color, and a brown bowler. Dark trousers and shoes. Middle class, I thought, or a poor one, trying to ape his betters."

"I'll bet you've answered these questions a hundred times."

"Two hundred," the man wheezed.

"Is there anything else you can recall?"

"No, sir. That's the lot."

"Thank you, then. We'll let you rest. If I may ask it, I would like this conversation to remain a secret."

"As you wish, Mr. Barker, sir."

Barker stopped and turned back to the supine figure on the bed.

"You know me?"

The fellow gave a brief cackle. "A cabman, not knowing the best tipper in London? I knowed you the moment you walked in. Mum's the word, Guv'nor. Ain't a policeman or reporter alive that'd make me peach on you."

Barker reached out and offered a hand to the injured man. The man raised his own, and my employer grasped it firmly.

"I want you to know something before I go. I put your horse down myself. I was there at her side. There was no way to save her. Her injuries were simply too severe. If I thought she had a chance of surviving, even out of harness, I would have waited, but there wasn't. She was crazed and injured, and it was a kindness." He turned to me. "Come, Llewelyn. This gentleman deserves his rest."

We left the old cabman to his solitary grieving.

10

I FINISHED PACKING MY CLOTHING INTO THE DIS-
reputable pasteboard suitcase I'd owned since before Barker had
first hired me. Within an hour, we'd be at Euston Station, the
London and North Western Railway terminus, on our way to
Liverpool. I felt uneasy, as if I were about to go into battle. The
chances I would get killed today were slight, I told myself. I
wouldn't allow myself yet to think of tomorrow.

I came down the stairs and set my suitcase by the door. I
hadn't seen Mac since he'd opened the curtains that morning. In
fact, the place was as quiet as a tomb. I went into the dining room,
where Dummolard was laying out breakfast. He had outdone
himself, creating a country hunt breakfast for Barker and me.

I sat down and helped myself to the coffee but thought it best
to wait for my employer. As I was taking my first sip, I heard the
click of the door of Mac's private domain in the hall, and Barker
suddenly came into the dining room.

Mac had put some concoction into Barker's hair, turning it
varying shades of gray, so that each strand resembled a bit of
wire. The front was plastered back; but behind his ears, it was

thick and unkempt. His beard was equally shot with gray, and not even his mustache and eyebrows had been spared. In place of his usual spectacles were a smaller pair, black as night, exactly like the ones van Rhyn wore, with dark lenses and glass side pieces. He wore a tweed suit of European cut, and I could tell that Barker had neared his goal of gaining half a stone in weight. In his hand was a tall walking stick, or short staff, inlaid with ivory.

"*Guten Morgen, Herr Penrith,*" he said to me.

"Good morning to you, Mr. van Rhyn," I replied.

"I think it appropriate that we pray over this meal," Barker said, and I bowed my head. He did thank God for the meal, but also he asked for success in our endeavor and a safe journey home. It only served to reinforce my fears that we were about to embark upon a most dangerous assignment.

The table was immaculate with white linen, heavy silver that I had never seen before, and Blue Willow transfer ware, laden with far too much food for just two men. Platters of eggs, bacon, bangers, kedgeree, potatoes, grilled tomatoes, toast, jam, marmalade, and coffee all fought for space on the sideboard. As I got my first cup in me, my appetite began to grow. I dared the toast first, then the bacon. It was excellent, so I thought I might have some eggs to go with it. The potatoes looked particularly good; and I wouldn't want to insult the cook, who had gone to so much trouble with the kedgeree. Before long, we had sampled every dish and even gone back for seconds.

Afterward, when we had shaken hands with Mac and Dummolard, and given Harm a parting pat on the head, I felt positively moribund. We stepped into the cab in danger of breaking the springs, and rolled off toward Euston Station.

"I think the next time we leave the city on a case, it should be a spur-of-the-moment decision," I muttered.

"Agreed," said my employer, for he had wielded his knife and fork as well as I.

We arrived at Euston Station in plenty of time, and boarded our train. I'd seen the northern trains before, with their pretty milk-and-claret paint scheme, but I would have preferred better circumstances for an excursion. I procured a copy of *The Times* at one of the news vendors, and spent the journey studying it in the smoking car, where Barker sat with his pipe and cogitated. The window was half closed. It rained most of the journey and no one dared disturb the Welshman reading his newspaper or the German poisoning the car with his heavy pipe fumes, so we had the carriage all to ourselves. When we arrived in Liverpool, my suit and my newspaper were crumpled and damp and smelled of tobacco smoke.

Barker reached into the cavernous pockets of his coat and produced a packet of papers, which he handed to me.

"I had these made for you," he said. "They are identification papers in the name of Thomas Penrith."

"Are they forgeries?" I asked as I glanced through the passports, which looked as authentic as any papers I had ever seen. Wondering where he could have procured such things, I thrust them into my pocket. Somewhere he had a fellow at his beck and call who was a maker of false papers. It was an odd business we were in. No shipping merchant or exchange clerk would require knowing such a person.

"Either that, lad, or I found another fellow named Penrith who is an explosives expert," he said. It was the closest he had come to jesting, and I took it as a good sign. He didn't appear to be worrying over the case. If anything, he was looking forward to it.

In the ticket office in the Lime Street Station, Barker asked the clerk—a portly, friendly-looking fellow in a blue coat and peaked cap—if he might use the telephone. And might the clerk recommend a good hotel in the area?

"Midland Hotel, sir, right around the corner," the clerk said, before leading us back to a cluttered desk where the telephone stood, surrounded by timetables, papers, and tin teacups.

"If he is like Parnell, he'll only want the best," Barker growled. He asked the operator for the hotel, and was connected through.

"Good day," he said into the mouthpiece. "I have an appointment with Colonel Dunleavy today, and I wanted to make certain that he is in. . . . The dining room, you say? No, you need not tell him. Thank you."

He replaced the receiver and turned to me. "Luck is with us, lad. He is indeed staying at the Midland Hotel. I must send a telegram, but afterward, let us go and see if we, too, can get a room."

My first view of Liverpool was grim and gray. A city does not look its best in the rain. As we stepped out of the station and into the road, the aspect of Lime Street reminded me of a watercolor painting, all washes and colors blending together. There were puddles in the gutter, and rain dripping steadily from the eaves.

The Midland, while not as intimidating as Claridge's, was certainly imposing. It rose five stories, with turrets offering a jagged skyline, but down on the street, it had window panels like a cozy tearoom to draw people in. Inside, the hotel was opulent. It was also exclusive. The clerk was not going to let just any pair of disheveled, slightly disreputable-looking persons such as ourselves into the establishment.

"I'm afraid we're full up, sir," the clerk said dismissively.

Barker was not to be dissuaded. He cleared his throat loudly and covertly passed a banknote across the desk to the clerk. Not a pound nor a fiver, but a full ten pounds, the price of a room for a week.

"Your name, sir?" the clerk asked, suddenly solicitous. His very demeanor had changed. One would have thought Barker a long-lost uncle.

"Johannes van Rhyn."

"You are from . . . ?"

"London. Well, Berlin, originally, but that was years ago. I lived in Budapest and then in St. Petersburg for a year, and . . ."

"London will be fine, sir. And your occupation?"

"I am an industrialist," Barker said, puffing out his chest.

"Thank you, sir. You are most fortunate. A suite of rooms has just been vacated. We can put you in Number 47."

"*Danke.* Is that rascal Dunleavy about? I have an appointment with him this afternoon."

"The colonel is in the dining room, sir."

"Excellent. Have our bags sent up to our rooms. We shall have a meal after our little journey."

We made our way into the dining room, but Barker made no attempt to spy out Alfred Dunleavy. We were shown to a table, and he made something of an act of being cantankerous, refusing the first one. Once seated, he ordered tea and roast beef and said loudly, "Well, Thomas, we are here."

"Yes, sir," I said, trying not to look around. I wondered what Barker was about. Casually, I glanced around the room. I couldn't see any terrorists, but, then, they don't exactly wear uniforms or have insignias on their lapels.

"Mr. van Rhyn!" a voice suddenly cried. "Telegram for Mr. van Rhyn!"

"Over here, my good fellow!" Barker called out to the young porter, whom he tipped a shilling. He opened the message and perused it, with the note close to his eyes. From where I sat, I could see it was blank. He had sent it himself from the train station. What was he up to? I wondered.

Our meal arrived, and without a word we ate. It was classic hotel dining room fare, the meat cut from a large joint on a serving table in the room, but I had no interest in it as I had eaten so well at breakfast. Barker had that look about him of a man waiting for a fish to rise to the bait. It did not take long.

"Pardon me, gentlemen," a polished American voice drawled behind me. I looked up to see a man in his mid-fifties with white hair, worn rather long, and a short beard. He affected a breezy manner, but his eyes glowed like banked coals. "I hope you will forgive my rude interruption of your meal, but would I be addressing Mr. Johannes van Rhyn?"

"Perhaps," Barker responded in his assumed German accent. "To whom do I have the pleasure of speaking?"

"My name is Colonel Alfred Dunleavy, and I am a representative of the Irish Republican Brotherhood," he said, putting out a hand.

"I am indeed Johannes van Rhyn," Barker said, taking the offered hand.

"I am very gratified to hear it. Mr. van Rhyn, we had heard rumors that you'd been snatched away by the British government and taken to a secluded place at Her Majesty's expense."

Barker nodded. "*Ja*. That swine Parnell informed on me, I think, because I would not agree to his terms. My solicitor was able to gain me a temporary release, and I have taken the opportunity to decamp. I am traveling to Dublin, then making my way to America. I have made too many enemies in Europe. It is time to see the New World, don't you think, Mr. Penrith? Excuse me, Herr Dunleavy, I would like to present Thomas Penrith, my assistant."

"A pleasure to meet you, sir," the American said, briefly shaking my hand. "I assure you, gentlemen, that I concur with your opinion of Mr. Parnell. But before you slip through our fingers, allow me the opportunity of delaying your departure for just a while longer. I'd like to present a proposal to you."

"I might be willing to entertain an offer. What do you have in mind?"

"May I arrange an appointment with you this evening in your rooms? I'd like to speak with my associates. Would ten o'clock be suitable?"

"Certainly, sir. We would be delighted."

"It was most fortuitous that you should choose this hotel to stay in."

"I heard it was the best," Barker said, shrugging. "And one has but one life, after all."

"My sentiments exactly, gentlemen. We will speak later. I'll leave you to your meal. Until then." He bowed, and left the dining room.

"That was simple enough," I said, returning to my food.

"I hazarded a guess that Dunleavy would be as fond of spending the Irish-American money as Parnell and that he would choose a hotel close to the station. Keep your wits about you, lad, and do not look around. If Dunleavy is the old campaigner I think he is, he shall send a confederate to watch us. He cannot be certain we are whom we claim to be, but by turning us down, he might have missed a great opportunity. He will alert his associates and have us watched."

"What shall we do?" I asked.

"We shall eat, and then go to our rooms. We are not tourists here to see Liverpool."

As we were nearing the end of our meal, a man came in casually and ordered a cup of tea. From the quick glance I caught of him as I summoned a waiter for a new fork, I saw that he was close to thirty with curly hair and a sharp nose over a small mustache.

"Is that the man?" I asked in a low voice.

"Doubtless," my employer answered. "From where I am seated, I can see that he is missing two fingers, a sure sign of the amateur bomber. Also, he's looked at us twice since he came in."

The fellow followed us out of the dining room and up the stairs, staying some distance behind us. When we were safely in our rooms, I heard his footsteps pass a half minute later.

"That was . . ." I began, but Barker put a finger to his lips. I looked over at the bottom of the door, where a sliver of light shone in from the hall. After a moment's pause, a flicker of shadow moved across the light.

Still standing in front of the door, my employer pulled back his arm, and then smote the door very close to eye level. I could picture the fellow in the hall with his ear pressed against the other side. I heard feet stagger back and then run swiftly down the hall. Barker wasn't going to let these fellows think that the prickly van Rhyn was going to be that easy to handle.

11

<hr/>

IT WAS NEAR ELEVEN WHEN THEY FINALLY appeared at our door. The odor of alcohol that I smelled on Colonel Dunleavy told me our rooms had not been his first stop of the evening, but his associates seemed sober enough. There were two of them, and one was the fellow who had followed us earlier.

"Gentlemen!" Alfred Dunleavy bellowed when we opened the door. "We come bearing gifts."

I need hardly mention that the gifts were all of the liquid variety. Each of the colonel's subordinates carried a wooden crate full of bottles, which they set down on the largest table in the room. There was a bottle of schnapps, bottles of Irish and Scotch whiskey, and a dozen bottles of ale. Rather than risk having the whiskey forced on me, I took a Guinness.

"I've never been to Liverpool before," I said. "What's it like?"

"I believe you'll find the town has much to recommend it, sir," the third man spoke up. "It combines the rowdiness of Dublin with the anonymity of London. You'll feel welcome."

"I am Johannes van Rhyn," Barker announced, putting out his hand. "And you are?"

<hr/>

"Eamon O'Casey," the fellow said, shaking it firmly. "This is Niall Garrity."

O'Casey was a young, capable-looking chap with a confident manner and an athletic build. He looked like a university student, the kind who takes a first in his studies and has a blue in rowing. As it turned out, that is exactly what he was. He had recently graduated from Trinity in Dublin. With his square jaw and frank, hazel eyes, I could see him succeeding in whatever he undertook, and he must have caught the eye of many a girl in Dublin or in Liverpool, for that matter.

As for Garrity, I noticed right off the missing two fingers. He reminded me of Cassius in *Julius Caesar,* the one who had "a lean and hungry look." He looked young enough to be a youth in the eyes of the cabman John Farris. His sharp eyes over a broad arrow of a nose gave him a devilish appearance.

In a moment or two we were all seated, Barker with schnapps, Dunleavy with a full glass of whiskey, Garrity with a bottle of ale. O'Casey, I noticed, was not drinking. I wished I could have emulated his abstinence.

Dunleavy spoke up. "Gentlemen, it was most fortuitous that we should find ourselves at the same hotel, but you must understand that I and my associates are suspicious of coincidences. British agents have attempted to infiltrate our ranks in the past. I wonder if I might prevail upon you to see some identification."

Barker and I reached into our pockets and handed over our passports. Dunleavy held them out at arm's length and read them. "You are quite well traveled, Mr. van Rhyn—France, Russia, Italy, Montenegro; in fact, all across eastern Europe. That is quite satisfactory. I wonder, sir, if I may presume upon our new friendship a little further and request that you remove your spectacles?"

A slow smile spread across Barker's face, the coldest, most lethal smile I'd ever seen him give. "Be careful what you ask for,

Herr Colonel. The last fellow who forced me to remove these met with an unfortunate accident. He was trying to light his stove and it exploded. Apparently, something had happened to the valve and it was leaking gas. Killed him and his dog A terrible tragedy. I liked the dog."

The three Irishmen looked at one another uneasily and silently agreed to let the matter of Barker's spectacles rest. They turned, instead, to me. Apparently, I was still fair game.

"So, Mr. Penrith, how long have you been working for Mr. van Rhyn?" O'Casey asked.

"Half a year now, I'd say."

"I take it," Garrity put in, "that you are something of an explosives expert yourself."

"He was trained by Mr. Nobel at his factory near Glasgow," Barker spoke for me. "And I have taught him much of what I know. He is a fast learner, but, then, he has had to be. You see, gentlemen, I have a degenerative ocular disease. I can no longer see the fine measurements on a beaker. Thomas is my eyes now. I cannot do without him."

"Where are you from?"

"Cardiff, originally. I've been living in London."

Garrity leaned forward in his chair. "What are your politics, Mr. Penrith? How do you feel about the English?"

"My country is no more free than yours, Mr. Garrity. I find calling the Queen's whelp the Prince of Wales to be the grossest of insults. Anything I can do to relieve them both of power shall be good for my people."

O'Casey turned to my employer. "You are a very famous figure, Mr. van Rhyn," he said. "One might almost say legendary. There are a lot of stories about you being passed around among the factions. Is it true, for example, that it was one of your bombs that blew up Czar Alexander the Second three years ago?"

"I was in Russia at the time, but the anarchist responsible was capable enough of building his own bombs. We consulted, but that was all. It was enough, however, to have Czar Alexander the Third's parliament declare me an enemy of the state and to escort me to the border."

"I see," O'Casey said. "And were you really a member of Le Cercle de l'Anarchie, which threatened Louis Napoleon?"

"Monarchies, even such enlightened ones as his, are relics of the Dark Ages, gentlemen," Barker pontificated. "The sooner they are exterminated, the better for society."

"You were a member, then."

"*Ja,* Herr O'Casey. I was a member."

"Then you would be sporting the society's tattoo on your forearm."

With a sigh, Barker pushed back the sleeve of his jacket and unbuttoned his cuff, exposing the back of his thick forearm. There, a few inches up from the wrist, were three crude black lines, crossing themselves to roughly form the letter *A.* I had sat with Barker in the steamed heat of his bathhouse many times, but I hadn't noticed such a mark before. Was it new, or had a former case required him to join that organization?

"Are you satisfied now, gentlemen, that I am whom I claim to be?" he asked, buttoning his sleeve. "This exercise is getting tedious."

"Of course we are, sir," Dunleavy stated, anxious to make peace. "Forgive these young fellows' doubts, please. It seemed too good to be true that we should come upon you just at this time."

"And what time would that be, sir?" Barker asked.

O'Casey gave a smug smile. "A week after we bombed London."

So, they admit it, I told myself. *Barker was on the right track. I should have known such an old hunter would find the scent.* My employer broke into a laugh.

"Ho, ho, so it was you! I should have suspected. Well, gentlemen, I don't know what you need of my services. Two attacks in one night! You are doing well enough on your own. From what I read in *The Times,* London has certainly sat up and taken notice."

"Aye, but the dynamite we're using is rubbish," Garrity said. "It failed to go off at the Ship Street Barracks in Dublin last month. We made two earlier attempts that failed in London, and a bomb we left in Trafalgar Square the same night was a failure as well."

"What kind of explosives are you using?"

"Atlas. American made," Dunleavy answered.

"I am familiar with the brand. It is industrial grade. Where did you get it?"

"It was donated by an American Irishman from Cincinnati and shipped here on a freighter, hidden in a shipment of raw tobacco."

"There is your problem, gentlemen. Chances are it had been sitting in a warehouse for years until the fellow needed to get rid of it. He knew you were desperate and convinced himself he was doing his bit for Irish freedom in the Old Country. Then it had to endure an ocean voyage with all that salt air. I would wager that the cakes are sweaty and that there is a waxy residue in the bottom of the case."

"Yes, there is," Garrity admitted.

"Then it is a marvel you haven't blown yourselves up. What you have is highly unstable. The nitroglycerin has separated partially from the kieselguhr base. It can explode at any minute, or the liquid can leak onto the wires around the primer, rendering the entire bomb inert. I strongly advise that you dispose of whatever you have left. A bomb is a tool and it should be reliable, like any other. It must go off when you want it to, or you have no control over it."

"Up until now," O'Casey admitted, "it's been 'throw it all together and hope it works.' No offense intended, Niall."

"None taken. We could really use your expertise, Mr. van Rhyn. You could help us strike a strong blow for the Irish cause and make us all heroes. What do you say?"

"I say you are already heroes, Herr Garrity. Five years ago, I aided a group in Montenegro who were fighting Turkish tyranny. Now they live in a free country, thanks to young men just like yours. Provided we agree upon the terms, I will gladly help."

Dunleavy poured another glassful, his fourth, and studied us shrewdly. "We are not wealthy, Mr. van Rhyn. We are dependent upon the aid of various Irish organizations in America. What sort of terms are you proposing?"

"It is not money I have need of, Colonel. I desire to have a permanent laboratory, without the fear that my door shall be kicked in during the night by the secret police. I have been incarcerated six times in the last four years, and I have had enough. My eyes are slowly failing me, and I am getting too old to jump from one country to another. I want a home and a place to continue my work. My work, gentlemen! A man is nothing without his work."

Dunleavy drained his glass again and set it down. "As a military man and a politician, sir, I've had to make several promises I was not sure I could keep, but what you ask is not too much. Aid us in our campaign against the Queen, and you shall have your laboratory."

Barker slowly put forth his hand. "A gentlemen's agreement, then?" he asked. The colonel took his hand and shook it solemnly. I looked over. O'Casey and Garrity had broken into grins.

"*Gut,*" Barker said, filling his glass with more schnapps. "I was intent upon leaving the country, but you make me take heart again. I believe I shall stay. It would be a shame to leave now when things are just beginning to get interesting. And as a German, I am, of course, concerned about English arrogance, especially regarding the seas. It is necessary that the Germans, the Irish, and the Americans show England that they shall not be cowed by its imperialist expansion. Who better than the Germans to be your allies, gentlemen?"

I thought he was laying it on a bit thick, but it was obvious these Irish radicals were impressed by his speech. They would ally themselves to Satan if it meant they could have their own country. It occurred to me, then, to wonder what would happen if they succeeded. A country just thirty miles away led by bombers and anarchists would not, in my opinion, be a stable ally; and should they truly form an alliance with Germany, where already there were rumblings of discontent, it would form an imminent threat to English security. That is to say, to my security. If we didn't stop these people, I could find myself with a rifle in hand on some foreign battlefield or, worse than that, in our own country. It would be 1066 all over again.

"Mr. van Rhyn," Dunleavy said, "we have done a desperate thing. We have planned a second attempt upon London within the month, using the very dynamite you have urged us to destroy. We are committed to this venture and shall go forth with our campaign, but if this dynamite is as dangerous or worthless as you say it is, we must find another source. Nowhere in these godforsaken isles will they allow an Irishman or an American to purchase dynamite, blasting caps, chemicals, or even so much as base materials. The Special Irish Branch and Scotland Yard are watching, hoping to catch us in the attempt. This dynamite is all we have in the way of munitions."

"You have adequately described some of the obstacles in our path," Barker stated, "but allow me to ease your mind upon a few points. First of all, Mr. Penrith and I are very obviously not Irish and would be able to purchase materials forbidden to you. My name, as well, might open some doors, though it might close others. Rather than attempt to purchase the ready-made dynamite or nitroglycerin, the two of us will be able to make them ourselves. We would then be able to fashion our own bombs. I would suggest we purchase the equipment elsewhere, such as Amsterdam or Paris, where the officials are not so vigilant."

"They're vigilant enough," Garrity complained. "I've been trying to buy materials for weeks."

"You just leave that matter to Mr. Penrith and me, Mr. Garrity. I believe we can work around it. Within thirty days, we'll have these Londoners dancing a jig again."

"Arrogant English aristocrats," Dunleavy slurred. The drink had finally gone to his head and loosened his tongue. "Let's see how they feel when half their monuments are in rubble. Let's see how they feel when we blow their Queen's head off her shoulders!"

"He's had too much," O'Casey apologized, and he and Garrity helped lift Dunleavy out of his chair. "If I may, I'd like to call on you gentlemen in the morning."

We shook hands quickly, and they maneuvered the American out into the hall. I could still hear him as they escorted him down the corridor.

"We won't stop till the town's in ruins. Dublin will be liberated from English oppression. And who shall be its new leader? Alfred Dunleavy, that's who! What do you think about that, Mr. Gladstone?"

12

THEY LET US ALONE THE NEXT MORNING, AND WE
went into the dining room for a good breakfast. I thought it possible the colonel was sleeping off the effects of the whiskey he had consumed. It felt strange not attending a service on the Sabbath, but Barker explained that he could not risk having van Rhyn, that old anarchist, seen in a Baptist church. We read the newspapers until eleven thirty, when there was a sharp rap upon our door. It was Eamon O'Casey with a gnarled wooden stick in one hand and a gladstone bag in the other.

"Fine morning, gentlemen. The sun is out," he announced.

"It is," Barker agreed, finishing his tea. "How is the colonel?"

"He is just getting up, but he requested to speak with you in the smoking lounge at twelve. He has asked me to express his apologies for being a bit concerned in his liquor last night. The month has been a rather strenuous one for him."

Barker nodded. "And where is Mr. Garrity this morning?"

"He should be halfway to Dublin by now. He's not an actual member of our faction but an officer of the Irish Republican

Brotherhood, and he acts as an advisor to the various factions, as well as constructing explosives for us."

"Ah. And what is in the bag?" Barker asked. "Surely you are not carrying the dynamite around with you openly, I trust."

"Faith, no." O'Casey chuckled. "It's just my uniform. Most of us faction lads are in a hurling club, and though it's off season, we keep in shape by playing unofficial games. We begin one in about an hour."

"What is hurling?" I asked.

"Hurling? What's hurling? Why, it's the greatest game, the only game. A fellow's only half a man if he hasn't tried hurling; and if he has tried it, it's in his blood, and there's no going back. Why don't you come with me and meet the boys, Mr. Penrith, while the older gentlemen strategize? It'll give you a chance to see something of Liverpool, such as it is."

"Well, I don't know . . ." I said, looking at my employer.

"Go ahead, Penrith," Barker said to me, and made a little gesture with his fingers that I interpreted to mean I was to stay alert and be his eyes and ears. "You've been restless all morning. You young pups go and play your games."

"Very well, sir, if you are certain you don't need me."

Outside, O'Casey rested his stick comfortably against his shoulder as he took the stairs down to the lobby two at a time.

"How was the ale last night?" he asked.

"It was fine. I noticed you didn't drink. That's unusual for an Irishman, isn't it?"

"I'm in training," he explained. "I'm captain of the local hurling team. I've never been a drinker, though. I've seen too many good Irishmen ruined by it."

"What did you read at university?" I asked.

"Politics and economics. If I can see how other governments have dictated policy, perhaps I can help my own country. My father died in his pursuit of Ireland's freedom. He was a great believer in Malthusian reasoning, that war, famine, and disaster are inevitable, since population increases geometrically while crop production increases arithmetically. It was the whole reason for the Irish famine in the first place. He was evicted from his own land and forced to go to Dublin for work. It is now my duty to carry on his dream to free Ireland. He was a barrister, who often took on cases against Her Majesty's government, cases he felt were unjust to the Irish people. Eventually he was arrested on a vague charge of sedition. They put him in solitary for months. He starved himself to death in Kilmainham Gaol, in protest against the tyranny of the English government."

"How did you fend for yourself after your father's death?"

"My sister and I were befriended by an Irish patriot who stepped in and acted as a mentor to us. He helped pay for my schooling and took us under his wing. He helped set us on our feet here. But that's enough about me, Mr. Penrith."

"Tell me more about this hurling."

"It is thousands of years old and was invented as a way to keep the Celtic warriors in shape between battles. There is a large field with goals, like for football, and two teams of fifteen players. Each of us has a stick called a *hurley*, and the purpose is to get the ball, or *sliotar*, into the opposing team's goal for three points, or over it for one point. You can hit the ball to your own team members or balance the *sliotar* on the edge of the *hurley*, which takes a little practice."

"So, who's the wee curly man?"

We'd been progressing down Renshaw Street, when suddenly, there was a man at my elbow, walking as casually as if he'd been there all the while. He was a big fellow, too, with brawny shoulders and a red, meaty face under his cloth cap. I would put him in his late twenties. He had a stick over his shoulder almost identical to O'Casey's, and the handle of his bag was looped around the end. For his size, he moved so silently, he'd been upon us before I saw him, despite all the training I'd received. Either this man was good, or I was not paying enough attention.

"Fergus, this is Mr. Thomas Penrith, Mr. van Rhyn's assistant, whom I was telling you about. Mr. Penrith, this is Mr. Fergus McKeller, the best right forward you've ever seen."

"Pleased to may-tcha," McKeller said.

"I was just explaining the rules of hurling to him," O'Casey said.

"That's a good thing, then. It sounds like there's been a serious breach in your education, Mr. Penrith. It all comes of having the terrible misfortune of not being born Irish."

"We'll soon set your woeful ignorance to rights," O'Casey agreed. "You can watch us play the English today, and if you're interested, I'll teach you the game."

We crossed Upper Parliament Street, and entered Prince's Park. Traversing it, we came to a pitch marked out in chalk, with goals set up, and a clubhouse for the players to change.

"Eamon," McKeller snorted. "Will you look who's here?"

My eyes followed his to a tall, thin fellow wearing a black suit with a large red tie. He had a wave of black hair that flopped down over his pince-nez. He caught sight of us and waved.

"Jesus, Mary, and Joseph," O'Casey muttered under his breath, but went over to shake the fellow's hand.

"That's Willie Yeats," McKeller explained. "He's a Dublin boy who's sweet on Eamon's sister. Comes over on the ferry as often as he can afford. Tries to ingratiate himself with us."

"He's not a part of the faction, then," I stated.

"He is, and yet he isn't. He's delivered a message now and then for Colonel Dunleavy and attended a meeting or two. He knows about us, but he's not the type you'd trust to set a bomb, if you know what I mean. Studyin' to be an artist, and doesn't know one end of a *hurley* from the other."

I didn't know this myself either, but I wasn't going to bring that up. I went forward and met the young Irishman, while O'Casey and his friend went to change.

"I have a message for you from Colonel Dunleavy," he said to me. "Your things are being moved out of your rooms at the Midland and taken over to the O'Casey house."

"I wasn't told of the arrangement before."

Yeats shrugged his thin, loose-limbed shoulders, and I realized that was all the information I was going to get.

"Do you play?" I asked, pointing at the field, where the hurlers had begun to warm up and hit the ball about.

"My good Mr. Penrith, I am quite useless at the game, and my hands are too important to me to risk being battered with a stick."

"Ah, yes. McKeller said you are an artist."

Yeats smiled, as if at a private joke. "Not much of one, I'm afraid. It is my father who is the artist. Actually, I prefer to think of myself as a poet."

"Ah, I love poetry," I said. " *'The poet's pen turns them to shapes, and gives to airy nothing a local habitation and a name.'* "

"You've read Shakespeare?" he asked, a surprised look on his face. It was an odd face, handsome at some angles, not so at others.

"Yes, I studied him in school. And not long ago, I read a book about your Celtic legends."

Now he looked interested. "Was it *Ancient Irish Myths and Legends?*"

"Yes, I believe that was the title."

"How fortunate to find a copy! There's not much written on the subject so far. It's mostly oral traditions. To tell you the truth, I've been collecting the old Irish fairy tales myself for months. I'd like to publish a collection of my own some day. Which was your favorite?"

"I think the one about the Giant's Causeway. That was Finn MacCool, was it not? Does the Causeway really exist?"

"It does, though I have yet to see it myself. You can find a postal card of it in any shop in Dublin."

"I should like to see it sometime," I said. I wanted to question him more thoroughly about his poetry and the old legends of Ireland, but just then the players were beginning the match.

Hurling, as it turned out, was a rather simple game for anyone who had ever played football or hockey. The object was to get a ball into a goal at the far end of the pitch. There was a goalkeeper, several defensive players in back, mid-fielders, and forward offensive players attempting to score. Points were awarded for putting the ball over the crossbar or into the goal.

That is the game in theory. In practice, it is two groups of men beating one another with sticks. They smote shins, pounded each other on the backs, and barely missed cracking skulls, all in an attempt to get at the ball. It seemed as if a brawl was attempted, and, somehow, a game broke out. I could all too easily see how it had begun as a way to keep warriors in condition.

The game continued for over an hour. The members of O'Casey's front line, including O'Casey himself, were formidable, and many was the time the ball shot over the goal. The middle line was good as well, smartly turning the ball back to the forwards. The team's weakest link was its goalkeeper. The fellow was terribly outclassed, the ball flying by his right ear, his left, between his hands, and behind his back. Every point made by O'Casey's team was matched by another as the sphere flew unerringly into the goal. It was only by O'Casey's ferocious efforts in the final minutes of the game, that the Irish team emerged triumphant by a mere three points. Another few minutes might have tied the game again.

It being Sunday, the pubs were closed, but we were taken to a friend's home after the scrimmage. The drinks were provided by the other team, who seemed not to bear any ill will for the various contusions, scratches, and missing teeth engendered by the competition. Their blue jerseys stood intermingled with the faction's green. Everyone drank far too much stout, save O'Casey, who drank only water, and Yeats and I, who nursed a lone pint each for most of the evening. Yeats pestered O'Casey until he agreed to let him come home with us.

Finally, we arrived at the O'Casey residence—Eamon, McKeller, Yeats, myself, and two mid-fielders who were twins by the name of Bannon. It was a tall, thin, four-story house, like many in Liverpool. O'Casey invited the others in, and after the hurling equipment had been deposited in a heap, we entered the parlor. The first thing I noticed as I stepped into the room was Cyrus Barker, sitting across from Dunleavy, with several pieces of paper and cups of tea between them. A conference had been going on. The second thing I noticed was the young woman pouring tea. Now I could see why Willie Yeats had been so eager to come back with us.

13

I SAT DOWN BESIDE BARKER, HOPING TO DIS-
cover what he had been doing while I was off with the younger
faction members. I knew if there was anyone who could ask the
right questions of Dunleavy and open him up, it would be the
Guv. I didn't want to do anything that might arouse suspicion, not
merely because it was dangerous but also because I didn't want to
jeopardize Barker's plans and thereby endanger the Royal Family.

My nose caught the scent of lilac water, and a small, pale hand
settled a teacup in front of me. Something—instinct, if I had it—
told me not to say a word to O'Casey's pretty sister but to concentrate on the meeting. I knew not how she was mixed up in all
this. Women and their intuition are a deep subject, and if it were
possible that anyone might penetrate my disguise, it could be she.
After all, hadn't I read in the Carleton book that women could be
as deeply involved in factions as men?

"Maire," Eamon O'Casey said, and raised his chin in a dis-
missive gesture. She finished pouring the tea, and as she passed
by Yeats, said something low in his ear. He trotted after her.
Lucky beggar, I thought. I would have liked to follow her myself.

Colonel Dunleavy turned easily in his chair and regarded the young men about him like a benevolent father. His dove-gray suit, with its buttons of brass, gave him a military appearance, and with his white teeth and chin beard, he cut a commanding and persuasive figure. I could see how he was able to gather loyal men about him.

"Good afternoon, boys," he said. "Did we emerge triumphant on the field of battle today?"

"We did," McKeller piped up.

"Good. I told you these English lads didn't stand a chance against you. You gentlemen are the tip of the spear that four million people in our homeland are holding. You are the best of the factions. But this shall be as nothing compared to the defeat we will deal the English government three weeks from now.

"London will be knocked off her pins. We will alert the other factions of the I.R.B. afterward, but by the time they arrive, we shall be in charge; if they wish to participate in the New Ireland, they shall have to line up behind us. I need hardly mention that the pacifistic, Queen-courting Mr. Parnell will not be receiving any post higher in our newly formed government than rat catcher."

That elicited a few chuckles from the young men in the room. Parnell had little to recommend himself among this radical element of the Irish Republican Brotherhood. All the young men were leaning forward in their chairs, listening eagerly to the American colonel's words.

They looked like soldiers, I thought, or worse, zealots ready to die if their plans did not work. Dunleavy's impassioned remarks made the quest for Irish freedom seem like a search for the Holy Grail.

"I know you gentlemen have voiced concerns regarding the dynamite we've been using," Dunleavy went on. "That is with good reason. It has failed to go off on several occasions, and Mr.

van Rhyn, who is an explosives expert, has warned me that it is most dangerous. He has agreed to rid us of it safely and to provide new infernal devices. He assures us that he has made more nitroglycerin than Mr. Nobel himself. Normally he does not respond to requests to demonstrate his extraordinary abilities, but for once, for our eyes alone, he is willing to bend his rules. He and his assistant, Mr. Penrith, have promised to give us a show of their skills within the week."

A show within the week? I couldn't help but shoot a glance at my employer, but he was sitting coolly in his chair, fingers laced across his ample stomach, as immobile and aloof as a statue, save for the smoke rising from his pipe. I wasn't sure I was proficient enough for some sort of demonstration, and I had no idea what kind of skills Barker possessed. Feverishly, I began going over the various formulas in my mind and what materials were required for each and just how we were going to obtain them. Dunleavy introduced my employer, who addressed the group.

"I am not a public speaker, gentlemen," Barker said. "I am a simple bomb maker, with a knack for tinkering and a fascination with destructive force as a means of progress. Your country stands on the threshold of the modern world. Great changes will occur before the new century begins, and I have decided to stake my life and future upon Ireland. The age of swords and cavalry charges shall soon be over, and we shall be the ones to usher in a new era. I look forward to meeting each one of you and to working with you for the worthy cause of your country's freedom. Thank you."

"Mr. Penrith," Dunleavy said. "Would you care to say a few words?"

"Me?" I asked. I hadn't expected to give a speech. "No, sir. I merely wish everyone to know that Mr. van Rhyn's goals are my goals. If he has thrown in his lot with you, I'll give all that I have to help you."

"Thank you, sir," Dunleavy said, flashing a munificent smile upon me. "There you have it, boys. If Her Majesty's government sees fit to ignore our little warning, as they appear to have done, then we have no choice but to teach them a lesson. Go on with your private lives and continue to train yourselves, but be ready within the week for a demonstration that would make the Prime Minister weak at the knees if he could see it."

That was our introduction to the desperate men who had bombed London. They all stood and shook our hands, full of confidence in their leader and his plans. The two men O'Casey and McKeller had brought with them, Padraig and Colin Bannon, shook my hand before leaving. They were thin, tough-looking fellows in tweed caps, twins who smoked short clay pipes and spoke little.

"Glad you happened along when you did," Fergus McKeller said, grasping my hand. His hand was like a vise, clamping down and beginning to crush mine. It was the sort of trick one saw in the school yard, but effective for all that. If I didn't put an end to it, he would attempt it every time I met him. Luckily, Barker had shown me a trick or two. I reached across and casually pulled back on his little finger. It is the weakest part of the hand, with the tensile strength of a carrot. Evidently, McKeller agreed. He let go, gave me an evil grin and a wink, and went over to confer with his friend O'Casey.

"I'll show you to your room, gentlemen," Miss O'Casey murmured behind us, and my employer and I gathered our belongings and followed her up the stairs. She seemed a demure, proper young woman, but having led a bachelor's existence in Barker's household, I couldn't help but notice the rustle of her dress and the gentle sway of her form as she climbed the staircase. I heard the Guv clear his throat behind me. It was a none-too-subtle reminder to keep my thoughts on the case.

Our room wasn't Claridge's, or even the Midland Hotel, but it was serviceable. It was a long room with two narrow beds, two chairs, a wardrobe, and a large bureau. There were feminine touches in the room, such as an embroidered coverlet. I hazarded a guess that the girl had made them all.

"You have no objection to my leaving the window open a little, Miss O'Casey?" Barker asked. "I prefer fresh air in the evenings."

"Of course," she said. It was my first chance to get a proper look at her. She was a beauty, with fair skin, lightly freckled across the nose, fine blue eyes, and a head of thick auburn curls. She wore a plain black dress with an apron tied around her waist, but even in severe clothing, she was still quite charming. In this some-what shabby house, she had the kind of beauty society girls in London struggled hard for and paid fortunes to attain, and very rarely succeeded.

"And tobacco?" Barker continued. "May I smoke in this room?"

"Provided you're not in the habit of falling asleep while doing so. I shall leave you to settle in."

After she left, the Guv looked after her, and favored me with a cold smile. "I would say she is not the sort of woman to be tri-fled with," he pronounced. "In her own way, she is part of the faction. There is a desk downstairs which is too dainty to belong to anyone else. On it is a Gaelic grammar book. She is part of the movement to return Ireland to its native language."

"Why have we moved here, sir, if I may ask? I would have thought that you'd wish to stay close to the faction's leader."

Barker sat down in one of the overstuffed chairs, and put a foot up. He spoke in a low tone so he wouldn't be overheard. "You have to understand the situation, lad. We have to remain adaptable and react quickly to any new information. Dunleavy was grafted onto this faction, but McKeller, O'Casey, and the Bannon brothers have likely been friends since childhood. They function as a team. Perhaps they were fortunate to find such a well-known spokesman as the colonel, but he, too, was fortunate to come across a group of such earnest, radical-thinking young men. I need to get as close to the inner workings of the faction as possible.

"The last two hours with Colonel Dunleavy have been very informative. As I previously mentioned, he fought for the Confederacy. I would say that he possesses bravery, spirit, and a natural ability to influence others. I do not think, however, that he is a very intelligent man, and that worries me. Either his threat was made on the spur of the moment, and he is attempting to deliver what he has promised, or the plan to bomb London was calculated by someone else. I don't care for either of the choices. I wish I could convince myself that this was solely his doing."

"What makes you think him incapable?" I asked.

"I suspect that through much of his youth he got by on family money. I would hazard a guess that he is the youngest son of the Dunleavy family and hence was relegated to the military. Alfred Dunleavy appears to be a very spoiled man. I imagine he started debauching himself in military college and hasn't stopped since. The loss of his side in the war was a deep blow to him, and was followed by his family's financial losses. He was trained for nothing but war and drinking, and being of Irish descent, he naturally drifted to the radical fringe, where he joined in a mad attempt they made to hold Toronto for ransom in 1868. It was a failure, as well, and serving on losing sides must haunt him. Note his fondness for Confederate gray. Dunleavy was imprisoned four years for his part in the affair, and he is very proud of it. It is his continuing entree into Irish-American politics and the coffers that go with it. He spoke of a book he is writing, his memoirs, but if he were an astute man, he'd have finished it long before now and used it to his advantage."

"You've formed an opinion of him quickly," I noted.

"It is important in our work, lad, to be able to evaluate men quickly, and to make a few constructive inferences. The most important thing right now is that I believe that this plan is brilliant, and I do not think him a brilliant man. Therefore, it is possible someone else is doing the thinking for him."

"Could it be one of the faction members, like Garrity or O'Casey?" I asked. "It would be a good combination of their brains and his name."

"You could very possibly be right," he admitted. "If everything goes according to what Dunleavy said, he could find himself the first official leader of Ireland, with both the younger men standing in the wings. Between the three of them, they could have Irish politics sewn up for the next twenty years, at least."

"If it isn't them, then who could it be?"

"First of all, it could be one of the men we spoke of earlier: Rossa, Davitt, Cusack, or O'Muircheartaigh. The latter, I've said before, is a master strategist, but I cannot picture him sharing his plans with another faction when he's got one of his own."

"I see."

"What do you think of the Bannon brothers as candidates?" he asked.

"Them? I hardly think so," I said. "They seemed rather slow, and those clay pipes of theirs . . ."

"Not necessarily, lad. Pipe smokers are often strategists, and the more silent they are, the more I wonder what they are thinking."

"Well," I said bitterly, "you've narrowed it down to just about everyone in this business *but* Dunleavy."

"Yes, but there is still time yet. Not plenty of time, but time enough. If it makes you feel better, by all means, include the colonel as a suspect. It's still conceivable that the old fellow had a rare stroke of genius."

For now, we had more immediate things to worry about. We had one week to dispose of the unstable dynamite and somehow provide new explosives in exchange. I wondered if Barker was really planning to give them better and deadlier bombs. It was just the sort of thing he would do, confident that he could get them away from the terrorists again when the time came.

Barker slept in his spectacles and snored through the night on his back. The next morning, he was rested and refreshed, which was more than I could say of myself. I began to unpack my old pasteboard suitcase, opening a bureau drawer in the room.

"Don't get too comfortable," Barker said. "We shall be moving again tomorrow."

"Again? Where to?" I asked, my hands full of shirts.

"Across the Mersey and into a northern corner of your native Wales. Dunleavy says the dynamite is hidden in a barn near an abandoned lighthouse at Colwyn Bay. It is very remote. I believe we can stage our demonstration there."

"But if we know where the dynamite is, why don't we simply inform Scotland Yard? They can't very well attack London with nothing but those sticks they carry."

"True, but if these Fenian terrorists are thwarted once, they shall merely come again later and more prepared. I'd have them arrested on the spot if I thought a good barrister couldn't help them wriggle out of it. They must be caught red-handed."

I must admit my face fell. I do not have Barker's manner, and all too often I show what I am feeling.

"Buck up, lad," my employer said. "I shall insist that we have complete privacy while preparing the explosives. You look as if you could do with a day or two in the country."

I suspected that meant that when we blew ourselves up, we wouldn't even have the opportunity to take a few terrorists with us, but I kept my opinion to myself.

"First, we have work to do in Liverpool," he went on. "We must see what kind of supplies we can gather. We shall be purchasing these items, though Dunleavy promises to reimburse us when the funds arrive from America."

For the most part, London is a conservative, Anglican city, with dissent saved for unionist organizations, and the Speaker's Corner of Hyde Park. On the other side of the Irish Sea, Catholic Dublin is a single dissenting voice, unified against England. Liverpool is both at once, oil and water that will never mix. One street has signs imploring one to vote for the most recent Fenian candidate, while the next bristles with Orangist ribands and placards. Liverpool is London's spinster sister, querulous over issues, passionate but changeable, willing to go whatever way the wind may blow.

Dunleavy had returned to his hotel room, intent upon soliciting aid from one of the local city councilmen. Much of his time seemed to be spent looking for money. I would have thought in such case he might have moved to a less expensive hotel than the Midland, but I supposed in order to secure such funds, one must not look as if one were in need of them.

Miss O'Casey was intent upon ensuring that Cyrus Barker didn't starve while in Liverpool. She fed us a breakfast consisting of eggs, bacon, sausage, black and white pudding, tomatoes, and toast. Dummolard couldn't have done any better.

With O'Casey's aid, my employer had compiled a list of places for us to go. At an ironmonger's in Hanover Street, we filled several baskets, purchasing spools of wire, a dynamite plunger, buckets and paddles for mixing chemicals, and sundry other equipment. We collected more than was necessary to blow up Dunleavy's old dynamite.

Before the day was out, we had visited a whitesmith, a chemist's shop, and a chemical warehouse. I couldn't help but wonder at how easy it was to purchase such terrible things when one has the means to do so.

14

———◆———

I BELIEVE THAT IT IS PART OF HUMAN NATURE, when one is about to set out upon a journey, to want to know the destination. Few of us in our lives step up onto some random train and leave their arrival to fate, but that is exactly what I was doing. Barker knew, of course, but I would sooner get an answer by speaking directly to the engine which was sputtering and steaming by the platform in Birkenhead Park Station, across the Mersey from Liverpool. It was the ninth of June, 1884, and we had been in the city for three days. We hadn't been discovered so far, but if we made just one mistake, Barker and I would be occupying two of those pine boxes Mr. Anderson had been so fond of describing. Beneath the casual veneer of the Irish faction members lay the hearts of cold-blooded murderers. Of that I had no doubt.

We had crossed on the ferry, and were now seated in the railway carriage. I like that feeling when the engine is first propelled forward by the steam pressure, and the carriages stretch out one by one at their couplings and creak and groan and squeak, until your own compartment shudders and slowly begins to move and you realize you are beginning a railway journey. At least we

———◆———

might be alone for a few days to puzzle out all the information we'd discovered.

Alfred Dunleavy was escorting us to our new encampment. As usual, he was sitting with Barker and chatting into his ear, discussing everything but revealing nothing. I took a moment to regard him. The man hadn't spoken more than a few words to me since this mission had begun. That was suspicious in itself, since the success of at least part of the operation came down to me and my abilities. Barker had questioned the man's leadership, and suggested someone else might be in charge. If not him, then whom? Parnell, keeping his terrorist scheme separate from his political plans? Garrity, running the operation from Paris? Or, closer to home, was O'Casey running the whole thing himself? It was possible, too, that Dunleavy was playing the blustering bureaucrat to cover up a more astute brain than we realized, an old card player's trick.

I shook my head and looked at Barker, who sat patiently while Dunleavy rambled on. In our last adventure, I'd had occasion to wonder if Barker knew what he was about, which only went to show that it was I who was ignorant. This was Barker doing what he did best. This was Barker being Barker, and reveling in it. The leader and mastermind of this cell could be anyone, but I had no doubt that the Guv would get to the bottom of it.

A little more than an hour's ride up the coast from Liverpool to Colwyn Bay, the train pulled up beside a small country halt. We alighted and were met by a youth with an open trap. I sat in the seat facing the back of the trap, behind Barker and Dunleavy, along with our boxes of supplies. The colonel had finally run out of things to say. I would have enjoyed the ride had I not been seated next to the explosive materials and over the back axle. As it was, I felt every pebble and pothole during the thirty-minute ride to our destination. The only consolation was that we were not transporting nitroglycerin.

We eventually arrived at a small cottage of cob and thatch, standing beside a boarded-up barn and several outbuildings. They were up against the sea, beside a vacant lighthouse built of Welsh granite. Smoke was rising from the cottage chimney, and it was obvious we were not alone.

"Who is here?" Barker asked suspiciously as we got out of the trap.

"I've engaged a housekeeper and cook for your comfort," Dunleavy explained.

"Bah!" Barker cried, playing the hardened revolutionary. "Send her away! We have no need of comfort. Mr. Penrith and I are accustomed to taking care of ourselves, and we do not believe in servitude. There will come a time, Mr. Dunleavy, when the servant classes shall overthrow their oppressors, and all men and women shall live as equals!"

"Very well," Dunleavy said, a smile on his hawkish features. While we waited, he got down and went in to speak to the housekeeper. I got the impression the American revolutionary did not share Barker's views and would very much like a large mansion full of servants. In a few moments, a squat woman came out and got into the trap, clutching a wicker basket in one hand and a jingling kerchief full of coins in the other.

"Is there enough food and water for several days?" Barker asked.

"There is," Dunleavy assured him, "and to spare."

"Then we shall not take up any more of your valuable time, sir. Mr. Penrith and I shall settle in on our own."

"When will you be ready?" the American asked.

"Give us a few days. Let us say Saturday. Bring your compatriots, if you wish. No doubt Mr. O'Casey, in particular, shall be interested in the proceedings."

Dunleavy nodded, shook our hands brusquely, and climbed into the trap in front of the housekeeper. The driver set our crates and carboys down on the ground.

Once the trap was gone, Barker and I went in to inspect our new quarters. Inside, there were thick beams overhead, a large fireplace with a swing-out hook for cooking, and stacks of dried peat for fuel. The furniture was old, but the housekeeper had wiped off the dust, and mended damage due to mice. It wasn't a palace, but it was comfortable enough for two bachelors.

Away from prying eyes and ears, Barker threw himself into a chair and put his feet up on a low table. I lit the fire, more to have something to do than because we needed it.

"You seemed short with Dunleavy, sir, if I may say it."

"Yes," he responded. "I've been closeted with the fellow for days now. I don't want him to think he has it too easy with van Rhyn. That old German can be prickly at times, as I'm sure you noticed at Aldershot."

I looked into a small larder. There were tinned meats, a brace of rabbits, dried fish, eggs, and several loaves of soda bread. A sack contained the inevitable potatoes and peas, and a mince pie sat beside containers of tea and coffee. Being Irish, Dunleavy had also seen that plenty of stout and Irish whiskey were on hand. Apparently, he thought nothing wrong with combining alcohol and explosives.

"There's plenty of food," I said. "Who will cook?"

"Have you ever seen me in a kitchen?" he asked.

That set me back a moment. Come to think of it, I hadn't seen him in the kitchen in London. Not ever. Can a man own a house without ever going into his own kitchen? This must be another of his eccentricities, such as his dislike of handling or discussing money. A couple of months earlier he had handed over his wallet, checkbook, and ledgers to me and hadn't mentioned them once until this case began. I could have been systematically emptying out the agency accounts, for all he knew.

"No, sir. Perhaps it was precipitate to send away the housekeeper."

"I was tired of speaking in that German accent and whispering to you," he grumbled. "These infernal whiskers are itchy as well. I want to relax, I want my green tea, and, by thunder, I want my little dog!"

I thought it best to soothe him. "She left a passable Ceylon tea here. I'll put the kettle on. I think I can cook well enough for a few days, at least. Shall I start preparing dinner?"

"No, let us reconnoiter. I don't want any surprises."

Barker and I left the cottage and began peeking into the various outbuildings. Having been inactive for several days, my employer exercised his muscles by prying the boards off doors and windows. The barn looked suitable for our work. The roof was sound, and someone, the old woman perhaps, had swept and laid down new straw.

A second building, which may once have been a granary, had been converted to sleeping quarters with two rows of bunks. Barker looked about, even stripping the covers from one and bringing the pillow to his nose.

"Not new," he deduced, "but not very old, either. I believe they planned and prepared the last operation here."

The next building was a privy. Barker gave a low grunt. I knew he was comparing it unfavorably to his luxurious bathhouse.

"I suppose one could bathe in the ocean," I suggested.

"In the Irish Sea in June? Are you mad? I'm not a seal."

Van Rhyn wasn't the only one who was prickly, I thought to myself, following my employer down the path toward the old lighthouse.

The door was nailed shut, but the bottom had rotted away. When we had removed the boards and stepped inside, something skittered across the room into a hole, and I could hear doves overhead.

"Stoats," Barker said, kicking the dirt.

"I'll have to clear them out before we blow it up."

"You're a soft-hearted anarchist, Llewelyn. London's fate hangs in the balance, and you're worried about a few rodents."

"Doesn't the Bible say something about caring for little creatures?" I countered.

Barker gave one of his rare smiles. "Proverbs twelve ten says, 'The righteous man regardeth the life of his beast,' but I don't think that applies here. For the time being, I'll help you clear out this place."

I climbed the steps to the second floor. My mind was calculating probable wall thickness to height, how much charge to use, and where.

"What do you think, lad?" The Guv's voice echoed up the stairwell. "Fuse, timer, or detonator?"

"Detonator, I would think," I said. "Do you have enough materials to blow it?"

"More than enough, depending on what effect we wish to produce. We can wire along the base and topple the entire structure into the water. We could run small charges through the building, which will cause it to shiver into rubble, or blow the whole structure to smithereens, but that might be a danger to spectators. It would also be very loud. We do not want to alert the neighbors, even in such an isolated spot as this."

I returned to the ground floor, and we stepped outside again.

I paused. "Hmmm."

"What is it?"

We were facing the rocky coast, and the waves crashing against it. "I haven't been in Wales in two years."

"How long has it been since you communicated with your family?" he asked, as we began moving down the path again.

"Not since prison days," I admitted.

"It's not my business to pry into your private life, lad, but isn't it time you put your mother's heart at ease?"

I looked down and kicked a small rock in front of me. "I'm not ready yet," I said. "I'll know when the time is right."

We began moving our supplies into the barn, and for a moment I thought our plans had gone awry. There was no tool with which to open the crates. It would be embarrassing if they came on Saturday and found us still sitting on sealed boxes. Then Barker reached into his sleeve, pulled out a ten-inch dagger, and began prying up the lid of one of the crates.

"I'd forgotten how well armed you are, sir. Do you still carry your calling cards?"

Barker reached inside his coat pocket and pulled out a penny. With a flick of his wrist, he embedded it into one of the beams overhead. He usually kept a handful in his pocket, their edges filed to a razorlike sharpness. They were not deadly, unless they struck a vital area just so, but they certainly took the fight out of most adversaries.

Barker finished opening the crates, and we removed the straw. We had primers and fuses, carboys of acid, and cakes of dynamite.

"Everything but Christmas crackers," I remarked.

"Yes, well, you can play with your infernal engines later, lad. For now, we must inspect the old dynamite."

In the corner of the barn we found a large packing case, showing evidence that it had been opened, then nailed shut again; straw hung down on all sides under the lid. I noted immediately that the raw wood of the case was stained near the bottom. Barker and I glanced at each other and crossed over to it. Both of us knew that it could only be the much-discussed crate of dynamite. The remark of van Rhyn's, that nitroglycerin sometimes went off out of sheer bad temper, came back to me.

My employer took his knife, carefully slipped the blade under the lid's edge, and pried open the case. It had been half emptied, but at the bottom were dozens of identical cakes of explosives.

Most of them had a waxy residue on the outside. Reaching in, I found that it had glued most of the cakes together.

"Do you think it is inert?" I asked.

"Most of it appears viable. I think we must separate the cakes, and scrape some of the wax from the fuses. We must be careful, of course, or this Welsh coastline will look like another Krakatoa. I daresay inserting one of the new sticks into the mass would have the effect of livening up the others, much as adding a new bull to a herd of cattle."

Barker took his pipe, and glanced at the beach. "I believe I will take a walk and clear my head. I have much to think over. You may begin to prepare dinner."

There was no getting around it. As far as explosives are concerned, I have a certain talent, but when it comes to cooking I'm completely inept. Five minutes into the preparation, and I was considering giving up rabbit forever. I don't know how butchers do not become vegetarians. It was all I could do to make a stew without getting clumps of fur in it. About forty-five minutes later, I swung the big pot out from the fire on the iron bracket, and spooned the bubbling mixture into a wooden bowl. Everything appeared to be cooked through, and it at least somewhat resembled stew.

Barker dipped in a spoon and brought it to his mouth. I was in a very unenviable position. He was close friends with two London chefs, Etienne Dummolard and Ho, and was part owner of at least one of their restaurants. My only hope was that Dummolard was correct in his assertion that Barker had almost no sense of taste. My employer chewed slowly and swallowed. After a few seconds, he nodded and took another bite. I let out my breath. As long as I hadn't poisoned him, everything was fine. I dared a nibble of the stew myself, then regretted it. My taste buds were perfectly intact. I put a carrot in my pocket and left Barker alone, chewing on the stew and staring abstractedly into space.

After dinner, we went back to the barn and began to remove the old dynamite from the crate. Barker took out his knife and began scraping the waxy buildup from the cakes.

"Careful," I warned.

"Don't worry, lad," he said. "I rather exaggerated the dangers of the decayed dynamite for Dunleavy's benefit."

We began getting out the equipment to set up our makeshift laboratory, and fell into conversation about what to blow up and how. Nothing of any import occurred during the next several days. Barker wished to put on a demonstration using several types of explosives: dynamite, picric bombs, timed and fuse bombs, anything that we could put together. Barker and I debated whether to test our explosives on a nearby dolmen. It was some-one's tomb, after all, and had remained untouched for a thousand years. It seemed a pity to destroy it.

Barker continued taking walks along the shore, and eventually, I joined him. A family of otters amused us, and I was glad they were there, for their antics diverted us. It was not easy living in such close quarters with Barker. When I am with Israel Zangwill, we can talk for hours over nearly any subject, but Barker prefers contemplation to conversation. The week passed slowly and quietly.

They arrived Saturday morning, the whole lot of them: Dunleavy, Yeats, O'Casey, McKeller, and the Bannon boys. Even Maire O'Casey had come, which I considered entirely improper. I thought it wrong of her brother to include her in these illegal pro-ceedings.

"Hello, Penrith," Willie Yeats said, pumping my hand. Though he still wore a flowing tie over his celery-stalk collar, he'd traded his city suit for country tweeds.

Fergus McKeller looked a bit moody, though I saw they'd brought a large picnic hamper, and a barrel of stout in the cart.

All that was left was the entertainment, and our demonstration would be it.

The moment she arrived, Maire O'Casey took over the kitchen, where she deputized Yeats and one of the Bannons, I believe it was Padraig, to peel potatoes. I showed her where everything was and hoped she didn't ask about my puny attempts at cooking.

"I'm rather shocked to see you here," I admitted to her when we were alone. "I thought your brother would keep you out of this."

"I am a sister and the daughter of republican patriots, Mr. Penrith. My father was a great man and a true patriot. I would not have you think me a coward."

I felt myself blush at the word. "Certainly not."

"I do more than merely feed the lot of you. There are many ways to contribute to the cause, such as writing poetry. Willie is very talented at that."

"Did I hear my name?" Willie Yeats spoke up from the corner, where he was peeling. I felt a trifle envious of him, and I suspected he was jealous of me.

"We were talking about your poetry," Maire went on. "It's marvelous. You should read it, Mr. Penrith. At times it is so simple, any peasant can read and understand it, but it has such a mystical and intellectual quality to it, one would have to be a Blake to interpret the deeper meanings."

"Oh, really, it's just scribblings, you know," Yeats said.

"Scribblings! Willie Yeats, you say that again, and I'll take one of Eamon's sticks to you. Someday you shall go far with those little scribblings."

What can one say after such praise from a beautiful girl? Yeats puffed out his thin chest like a carrier pigeon, while I felt insignificant indeed.

"I've written a new one, Maire, about Queen Mab and the

fairy world. Perhaps I can bring it over in a couple of days, when I return from Dublin."

"I should love to read it, Willie."

Yeats bowed and walked off in stiff, long strides.

"Why does he walk like that?" I asked under my breath.

Maire gave a smile for the first time since I had met her. "Ever since he took me to the theater in London a few months ago, he has emulated the gait of Mr. Henry Irving."

I couldn't help it. I choked and began coughing. Maire tried to hide her own giggles behind her hand, but it was too late. Yeats turned around and scowled at us. I noted that his walk after that was far less theatrical.

About an hour before sundown, the time for the big event arrived. I went over to the lighthouse and rechecked the various charges and the wires hooked up to the new detonator for probably the hundredth time. If Barker's plan went off as hoped, we would give them a show they wouldn't soon forget.

As if on cue, everyone came together and perched on a ring of rocks that had once formed the base of an ancient home or fort. We sat in a semicircle, facing the sea, while Alfred Dunleavy stepped up on a tall, flat rock and addressed us.

15

"**S**ONS OF IRELAND," DUNLEAVY BEGAN, CLUTCH-
ing the lapels of his military coat, "I thank you for taking time
away from your daily lives and coming all this way for a demonstration. I must admit to you that I had grown a little discour-
aged lately regarding our situation with England. Mr. Parnell
does little save flatter society matrons and squander our precious
funds, while Gladstone stands like a farthing in a crack, refusing
to fall either way. I was sure that our little attack upon London
would topple him, but apparently he's set in stone. They are a
flinty-hearted race, the English. We had shot our bolt, and they'd
absorbed it, almost without a trace, and our supply of precious
dynamite was old and faulty. What would we do next? I wondered.

"Then, as if by Providence, whom should I meet but the great
Johannes van Rhyn himself. His reputation as a bomb maker and
revolutionary is legendary. He understood our struggles and
offered his services to us. I took heart again. With such expertise,
surely we cannot fail!

"But, I see I have forgotten Mr. Penrith. He began as an

apprentice in the revolutionary trade under Mr. van Rhyn, but even the maestro will admit that in some matters, the student has surpassed his teacher. He was trained at Mr. Alfred Nobel's own factory near Glasgow. When looking at Mr. Penrith, one is first struck by how young he looks. Yet he is a seasoned veteran in the war against tyranny and as anxious to help us as Mr. van Rhyn. We are privileged to have such a fine young man with us today."

Everyone applauded. I could feel the heat of my blushes around my collar.

"These two gentlemen have worked for days to set up a display of their abilities for us all. Foreign governments would have traveled far to witness these marvels. And you can believe that after seeing such a sight as this the representatives of Her Majesty's government would be shaking in their boots. But none of them may see it, for this demonstration is for our eyes alone. I must ask you, on your oaths as protectors of Ireland, to keep absolutely silent about what you see here today for a while, at least. Someday, perhaps, this event will be spoken of with pride and hushed tones in the pubs of Dublin and Cork, Boston and Chicago, but for now I ask silence.

"Speaking of silence, it is time for me to stop rambling and to turn this rude stage over to the gentleman who has done more for the cause of freedom than I ever shall. Gentlemen, and lady, I give you Johannes van Rhyn!"

Barker stood and bowed gravely. He cleared his throat and began in that bass rumble of his. "Mr. Penrith and I have collaborated in preparing for you a demonstration of some of the latest advancements in infernal devices. Perhaps you will allow me a moment to light a cigar, because I shall need it for my work."

After Dunleavy's introduction, my employer was deliberately lowering their expectations. They were expecting a show and he appeared ready to deliver a lecture instead.

"Mr. Penrith, the sphere, please." Barker took the bomb and

held it aloft for all to see. *"Danke.* This black sphere I hold in my hand, gentlemen, should be recognizable to you all. It is a picric bomb, full of the acid of the same name. One just like it was used to end the life of Czar Alexander the Second in St. Petersburg."

Barker used his cigar to light the fuse, and it sputtered to life.

"I am not a dynamiter, of course," he said conversationally, as the fuse vanished inch by inch, "nor am I as young as I once was, but I hope to throw this far enough so that the shrapnel does not harm any of you."

My employer leaned back and hurled the bomb, watching as it arched to the left. It bounced and rolled across the clearing like a *sliotar* before finally striking a rock. There was a loud crack and flash, and clods of earth and rock showered down. Everyone cried out in fear and wonder. The bombers were more accustomed to leaving their deadly devices to explode after they had gone. Now they were seeing the results of their art firsthand.

"Here now are three sticks of dynamite Mr. Penrith has tied together. Dynamite is nitroglycerin which has been soaked into kieselguhr to render it safe, though not too safe, I fear, as the brother of Mr. Nobel would attest, were he alive to do so. Dynamite has been a boon to bombers everywhere."

He lit the fuses with his cigar and threw the bundle of dynamite among some clumps of sea grass. The explosion was louder and more powerful than the one before, blowing stalks high into the air. Miss O'Casey and Willie Yeats held their ears.

"Let us move on," Barker said in a professional manner. "I draw your attention to that ancient dolmen over there, close to the sea. We have taken the opportunity to build a low-grade bomb from materials we acquired, and attached it with a pistol and primer to a timing device. How much time have we left, Mr. Penrith?"

I had made my way to the dolmen and set the timer as he was

speaking. I came back, consulting the watch Barker had lent me for the demonstration.

"Forty-five seconds, sir," I called out, making my way back to the circle. Everyone was leaning forward. They were looking the worse for wear, I thought, with bits of grass in their hair and dirt on their clothes. Fifteen seconds went by. No one spoke. Thirty. Forty-five. A minute.

"It didn't—" Eamon O'Casey began, when the air was suddenly ripped by an explosion. The large rock atop the dolmen convulsed and split down the middle, like the veil in Herod's temple on Easter morning. The air was full of smoke and dust.

"It was late," Barker complained.

"I am sorry, sir."

"It is not an exact science, you see, gentlemen," the Guv explained. "The more complicated the bomb, the more things can go wrong. Complications can also lead to better results. Mr. Penrith has been playing with the old cakes of dynamite and has added a little something of his own to liven them up. So far, we have used fuses and a timer. I have here a commercial detonator. I would like to demonstrate how easy it is to use. Miss O'Casey, would you like to come forward and do the honors?"

"I?" the girl asked, looking reluctant.

"It is easy to use. Come, miss. Just put both hands on this rod of wood here. Now push down."

Gingerly, Maire O'Casey pushed down the plunger. The old lighthouse gave a convulsive leap in a massive explosion, rising it at least ten feet off the ground. The bottom half shivered into bits, but the top flew headfirst into the sea. The concussion blew past me and knocked everyone flat except the two of us, who had been prepared. Barker made some final comment loudly, but I had momentarily lost my hearing.

O'Casey recovered first, a look of awe and joy on his face. Dunleavy was next, blinking, his mind calculating what this might mean for Irish freedom. McKeller was still on the ground, but he was holding his sides and laughing. The Bannon brothers had been knocked all in a heap. Only Yeats did not look happy. He fumbled with his pince-nez, glowered at us, and rose.

Maire had received a small cut on her forehead from the debris, and he rushed forward to dab it with a handkerchief. From my position between O'Casey and McKeller, I couldn't see how she was. I was still stunned that Barker had used the girl for the demonstration. I didn't approve of her detonating the bomb, and would have voiced my objection to my employer had her brother not been shaking me hard by the shoulders and thumping me on the back.

"By the saints, that was absolutely bloody incredible! I thought you were going to launch that old lighthouse, like a Roman candle, right over London! With explosives like this, our mission can't fail!"

Fergus McKeller was still laughing so hard that tears were running down his ruddy cheeks. He finally sat up, his feet spread out like a boy at play in the dirt, then bawled over his shoulder.

"Colin! Padraig! Get up, ye buskers! Go find your fiddle and your whistle, and let's have us a ceilidh!"

Slowly, the group came to life again. Maire stood and checked her hair, then began to set out the food. Yeats brought more provisions from the cart, complaining that the horses were panic-stricken. Fergus McKeller hammered a spigot into the barrel of stout, while Colin and Padraig Bannon began to warm up their instruments. Before I knew it, I was in the middle of my first ceilidh. We Welsh are a more sedate group of Celts than our Irish brethren, thanks to the evangelizing work of John and Charles Wesley. I was wondering if a wild Irish revel might be too much for a born Methodist and his Baptist employer.

There was a sudden pop behind me, which I must admit made me jump. Dunleavy had opened a bottle of champagne, which he poured into three pint glasses already half full of Guinness. He handed one each to Barker and me.

"I understand that this drink was created upon the death of Albert, the Prince Consort," he explained. "It was decreed that day in Dublin Town that even champagne should be in mourning black. They call it a black velvet, and if either of you can still stand up after three of them, you're a better man than I."

We raised our drinks and gave the official toast, *sláinte*, but I was thinking I'd give a month's salary for a nice glass of milk, and I think Barker would have, too. Stout was fine, but I couldn't see myself making a steady diet of the brew.

I went into the cottage to help Miss O'Casey with the food. It was amazing how much she and her crew had thrown together in a short couple of hours, with not much more than a few old pots and an open fire. The feast consisted of colcannon, sprouts, tinned beef, peas, soda bread, a small ham, and rashers of bacon.

"It was a shame for the lighthouse to come down," Yeats commented from the inglenook. "I know it wasn't of any use to people anymore, but I liked the old building."

"As did I," I admitted. "We had to turn out some stoats and other small animals that were living there. I would have preferred another site, but Mr. van Rhyn insisted."

"So, Mr. Explosives Expert," Maire said, "are you going to stand here and bother my helpers, or are you willing to do some actual work? Start slicing that bread there, if you have a mind to, unless destroying is all you're good for."

Yeats grinned, and I began to slice. An hour or two before, we'd been making fun of Willie's absurd walk, and now I was the victim of her sharp tongue. I can't say I especially cared for it.

We began taking the feast out to the hungry men, who had already started drinking on empty stomachs. I barely had time to set down the pot of peas, when there was such a flashing of spoons about it, I thought I'd better get my own in quickly or I wouldn't get any at all. I asked McKeller why peas were such a favorite among the men in Ireland.

"It's simple economics, Penrith," he explained. "The less money you waste on food, the more you can spend on drink. A plate o' peas should be enough of a meal for any Irishman."

Having loaded plates for Barker and myself, I went back into the cottage, for I'd seen the kettle brewing on the fire. I took a tankard of tea and a plate to my employer, who had wandered to the bonfire the men had started and sat down on a rock.

"Thank you, lad," he murmured under his breath.

"It went off without a hitch," I whispered.

"Aye. I'm inclined to hope that Dunleavy shall open that purse of his a little wider now that we've shown him we know what we're about."

"That's cause to celebrate," I said.

"You really are starting to sound like an Irishman, lad." He sniffed. "I, for one, have no wish to partake in drunken revelry for its own sake. I believe I shall retire early. You may give them my excuses." His moral dignity intact, Barker took his plate and tankard and went into the cottage.

It was growing dark by now and the Bannon twins were in full swing, while McKeller danced a jig with all the elaborate concentration that comes from having had too much to drink. Eamon O'Casey was leaning against a rock, laughing at his friend's antics and clapping in time to the music.

"Maire!" McKeller roared. "Come have a dance!"

The girl demurred, but it was only a matter of convincing her. They all started calling her name, chanting it together, until she finally relented, allowing Yeats to escort her to the dance floor—a sandy clearing.

"I won't dance on sand!" She demanded, "I shall need a door, at least."

It suddenly became the most necessary thing in the world that they find her a good door. They finally took one in the main cottage off its hinges, despite Barker's protests, and set it on the ground.

Maire O'Casey stepped onto it as regal as a queen and stood for a moment, looking tall and cool. Her arms were at her sides, and she lifted her hem a few inches, displaying a pair of dainty shoes and trim ankles. She stood stock-still a moment, as Colin's fiddle and Padraig's pennywhistle tune began to build, and I realized I was holding my breath. There were no ribald comments from the men, no half-drunken singing. All eyes were on Maire.

She began, her feet moving lightly, clicking on the wood, hands at her sides, a look of concentration on her face. Her feet moved so quickly my eyes couldn't keep up, her heels providing a drumbeat for the rest of the music. The cool evening wind combed through her curling hair, which had fallen from its bun, and the fire played across it until it, too, seemed to be made of fire, a head of flames burning in the summer darkness. Her face was still frozen, however, her features chiseled in ice.

She leapt up high, like a roe, and one of her feet lashed out in a kick. Her dance grew more and more wild, spinning in a circle, and then slowly, her eyes moved downward and fastened on me. I felt my face heat up, and not merely because I was near the fire. I don't think I could have taken my eyes off hers if I had two men tugging on me.

Maire's icy reserve began to thaw as well. Her face took on a sheen from her exertions, and her eyes grew large. She raised her skirt up higher, displaying a glimpse of petticoat, as her feet flashed in a dozen directions, stamping on the door like a thousand hammers. She danced like a fairy, tossing her head about as her hair moved like a live thing. I was spellbound, hypnotized. Who would have suspected this mild girl could have such fire in her?

The wild dance suddenly came to an abrupt end along with the music. She froze into ice again in an instant, the only movement being the heaving of her bosom and the trickle of perspiration down her cheek. We all gave a wild cheer, jumping to our feet, and clapping. I beat Yeats to the punch, pulling the handkerchief from my pocket and presenting it to her. She thanked me, and made her way through the appreciative men toward the cottage, to remake herself into the image of the demure Irish girl, who had been preparing a humble dish of colcannon for her brother and his friends not a half hour earlier. Which, I wondered, was the real Maire O'Casey?

Anything after that, of course, would be anticlimactic. Solemnly, Padraig Bannon stood up and began to play some sad, familiar airs on the pennywhistle, and the men joined in and sang. They were songs of eviction, of the potato famine, forced emigration, and heroes who had been martyred for the cause of Irish freedom. There was something pure and simple in his playing that was almost unbearably tragic. I looked over at Fergus McKeller, now a half dozen pints into his evening. He was crying like a baby over the fate of his countrymen.

The party came to a slow end some time after one in the morning. Most of the men had fallen asleep on the ground outside around the fire. I carried plates into the cottage, but Maire was nowhere to be found. I threw more boards from the outbuilding we'd blown up onto the fire, enough to last the night. The firelight reflecting on the faces of the men asleep around it made them all look like youths, mere boys out for a night's camping together, rather than the hardened bombers they were.

By the time I went to our cottage, Barker's broad back was already to me, and he was sound asleep. I supposed I would have been sleepy, if I hadn't had some strong tea earlier. Tea has always affected me that way. I attempted to sleep, but gave it up after half an hour. I was wide awake and restless, so I got up and went outside.

The moon was full and clear, bathing the landscape in silvery light. It was exactly the kind of atmosphere I'd imagined when reading the book of Irish myths. One could believe in leprechauns and banshees on a night like this. The wind was cool, and I turned up my collar as I made my way down to the beach. I wanted a closer look at the remains of the lighthouse.

There was nothing but a circle of stones now, with a trail of rubble leading to the sea. *Well, that was good, then,* I told myself. I'd accomplished at least one part of Barker's objective. We'd proven we were great explosives experts. If someone had told me two months before that I'd be blowing up Welsh lighthouses, I'd have thought he was raving mad.

There was a sound behind me. My training took over. I turned in a crouch and raised my fists. It was Maire, alone. She had a thick shawl wrapped around her, and the pins in her hair just barely held in the wild curls I'd seen at the fire's edge.

"You're a dangerous man, Thomas Penrith," she murmured.

"Not half as dangerous as you, Maire O'Casey."

Then somehow, her hands were in my hair, and her lips were pressed against mine. Her cold fingers were clenched against the back of my head, which was spinning like a top. I wanted to inhale her, consume her. I wanted us to burn up together. Which was just what would happen if I allowed this to go too far.

16

I COULD HAVE GONE ON KISSING MAIRE O'CASEY forever, if she would have let me. The feel of her lips and the heady scent of lilac water in her hair are things that will linger in my memory forever. Finally, she put both hands on my chest insistently and ended our kiss. I murmured her name, and she silenced me with her cool hand.

"You quite take a girl's breath away, Mr. Penrith," she said, and I could feel her tremble with emotion, or perhaps it was only the chill of the night. She stepped back and gathered her shawl about her shoulders again. "I hadn't intended to . . . to . . . I had better go now."

She turned, and before I could stop her, she fled, bounding from rock to rock. I could still taste her lips and smell the lilac, but they were the only evidence that it wasn't a dream, that I wasn't still in the cottage with Cyrus Barker, sleeping. I didn't think she'd meant to kiss me. She was going to say something, to utter some commonplace remark about the party or the demonstration or about coming upon me alone so late at night, and then something happened. She was the match and I the dynamite. We'd gotten too close to each other, and a chemical reaction had occurred.

I walked along the shoreline for a while, but every couple of steps my mind and feet were arrested by the memory of what had just happened, and I'd stand and relive it. That had been no casual kiss. I think it surprised her more than it had me, and that is saying a good deal. It was half an hour before I finally thought to return to my berth, and I was still walking with my head in the clouds. That is my explanation for not noticing the train until it hit me.

It wasn't an actual train, of course, but it might as well have been. It ran on eight legs at a tremendous pace and struck with the force of a steam locomotive. I was knocked clean off my feet and didn't land again for a half dozen yards. I skidded along a rock and then was crushed in a tangle of arms and limbs and bodies. I tried to see what had hit me, under the silvery moonlight, but what I saw was something out of the book of Irish myths. That alone could explain the wild-haired, blue-skinned Celts that had stepped out of the past and now stood over me.

Eight rough hands seized me, ripping braces and buttons and pulling up my shirt while keeping my limbs pinned to the ground. I struggled as my stomach and chest were laid bare, and for a moment I wondered if I was about to be sacrificed by a secret cabal of Druids to their ancient gods. Then, a rain of blows from sticks showered down, as if my stomach were a drum to be beat upon, and all the fierce warriors began to chant: *"Bata, bata, bata, bata, bata, bata, bata, bata, bata, bata, bata, bata, bata, bata, BATA!"*

I cried out in pain as my ribs were pummeled. Then, as I lay prostrate, my four assailants proceeded to strip me almost bare, tossing clothes and shoes over their shoulders, as if I'd never need them in this world again. My reverie had suddenly become a nightmare. Finally, the moon slipped from behind a cloud, and I could see what calamity had overtaken me.

Eamon O'Casey looked down on me, his heel on my right

shoulder, his stick against my cheek. He was shirtless, though he still wore braces over his naked chest. All manner of designs had been drawn over his face and torso in blue paint, giving him the look of a South Sea island savage. I could see a Celtic dragon across Fergus McKeller's brawny chest; his braces hung about his knees. Despite his fierce war paint and bare breast, Colin Bannon still wore his respectable bowler, but he'd stuck some feathers into the band; and Padraig was got up as close to a Plains Indian as an Irish lad could be, with nothing but trousers and his waistcoat, and dozens of painted tattoos over his arms, chest, and face.

My first thought, absurd as it was, was that O'Casey had seen me kiss his sister and had come to thrash me, but that wouldn't account for the elaborate paint and the presence of the others. Then it occurred to me that somehow they had penetrated our subterfuge, and I grew truly frightened. Perhaps I really was about to be sacrificed, with Barker coming next. In either case, I was certain I wasn't going to get out of this alive, not by the serious and resolute expressions of O'Casey and McKeller glowering over me.

"Is the candidate ready?" a voice intoned behind me.

"He is ready," Eamon O'Casey declared.

"Move him to the sacrificial stone."

The four men carried me, struggling, to the fractured dolmen, where they held me down, a man to each limb. The fifth member of the group followed, and they parted as he stepped up onto the stone, stood between my splayed limbs, and placed a short length of wood like a wand against my breast. He wore a long black cloak that covered him to the ground, but his face was not obscured. It was Willie Yeats. Spectacles had been drawn onto his face in blue, with wavy lines radiating out in every direction. He looked like the high priest in some secret order, which, in fact, he was.

"What is your name, candidate?"

"You know very well what my—*Oof!*"

I'd received a thump from each of the four corners.

"What is your name, candidate?" he repeated severely.

"Thomas Penrith!"

"Mr. Penrith, you are about to be initiated into one of the most secret and sacred orders of the world: the Invisibles. Do you swear under penalty of death that you will not reveal or divulge anything that you see here tonight?"

My word! It was an initiation ceremony. I let out a sigh of relief. "I swear."

"Then repeat after me. I, Thomas Penrith, do solemnly swear . . . that I will hold secret all arcane ceremonies of the Invisibles . . . and if I dare to reveal these secrets . . . may my tongue be torn out by its roots . . . my breast opened . . . and my heart and liver removed and roasted on a spit . . . for being a blasphemous traitor. . . . Henceforth, I declare these men here . . . to be my true and only brothers . . . and I pledge undying loyalty . . . to my brethren . . . and to this hallowed society."

"And to this hallowed society," I finished.

Yeats poured a drink into my mouth, a mixture of stout and ash from the fire. While I was still sputtering, he turned his wand sideways, and thrust it between my teeth. I should have noticed that my left leg was free and Colin Bannon missing, but I was too busy choking to realize it until he had returned to perform the next part of the ceremony. I cried out as the red-hot metal ferrule of his stick burned the flesh of my shoulder. I knew Cyrus Barker had close to a dozen such marks, but it had never occurred to me how much each one of them must have hurt.

Willie Yeats reached into the pocket of his cloak and pulled out a small pot of blue paint and a brush. While I lay there, still groaning with his stick in my mouth, he began painting my torso in runes and symbols. I'm sure he loved every minute of it, playing the high priest and torturing his rival for Maire's affections, if in fact, he knew I was a rival.

"This is your new stick. It's called a *bata* in Gaelic. Does it hurt?" he asked with a devilish smile.

"You know it hurts!" I sputtered around the stick in my mouth.

"Would you like some cold water on it?"

I nodded. Cold water was just what I needed for my shoulder.

"He wants water, boys," Yeats said. Suddenly, I was dragged off the rock and, before I knew it, I was sailing through the air, until I struck the icy water of the Irish Sea. I hadn't meant salt water. My shoulder stung as if a thousand needles had been jabbed into it. Unsteadily, I crawled out of the sea onto the rocks. What had I been thinking when I assured myself this was just an initiation ceremony? I was hoping now to simply live through it.

Shivering, bruised, wearing nothing but sodden drawers, I came back up to the circle of smirking devils who awaited me.

"Is that it?" I asked. "Is it over?"

"Almost," O'Casey said with an evil look, handing me the stick I had just been branded with. "You just have to fight Fergus and me and it's all but over."

"But I've never fought with a stick before!" I protested.

"Aye, we know," he gloated. "This is to teach you the importance of knowing how. Fergus?"

"Call it!" He tossed a ha'penny up in the air, caught it, and slapped it against the back of his wrist.

"Heads!" Fergus called, delighted.

"Heads, it is, then. Your treat. But save me a little."

"I'll save you just enough to wrap a stick around," he said, and began to circle me.

I was about to get a hiding, while Barker was asleep a quarter mile away, which might as well have been London, for all the help he could render me. If my rapidly bruising ribs were any indication, this was going to hurt. I had had no more than a week's worth of lessons from Monsieur Vigny, and my experiences with fisticuffs, in prison and the school yard, had been generally unsatisfactory.

McKeller raised his stick behind him, waving it in small circles over his head. His other hand was out, his feet spread apart, ready to wage war with the ease of a seasoned fighter. I raised both hands in front of me and swung my stick around in an attempt at self-defense.

He lashed out before I could move and smacked the knuckles of my free hand. Pain blossomed as if I'd been stung, but I dared not drop the stick. I thrust the hand under my other arm and continued circling my stick. He swung across with a swipe that would have taken off my head had I not barely ducked out of the way.

The stick continued in an arc, coming back my way again with more speed. I wasn't going to stand there and get hit. I blocked and parried it, but missed his shoulder by a good foot. The malacca stick I had trained with was nothing compared to the knobby cudgels we were fighting with now, and I had nothing to protect me at all save my wits.

Fergus McKeller feinted at my head again, causing me to raise my stick just enough for him to wallop me in the ribs. The stick felt like an iron fist. I gasped and leapt back, but the ring of young men pushed me into the fray again. We circled about once more, McKeller with a grin on his face, assured of an easy victory. I was going to have to do something to show him this wasn't going to be so easy.

What could I use that Barker had taught me? He told me there were three basic kinds of fighters: the runner, who strikes quickly and dances away; the blocker, who blocks the attack and launches one of his own; and the jammer, who jams your attack as it starts and brings the fight to you. Identifying which fighter I faced would allow me to anticipate what he would do. McKeller, I decided, was a jammer. He wasn't afraid of my stick and didn't fear leaping into my territory. I'd have to teach him.

As if in answer to my thoughts, my opponent jumped forward, stick raised overhead, ready to hit me over the ear. Grasping both ends of the bata stick, I pushed it into his chest, knocking him back before his stick could hit me. Everyone laughed, and McKeller was left rubbing his chest, a lopsided grin on his face. He gave tit for tat on the next move, however, as his hand shot out and he lunged forward in a classic fencing move, the knob catching me square in the solar plexus. I gasped for air and rubbed furiously at the spot.

We circled for a few moments, swinging and missing, feinting and jabbing. I was hoping I'd earned a bit of respect from him. I dodged one of his attacks and caught him on the knuckles of his stick hand, which brought some colorful Irish language from his lips. My downfall, however, was in foolhardiness. I swung at his head; and in answer, he parried it solidly and gave me a riposte upon the ear that knocked me right off my feet.

"My turn!" Eamon O'Casey called eagerly, and he and McKeller switched places. Of the two, he was the more dangerous. McKeller relied upon his aggressiveness and his strength, but O'Casey was a scientific fighter. Watching me as I got up again, he padded about like a young panther planning a kill. He stepped this way and that lightly, almost on his toes, and reluctantly settled into position. His every muscle was coiled, and when I dared ·wave my stick at him, he knocked it down and lashed out, catching me on the other ear. Now it was I who cursed.

I won't embarrass myself any further by describing it. I attacked; he struck. I blocked; he struck. I ran; he came after me and struck again. I was hopelessly outclassed. I was also quickly growing black and blue. My lip began bleeding, but I wouldn't give him the satisfaction of quitting. He'd have to knock me off my feet before I admitted the point. Which he did.

I lay flat on the rocky ground, remarking to myself how many types of pain there are. The sharp agony from a blow on the elbow, for example, is far different from the deep ache from a whack on the lower limbs. A blow to the ears feels cold, as if a bucketful of water has been thrown on your head, but a handful of barked knuckles is hot, like a burn. These were the thoughts I was mulling over when both my opponents bent and looked down on my prostrate form.

"Both at once?" I asked, a bit of fight still left in me.

"Well, he's game enough," McKeller stated.

"What's this about?"

"Call it a test, Penrith," O'Casey said. "An initiation. We initiated you in the Invisibles. This is a tryout for goalkeeper of our hurling club. We'll need one badly once this is all over and we go back to Dublin. Are you interested?"

"I'll consider it," I said diplomatically.

"First non-Irish lad we've ever invited to be on the team," McKeller said, making sure I saw what an honor it was.

"Perhaps, if you stop beating me with sticks."

"Stop! Why, boy," McKeller insisted, "we was just getting started!"

"Very well," I said, "but I want you to know I'm taking names of those to whom I shall eventually give a good beating."

"Put me down," quipped McKeller.

"Me, too," O'Casey added.

"Is this a private gathering, gentlemen, or may I join?" a voice came from the shadows. All eyes turned as the blessed form of Cyrus Barker stepped forward into the flickering light of the bonfire. He was removing his jacket and pulling down his braces. "Perhaps, Mr. McKeller, you would enjoy sparring with someone closer to your own height and weight."

Everyone looked at one another. I was never so glad to see anyone in my life. Barker changed things. Barker leveled things.

"I dunno, Mr. van Rhyn," McKeller said. "You ain't a member. You haven't been initiated."

Barker turned to O'Casey. "In that case, I formally apply for membership in your organization. Here are my credentials."

He removed his shirt and singlet, revealing to the terrorists the dozens of entrées to other secret organizations he wore across his arms and torso. He flexed his bulging arms as he displayed Chinese figures seared into his forearms, Arabic script across his biceps, and a dragon tattoo on his shoulder.

"Get the paint pot, Willie," O'Casey commanded. "Colin, put Penrith's stick back into the fire."

"I have brought my own," my employer said coolly, handing his ivory-inlaid stick to Bannon. The tip of his cane, I noted, was much thicker than my bata stick.

He neither cracked a smile through Yeats's silly speech nor flinched when he was given a new brand on his arm. He solemnly swore to keep the secrets of the Invisibles, on pain of death. With the paintbrush, he covered his own chest and arms in Germanic script. Then he lightly sprung from the dolmen and picked up his cane.

"Are you ready, McKeller?" he asked.

"Aye, but no hooking with that cane of yours."

For once, McKeller looked almost afraid.

"Appeal to Mr. O'Casey, not to me," Barker stated, going into a crouch.

"Eamon, lad," McKeller pleaded. "Canes ain't in the bata rules. He needs a proper knob at the end."

"I'll allow it, Fergus," Eamon replied. "It's his stick and his choice."

Now it was my turn to see the big Irishman squirm. I looked over at Yeats and the Bannons. We all appeared to be looking forward to seeing Fergus McKeller taught a lesson.

Reluctantly, McKeller went into a crouch. He was a jammer,

as I said, and he immediately took the fight to Barker. My employer had anticipated the move, however, and stepped across at an angle, swinging his stick laterally. It caught McKeller on the temple. He let out an oath and backed up.

They circled again, the light and shadows playing across their faces. Barker made a feint, and McKeller roared in. The Guv stepped under his flailing arm and, as he passed, reached up behind him, catching McKeller on the shoulder. Before the Irishman could react, he fell backward over Barker, all his limbs thrashing, and landed on his head and shoulders in the sand. There was a short moment of grappling, and before he knew it, his head was squeezed between my employer's knees, the cane's handle around his throat. The Irishman dared not move.

O'Casey strode over casually to McKeller and looked down into his beet-red face. "You call that 'form,' do you? After all the training I've given you? Face it, man. You've just been outclassed, and rather handily."

McKeller tapped Barker's knee and was released. He rubbed his throat.

"I still think he shouldn't have used his cane. 'Twas no proper bata fight to my way of looking at things."

"Are you next, Mr. O'Casey?" Barker asked, bowing.

"Some other time," O'Casey said nonchalantly. "Where did you learn to fight, Mr. van Rhyn?"

"Here and there," came the reply. "There are some advantages to living a nomad's existence."

"Are we done now?" McKeller asked his friend. "This has built up a powerful thirst, and I want to be the first to pour my new little brother a drink. Great things, brothers. Always willing to lend you a shilling for a pint or two."

Barker went back to the cottage, and I had several pints with McKeller, while with time and night air, my wounds slowly blossomed, every blessed one of them. I have a conviction that the only good thing about alcohol is its use as an anesthetic. I don't think I was brave enough to face all those bruises sober.

By the time I climbed into bed a second time that night, I had no trouble at all falling asleep. Between the nervous exhaustion from the demonstration, the ceilidh, the sudden kiss from Maire, and the initiation—with its branding, ceremony, and beatings—it was a wonder I was still conscious. My last thought before I slid into sleep, as easily as one slides beneath the surface of a pool, was this: of the two sides, theirs and ours, who that evening had provided the best show? At best, I'd call it even.

17

THE NEXT I KNEW, IT WAS MORNING. WARM, PAIN-
fully bright sunshine streamed in from an open window, and the
room was full of the scent of Barker's tobacco, which at the moment smelled like burning seaweed. I tried rising, felt the effects of
too much alcohol and the pain from the initiation, and thought better of it.

Barker was leaning against his headboard, his ankles crossed,
his fingers knotted over his now-ample stomach, attempting to
blow smoke rings.

"Morning, sir," I muttered. I missed my room in Newington
and my privacy.

"How are you feeling?" my employer asked.

I got up, groaning, and went to the ewer and bowl in the corner. Somehow, the water began turning blue. It took a moment
for my disjointed brain to put it all together. I was still half
clothed and covered in paint like a savage. There were arcane
symbols all over my chest and face. Barker, of course, had washed
his off the previous night and looked as normal as, well, as he had
looked since this case began.

"How long were you there watching before you joined in?" I asked, as I wiped my face and chest with a towel.

"I wandered over during the initiation ceremony."

"Why didn't you stop them?" I demanded. The burn on my shoulder was a small, circular welt that stung like anything, and my mood was sour.

"Because I wanted you to be initiated, lad. Now we're in. We can relax, at least a little."

"You let McKeller and O'Casey thrash me," I complained.

Barker managed one perfect smoke ring, then spoke. "You'll live. Had they really intended to harm you, I would have stepped in. How was the rest of the night?"

"I don't remember much of it, I'm afraid," I said. "McKeller kept making toasts."

"As soon as this case is over, I shall put you in Brother McClain's hands at his Mile End mission in London. He's had some success with inebriates such as you. What did you do before the initiation?"

I let the remark pass. "I went out to look at the damage to the lighthouse, and I may have kissed Maire O'Casey there," I confessed. It was the last thing I wanted to reveal to him, but I knew it might affect the case and Barker's plans in some way.

He puffed on his pipe a moment before launching another perfect circle of smoke across the bed. "You may have? You're not sure?"

"No, I am sure. I kissed Maire O'Casey."

"I see. Interesting. Did she kiss you back?"

I concentrated on my memories of the night before. "Rather."

"You do realize that she is the sister of a young man who may have blown up Scotland Yard, not to mention our chambers."

"Yes, sir."

"You're pretending to be someone else, and if she found out who you are, she'd probably loathe you. You are the enemy."

"Yes, sir."

"And need I remind you my agency doesn't exist to find you female companionship."

"No, sir." The words stung worse than the burn. I despised myself for disappointing him.

"Miss O'Casey, like most beautiful young women, is a complication, and we have enough complications as it is. Keep your wits about you, Thomas."

I sighed. "Yes, sir."

"It's for your own good. Wash again. You're still blue about the ears." He got up and left me to my ablutions.

The group was slowly awakening. Rising from around the now-ashen bonfire, the young men broke their fast on the stale bread and stout from the night before. I decided to wait until we were in Liverpool again before I dared to eat anything.

Maire O'Casey was still using Yeats as a beast of burden. He was loading the hamper and some pots and pans into the cart. I wondered what sort of reception she would give me, after last night. As it turned out, it was none at all. I might as well have been a ghost for all the attention she gave me.

Sore, tired, miserable, and confused, I climbed into the vehicle beside my employer and counseled myself to be philosophical. This is life. One minute, you're the hero and the next, the goat. Yesterday, after the success of the demonstration, I felt I could do no wrong. Now, all I had to look forward to was a ride back to the railway halt with a group of sullen people and a train ride to Liverpool.

The next day there was another hurling match in Prince's Park. As I watched, I reflected on the fact that none of the faction members appeared to have occupations. O'Casey was enjoying summer holiday from Trinity, but who fed and sheltered McKeller and the Bannons? Were they all living on American money, like Dunleavy? McKeller suddenly entreated me to stand in for one of the players, but I'd have none of it just yet, nor of the drinking bout that occurred afterward when they won. Instead, after the game I jumped onto the first omnibus, heading back to the O'Casey house.

As I got off in Water Street, I passed a hansom cab sitting at the curb; hearing a voice I recognized, I glanced in. Two men were conversing, while the cabman and the horse waited patiently. One of the men was tall and the other short and stocky. I did not recognize the tall fellow, but there was no mistaking Inspector Munro of the Special Irish Branch. I could not believe he was here in Liverpool, a few blocks from our very street, merely sightseeing.

Suspecting I might be watched, I turned down a narrow alleyway to the next street and passed down it until I was near the back of the O'Casey house. There I squeezed between two buildings set close together, made my way to the back entrance, and went inside and upstairs quietly, so as not to alert anyone.

"Munro is in the area, not three streets from here," I tumbled out, as I entered our room, but as usual, Barker was ahead of me. He had a chair pulled up against the wall near the window and was peering out while smoking his pipe.

"I'm not surprised. I do not care for the fellow, but he is no fool, and he has great resources."

"What shall we do?" I whispered.

"We cannot alert the faction," Barker said adamantly. "If the Special Irish Branch has arrived, I would not willingly jeopardize their investigation merely to save my own. You and I should lie low as much as possible and avoid being taken. Do not leave by the front door, by all means, and stay away from windows. Did you notice any constables at the hurling pitch this afternoon?"

"No, sir, but I wasn't looking. If we get arrested, is there some way we could talk ourselves out of it? Munro will obviously recognize us if he sees us."

"He would, but in order to clear the way for his own capture of the faction, he would probably keep us incarcerated for days. I've seen suspects held by the S.I.B. for a month."

"A month!" I cried, my blood running cold.

"Oh, yes," Barker assured me. "Her Majesty's government takes treasonous acts very seriously."

"But we're innocent!" I stated. "We're working for the Home Office."

"Munro is not above his petty jealousies, and, as you are aware, he has a special antipathy for private enquiry agents."

"Oh, that's marvelous," I muttered. "On the one hand, we have to aid the bombers and not reveal ourselves, lest we be killed, and on the other, we risk arrest and incarceration for an indefinite period, even if Munro knows who we are."

"You put it most succinctly, lad."

It did not help our predicament that Colonel Alfred Dunleavy came bowling in the next morning through the front door as bold as you please, brimming with confidence about our upcoming assault on London. I wanted to warn him and O'Casey that the Special Irish Branch was in the area, but Barker warned me to silence. We were playing a very close game. Especially damning was a newly acquired map of London with all the bombing sites marked that Dunleavy had brought with him.

"Five men, gentlemen," he stated loudly enough to be heard in the street as he rolled out the map on the breakfast table around which I, Barker, and O'Casey sat. "Five heroes to bring London to her knees and to free Ireland from the chains of tyranny."

The bombing targets were marked with stars in red ink. This was the colonel's element, planning a campaign, a battle plan. Thirty sites were marked on the map.

"My word," I blurted out, glancing over Dunleavy's shoulder. "Buckingham Palace."

"Yes," Dunleavy enthused, misinterpreting my dread. "And the Houses of Parliament, the Home Office, the Prime Minister's residence, the Horse Guards, and Scotland Yard again. Whitehall shall be completely reduced to rubble. Then there is the Telephone Exchange, the Central Telegram office and Postal Exchange, the Bank of England—"

"Very good, Colonel," Barker stated. "I see you have marked all the major train stations, as well. Do you think St. Paul's is necessary?"

"To my way of thinking, Mr. van Rhyn," Dunleavy stated, "our biggest troubles with England began when they broke away from the Catholic Church."

"This is a very bold plan."

"With your new explosives, we can afford to be bold."

"So many sites," O'Casey stated. "However will we manage it with just five men?"

"Each man shall go out armed with two satchels. Each satchel will contain a bomb, already primed and set with a timer. Each man shall deliver a bomb, setting it in some out-of-the-way corner, if possible, and carry the second one to another location. All at once, ten bombs will detonate simultaneously. In the confusion, our bombers shall return, collect two more bombs each, and deliver them to additional sites. A half hour or more later, the second group of bombs will explode, and a half hour beyond that, the third set."

"So," Barker said, "the government will be crippled, along with the train stations, the post offices, telegraphs, and the banks."

"Yes," Dunleavy continued, "and the gas and water as well. We'll throw London back into the Dark Ages. Oh, and there is one thing more."

"And that is?"

"We're no longer targeting mere buildings, gentlemen. This time there will be casualties. It is time for the gloves to come off. That is why we'll time our first attack for six o'clock, when the businesses are closing and street traffic is at its highest. Let us see what kind of carnage and terror we can create then."

18

W E WAITED FOR TWO DAYS FOR SCOTLAND YARD
to appear on the doorstep. The wait was agonizing. Any minute, I
thought, Inspector Munro and his boys were going to kick in the
door, clap us in darbies, and haul us off to the constabulary for an
indefinite stay, all our plans in ruins and Barker's reputation in dis-
grace. After two days, however, we saw no sign of the Special
Irish Branch in the area. It was a good thing, too, for all this con-
finement was wearing on our nerves.

"I must get out of this house," Barker complained to me. "I
cannot think here. I believe we can risk relaxing our vigil. Miss
O'Casey!"

Maire O'Casey came in from the parlor, where she had been
studying Gaelic. Like the others, she never knew how close the
Special Irish Branch had been to discovering all of us. "Yes, Mr.
van Rhyn?"

"Mr. Penrith has expressed an interest in seeing the docks. We
shall take a walk and perhaps see a little more of the city. Would it
inconvenience you if we dine out?"

"Not at all, sir. As you wish it."

"Thank you. You are very kind to a pair of refugees. Come, Thomas."

My employer seized his ivory-inlaid cane and made his way out the back door and through to the next street while I followed. My duties as assistant to a prominent enquiry agent seemed to involve following Barker, never knowing where he was going or in what situation we would find ourselves once we got there. I was the apprentice, and he the master, but we were also each other's safeguard, there to help each other out of any possible scrape. Of course, so far, Barker had done all the helping.

We did actually go to the docks. I've never been one of those people who has romantic notions of the sea and ships. The life, when it isn't banal, with its thousand tasks to be done constantly, is often brutal and dangerous. The sea is a cold mistress, and she doesn't care a fig what happens to you. I had to remind myself, however, that my employer had grown up on it, rising from dock-hand through the ranks on various ships until he was captain of his own, the *Osprey*. I didn't know a belaying pin from a bo'sun's whistle, but it had significance to him, significance and a degree of comfort. When we reached Liverpool Quay and looked out upon the forest of masts and the bustle of men loading and unloading, I let him have his head and remained silent for a while, knowing that he had come here to think.

Half an hour later, we stood at a railing overlooking the ships, and my employer had not moved for fifteen minutes. I'd used the time reflecting on the enigma that is Cyrus Barker. Perhaps it was a makeup of his constitution, but, though he had surrounded himself with a number of friends and acquaintances—not to mention an assistant who lived in his very house—he was a very solitary individual. Sometimes, I wondered if I were an irritation to him, as I am inclined to blather. At least, for once, I knew to keep my mouth shut.

Slowly, he turned and clasped his hands behind him, as a ship's captain would, and I pictured him in command of his own vessel.

"We have accomplished several things so far," he said, as if in the middle of a conversation with himself. "We have located the faction, joined them, and gained their confidence. We've destroyed their supply of dynamite. Soon it will be time to gather the materials for the second attempt upon London. How do you feel about making our own nitroglycerin?"

"It certainly would impress the faction, but where would we get the materials? We would need a lot to make thirty bombs, as Dunleavy described."

"England is too tightly controlled for such large quantities. As he said, we may have to go as far as Paris for supplies. The fellow still puzzles me. After all this time with him, I still do not countenance that this plan is his. I think we should search his hotel room."

"Is it really necessary?" I dared ask. "I mean, we'd be going to a lot of risk, possibly for nothing."

"We might come up with empty hands, but we also might find something of value."

"If we can get in," I countered.

"Get in?" the Guv scoffed. "A simple matter."

It was indeed a simple matter, as Barker said. After a quick meal at a tea shop, we found ourselves in the hallway at the Midland Hotel, where he removed a skeleton key, or "betty" as he called it, from his pocket and inserted it in the keyhole. After an agonizingly long moment in which no one appeared in the hall, we heard the soft click of the lock, opened the door, and stepped inside.

"How did you know he wasn't here?" I asked, thinking it was a mercy Barker had not been a criminal. What other little contrivances did he carry about in his pockets?

"I asked him what he had planned for today. He's got a meeting with a Liberal Liverpool MP, trying to make him more sensitive to the Irish cause and to convince him to throw in the odd shilling."

Number 314 was a suite, with fresh flowers on the table. There was a pile of papers on the table that attracted Barker's immediate interest. He crossed to it and began looking through a stack of messages.

"Tailor's bill. Creditor. Creditor. Oh, dear. Dunleavy appears to be in a spot of financial trouble. Start looking but keep everything neat. I want to know with whom Alfred Dunleavy is communicating. Surely a fellow as disorganized as this must have left some sort of evidence behind."

We began to search. While Barker went through the papers slowly, I opened drawers, peered under the bed, rifled luggage, and searched among his toiletries. I discovered several things about the colonel. He had a fondness for Cuban cigars, his boots were made in a place called Chattanooga, and he used Parker's hair tonic. If any of these bits of information were helpful in answering some of Barker's questions, our quest would be successful, but unfortunately, they were not.

Barker suddenly seized me by the collar and dragged me swiftly to the window. He pushed me behind one curtain, and took his place behind the other. We heard the door open and footsteps enter the room. Dunleavy had returned unexpectedly.

What would happen if the colonel caught sight of us? Were he armed, he'd have us at a disadvantage. Obviously, he'd know we were spies and would pass that information to the faction. On the other hand, he couldn't exactly march us through the lobby at gunpoint.

I was very conscious of my breathing, feeling that it seemed extremely loud in the room. I looked over at my employer, but he was no more animate than a hat stand. Perhaps this sort of thing was a matter of course to him, but for me, it was a new experience. Any minute now, I expected Dunleavy to fling back the curtain, seize me by the lapel, and clap a pistol to my head. I knew how they treated traitors, and I had no hope that they would treat spies any better.

He didn't see us, of course. He'd come back for something or other, and when he found it, after a few minutes' search, he left the room again. *Confound the fellow and his lack of order,* I thought.

"Right. Let us continue the search," Barker said, as if the near capture hadn't happened. "What is this?"

There was a new letter laid atop the stack of bills. Barker snatched it up and read it before passing it to me. I spread it out on the table and read.

Buffalo, New York

Mr. Dunleavy,
We acknowledge your need of funds but regret to report that there may be some delay. As you know, much of our monies are divested in supporting candidates for elections, as well as in silver speculation. As soon as funds arrive, we shall send them along speedily.

Your humble servant,
Chester Finney
Secretary of American Hibernian League

Barker turned the note over in his hand. "This certainly does not ease Mr. Dunleavy's financial woes, does it, lad? The American gives him no idea if the money shall be forthcoming in time for the faction to proceed with the bombings they have planned. This throws everything askew. Mr. Anderson has given us no instructions on what to do if the faction changes its plans. Do we hand them over to Munro and let him decide what to do about them, or continue our deception a little longer, to see how

Dunleavy and his men proceed? I have no wish for us to remain on this case indefinitely. We must cast our nets a little farther. I believe the time has come to make a more thorough search of the O'Casey house. I do not see any evidence of plans or communications here beyond this note, but there is still the possibility that O'Casey has information. I've already searched his room, but I don't think we should overlook his sister's."

"You don't seriously think her mixed up in all this, surely."

"Remember what I counseled you, lad, about considering everyone a suspect until all the facts have been revealed? If she's innocent, nothing will be found. You look through Miss O'Casey's room first, while I distract her, and then you do the same while I inspect her brother's quarter again."

"Me!" I cried. "Why have me search? I don't even know what I'm looking for."

"No more than I, Thomas. I shall engage her in conversation, while you feign a headache and go up to the room to lie down."

Upon our return, we found Maire O'Casey in the parlor. "Did the two of you find lunch while you were out?" she asked.

"*Ja, Fräulein,*" Barker said. "We availed ourselves of one of your Aerated Bread Company tearooms. The sea air has not been so helpful for Mr. Penrith. It has brought on one of the headaches he suffers from time to time."

The girl gave an anxious look my way.

"It is nothing," I muttered, raising a hand to my head. "If you will excuse me, I think I shall lie down."

As I climbed the stairs, I heard Barker speak to Maire. "I see you have been studying your own ancient language. Is there much need for it these days?"

I found her room on the third floor. When I had first been hired as an assistant to a private enquiry agent, I had thought myself ill equipped, but since then, I have found some duties that I am suited for. I am a confirmed busybody, inordinately curious.

I began going through drawers, all the while keeping a sharp ear out for someone on the stairs. A chest contained only clothes. I looked through it swiftly. There was nothing concealed under her garments, save a lilac-scented sachet. In a small, white desk with Queen Anne legs, I found her correspondence, along with her own stationery and ink. She kept up with a few friends she had known in school. One had married and was living in Cork, and another was a servant to an English family in Londonderry. Just when I was sure that my suspicions were groundless and the most secret thing she owned were merely her undergarments, I found a small wooden box on a shelf, and it was locked.

There were hairpins on her nightstand, and almost without thinking, I bent the end of one over my thumbnail, then inserted it into the lock. After a few frantic twists, the lock sprung open. There were letters inside. I read over one feverishly, knowing I might be discovered.

> *Maire, it has been too many days since my eyes feasted upon your beauty. I count the hours . . .*

My eyes flew to the next one.

> *Maire, having just come from walking with you, I wanted to set down the impressions I have . . .*

Love letters. Unsigned and undated. Who could have written them? Well, of course, anyone could; she was a rare beauty. But who had? Was it Willie? A secret lover, perhaps, or an old flame? I scarce knew. I got to the bottom of the stack of letters and found jewelry; a coil of pearls, a diamond broach, and a pair of opal earrings. Who had given these to a poor Irish girl?

My mind gave a sudden leap. Was it Dunleavy? He was old, but such things had happened before. Was he out of pocket because he lavished jewelry on Maire?

I shouldn't jump to conclusions, I told myself. The jewels could have been handed down from her mother, and the letters . . . well, any pretty girl over twenty must have a boxful. Then, I reached the final letter and saw the inscription at the bottom. I locked the box once more, pocketed the hairpin, and left the room.

I wanted to sprint down the stairs, to fly, to slide down the banister, anything to get me down as quickly as possible, but I couldn't attract attention. It required all I possessed to come down the steps at a sedate pace. I wandered into the parlor, still holding my head.

"I say, Miss O'Casey, I wonder if I might trouble you for a cold cloth for my head?"

"I do hope you are not catching a fever, Mr. Penrith," the girl said, coming up and placing the back of her hand against my forehead. If I was feverish, it was more to do with the news I had to impart to Barker than any feigned illness. "A slight one, perhaps. I'll get that cloth for you."

She left the room and I moved over to her desk, where Barker was seated. He sensed I had something to tell him.

"Letters," I whispered. "Love letters. A stack of them, along with jewelry. Expensive jewelry, if I am any judge. And you can't imagine who sent them."

"Tell me," Barker murmured.

"Seamus O'Muircheartaigh."

19

BARKER SUGGESTED THAT MISS O'CASEY BREW A cup of tea for me, and while I sat and sipped, making small talk with the girl and feigning a headache, he flew up the stairs to the box and read her private correspondence. Normally, of course, doing so would be an unconscionable act, but then most girls did not receive declarations of love from dangerous criminals. Even then, talking with beautiful and wholesome Maire, I could not picture her with the hard, dry Mr. O'Muircheartaigh, who, for one thing, was almost twice her age.

I used Barker's diversion, and asked her to show me the Gaelic book she was using, but what I really wanted to do was to talk to her about what had happened at the lighthouse. Though it had only been one kiss, I felt betrayed. Willie Yeats was one thing, but that chilling fellow I'd met at Ho's was quite another.

"You are not paying attention, Mr. Penrith," she admonished lightly.

"Call me Thomas, Miss O'Casey. You must forgive me. This headache has put me out of sorts. Tell me more about your lessons."

Twenty minutes later, I found Barker standing in the window of our room, absently playing with one of his razor-edged coins, deep in thought. There was a smile on his lips. He had discovered an enemy's weakness, and was considering how to turn it to his advantage.

"Who would have thought it?" my employer murmured. "I would stake my life these letters are genuine. You missed an envelope at the very bottom of the stack. The letters are half a year old, from when the O'Caseys were living in Dublin. Seamus makes mention of meeting her at the O'Connell Bridge. He must have been seeing her in Ireland."

"How did they meet?"

"He doesn't say. Presumably, there must be some meeting of the I.R.B. factions. As far as I know, that is their only link."

"I cannot imagine she would encourage his suit," I said a trifle bitterly.

"I did not see any indication from the letters that she had. Twice he accuses her of being cool, and he only hints at a possible proposal of marriage, as if testing the waters. To be truthful, I hardly thought O'Muircheartaigh had it in him to play the romantic swain. Miss O'Casey has nothing to offer in the way of money or influence, yet he speaks of her as his equal. I can assume she has her beauty to recommend her."

"Oh, she has that," I stated.

"You should know, you rascal," he said. "But what does she possess that O'Muircheartaigh might want?"

"She possesses a presence and a keen mind," I said. "She has the ability to put an entire group of men in their place and to have them do her bidding. Surely that is enough, even for someone like him. Do you think him involved in this? Is he the faction's true leader?"

"One should never underestimate him. He is as silent and lethal as a poisonous spider. Think of this, lad: if a man speculates and is able to cause a war between two nearby countries, he could invest heavily in munitions and arms on both sides and make a fortune. Even if it never came to that, the mere rattling of sabers would be enough to drive the stock exchange prices through the roof."

"Good heavens!" I said.

"Exactly. O'Muircheartaigh would be the next Rothschild. I believe the possibility of hundreds of deaths on both sides because of an Irish insurrection means little to him. We must watch Miss O'Casey a little more closely. She could be the conduit for messages from London."

That gave me much to think upon, and none of it pleasant. I had been impressed by Maire's purity, as well as her beauty, and to think that she might be receiving secret messages with plans and monies quite sullied my belief in her. Perhaps Barker was right, and she was not the girl I thought her to be.

Dunleavy came to dinner, annoyance and petulance on his face. The money from the Irish Americans was being delayed, as Barker and I already knew, and he could not be certain it would arrive in time. I thought he was working himself into another drinking bout, and I was correct. He was churlish when none of us seemed disposed to drink with him. Finally, Fergus McKeller arrived, and we spent the evening watching Dunleavy alternate between complaining about his past failures and crowing about his future successes. Between that and the news about Maire, I went to bed feeling very low indeed.

Barker was standing at the window of our room. Something had awakened him, if he had been asleep at all. It was past ten, and we'd been upstairs for about half an hour.

"What is it?" I asked my employer.

"Someone has just left the house. It appears to be your Miss O'Casey. Throw some clothes over your nightshirt, and hurry."

It is not an easy task to go from sound sleep to fully dressed and out the door in three minutes, but somehow I managed it. I wouldn't pass inspection in Savile Row, with my collarless night-shirt thrust into my trousers, but at that point, I was glad to have each shoe on the right foot. We stealthily moved down the stairs, but once we were outside, Barker was off like a shot.

"Are you sure it was Maire?" I asked, still skeptical that she wasn't in bed, enjoying a well-deserved slumber. "Perhaps it was Dunleavy."

"The figure I saw was in a cloak, but only Miss O'Casey is that small. Hurry along, lad. Don't dawdle."

For the hundredth time, I wished I had my employer's long legs and his stamina. It took all I had to keep up with him, and he was sporting half a stone of extra weight.

We reached the intersection of Water Street and the Strand and headed deeper into the poor section of Liverpool.

"Could it have been another woman delivering a message?" I asked, still convinced it could not be Maire.

"Possibly," he growled. "This part of town has been a front for more than one faction, or so Dunleavy has informed me."

"So someone could have sent the O'Caseys a message," I insisted.

"Or Miss O'Casey herself is delivering one in return."

I pondered that for a moment as we walked along Strand Street. We were in the Irish slums now. Broken-down tenements stood on either side of the street. My attention was distracted by a beggar child, and when I looked up, the figure ahead of us had disappeared like a will-o'-the-wisp.

"Where did she go?"

Barker pointed to the left. "Into that court there."

It was a villainous-looking square. The worst section of Whitechapel could equal but not surpass it. The court was formed by back entrances to bawdy and public houses. Men leaned against the walls with dazed expressions or slumbered on the dirty ground.

"What's that smell?" I asked. It was cloying and slightly sweet.

"Opium," he answered, pointing. "She appears to have gone in that door there."

Barker plunged into a doorway. I followed. We were in a dark hallway, lit by a single, uncovered gas jet. The Guv'nor hurried down the hall until we came to a fork in the road, that is, a stairwell going up and down.

"Should we—"

"Ssh!" Barker put his hand on my shoulder, and we listened intently. He had a complete knowledge of the nervous system and how to attack various places he called pressure points. I hoped it was merely training that caused his thumb to press against one of the nerves near my collarbone just then. My fingers started to tingle.

"This way!" He was off down the stairs like a hound who'd heard the huntsman's horn. Under normal circumstances, nothing could have induced me to go down such a rickety-looking stairwell, but I didn't have the luxury of refusing. I hurtled down in the semidarkness after my employer.

We were in a hallway lined with doorways, with women standing in them. Fallen women they were, of the lowest order. The rooms were little more than cages. One glimpse of the first rouge-cheeked, scrofulous wretch, old beyond her years, was enough to keep my eyes riveted to the floor from then on. I hurried along behind my employer, despite the painted talons that brushed my sleeve or ran through my hair. It was a nightmarish world, the light from a silken shawl thrown over a gas lamp splashing scarlet over everything.

At the far end of the hall, Barker plunged down yet another stairwell. I began to feel as if we were descending through the various circles of Hell. We were now a full two stories underground. The wooden floor had given way to earth, and the walls were beamed like mine shafts. These appeared to be merely tunnels dug to escape the law. We reached the far end of one and found nothing but a dead end and a stone wall.

"We've been outfoxed," Barker said, turning and walking back. "Let us double back up to the next floor and see if the trail is cold."

I followed him up the last staircase and we stood a moment, debating what to do next. I certainly didn't want to go down the red-tinged hallway again.

"Cold as an Orkney winter," the Guv'nor declared. "Oh, well. It may have been nothing, as you say. Let us continue up this stairwell and see where it leads."

On the next floor, there was what passed for a reception hall of one of the illicit establishments. Luckily, the men and women there were too gin soaked to notice us as we passed among them and out of the building. I was glad to get the odors of patchouli and opium and unwashed humanity out of my nostrils.

"There's nothing else for us here," Barker decided. "Let's go back to our beds."

"That sounds like a good plan," I said. "Do you still think it was Maire?"

Barker shrugged. "Who can say? I thought it was Miss O'Casey, but she was a good distance away. It is even possible that we were deliberately lured out of the house, though the reason for such a ruse escapes me, unless they are onto us."

We were passing by the Strand again, and I was just about to make some remark, when there was a sudden clatter of shoes, and I was suddenly knocked off my feet. My head hit the cobblestones, and I tried to struggle, but there was more than one man on top of me. The familiar cold steel of bracelets closed about my wrists. I was thrown over onto my back, a bull's-eye shone in my eyes, and my throat felt the unwelcome weight of a truncheon. I couldn't see my attackers behind the lantern or what had happened to Barker, but if he was in a similar situation, we were in a fine mess.

"Sir!" I cried.

"Do not struggle, lad!" I heard my employer's low voice from a half dozen yards away.

A face came into the light, looking me over carefully. It was a meaty face with a brushy mustache and a blue helmet, a sergeant of the Liverpool police.

"We been waitin' for you two blokes to come back down here. Glad you could oblige us."

As Barker and I were hefted to our feet and prodded along, bruised and shackled, to the station in Wapping Street, I reflected on how that which you most fear will happen so often comes to pass.

Breathe in, I told myself. *Breathe out. In through the nose, out through the mouth.* Anything but dwell on the fact that there were darbies on my wrists again and a truncheon prodding me in the kidneys. *No more,* I told myself. *No more. I'd learned my lesson. I'd sworn I'd never give anyone reason to throw me back in stir. How did I get in this situation? We were just walking down the street, like normal citizens. We hadn't been doing anything illegal. We would have been safe if only we'd stayed in our beds, but our fool's errand had brought us in harm's way.*

We were tricked, I told myself. We'd raced out after her, and now we'd been jugged as easily as a hare. Barker couldn't reveal our identities and our reason for being in Liverpool. I knew we'd promised Anderson we wouldn't involve the Home Office, but back then, the chances of discovery had seemed so remote. *Surely,* I thought, *the emergency of the situation warranted disclosing who we were to the authorities.*

I looked over at Barker, wondering what he was thinking. He was marching along with his hands behind his back, his head down. He might have been wandering in Hyde Park, deep in thought, for all his appearance. I envied him his ability to retreat at any moment to some remote corner of his mind, as cold and mystical as Lhasa or Kathmandu.

Suddenly, Barker did something I'd never seen him do before. He tripped, sprawling face-first in the street. Barker never tripped. He was as sure-footed as a cat. As the men swarmed over him and yanked him again to his feet, I tried to read his expression. His cheek was bruised, and he looked disoriented. Was it defeat, or was he up to something?

We were herded into the entranceway of the constabulary building. A man waited for us as we neared the front door. He was approximately five and thirty, with a thin mustache like a brow across his upper lip and one of the squarest jaws I'd ever seen. He looked at us out of steel-gray eyes and over an aquiline nose. He was dressed in the military-looking green uniform of a Liverpool inspector.

"You've got them, eh? Good work, gentlemen. Take them to the questioning room."

I didn't like the sound of "questioning room." British officials are quick to give bland names to menacing places. The euphemisms complemented the chilling humor of the administrators.

We were taken into a room where, despite the fact that we made absolutely no struggle since it had all began, we were thrust roughly down into two chairs. The fellow in the green jacket came in and we were left alone with him and one constable, who had his notebook out. I noticed the inspector had a short riding crop in his hand.

"I am Chief Inspector Johanson," he stated. "You two gentlemen have been seen in the company of known Irish rebels. I demand to know your names."

Barker ignored the question and launched a barrage of his own in a thick German accent. "What is the meaning of this? Where have you brought us? Cannot a man walk in this city with-

---

out being attacked by the secret police? I demand to be released immediately!"

Barker was oscillating his head slightly, and it took me a moment to realize what he was doing. He was pretending he was blind. It was why he had stumbled in the street.

"You have not answered my question," the inspector warned. "Tell me your name, you." He held up his riding crop, threatening Barker, but my employer appeared to take no notice. Seeing that warning him didn't work, he struck the Guv a cutting blow across the face. Rather melodramatically, Barker fell out of his chair. He would have absorbed such a blow without comment under normal circumstances.

"*Schwein!*" he called from the floor, shaking in anger. "You strike a blind man, without warning? Coward! Why don't you simply go out in the street and kick children and old women?"

Realizing for the first time that his suspect was blind, Johanson hefted him back into the chair, though he offered no apology.

"Look, man, you are in no position to be calling names here. You watch your mouth or I'll give you another one."

"You strike me one more time, Inspector," Barker assured him, "and you shall be patrolling the quays as a constable by tomorrow. Do you think I am some common street thief you have caught in your dragnet? *Nein!* It is a whale. I am too big for your little boat. You want to know my name? I shall tell you my name. It is Johannes Otto van Rhyn! You recognize it? Good! Now run along. Get someone of authority in here. I do not talk to . . . to . . . What is the word, Thomas? The little fishes, you know."

"I think the word you want is 'minnows,' sir," I prompted.

"*Ja. Danke,* Thomas. I do not talk to minnows. Run along, Little Minnow. And I should like some tea if I am to be kept waiting long."

I could see a thousand thoughts running through the inspector's head. No prisoner had ever spoken so rudely to him, or they'd have been beaten soundly, but no prisoner ever had spoken with such authority either. Certainly, he'd heard of van Rhyn. The mysterious bomber's name had been in the newspapers several times. He was well known, indeed. Johanson might receive acclaim for capturing him. On the other hand, he'd struck him. Did Barker really mean that he could have the man demoted? If Barker spoke to the press and made it seem like the Liverpool police had beaten and mistreated a blind man, he might. These were deep waters, indeed. Johanson didn't want to get in trouble with his superiors. He did have a whale in his net. It would be a great deal safer if he'd simply step down the hall and speak with his supervisor.

"What are you doing?" the inspector snapped at the brawny constable holding the notebook.

The fellow looked up in surprise. "Taking notes, sir."

"Destroy that!" he ordered.

I dared put in my own oar. "Herr van Rhyn takes milk and two sugars in his tea, Inspector, and I prefer black, myself."

I could see he'd dearly like to have a swing at my head with that crop of his, but the political ramifications had suddenly filled the room. It was too hot in here. He needed to step out for some cool dock-side air.

"Stand guard outside!" he snarled at the poor constable. "I'm stepping down the hall to talk to the superintendent. Inspector Munro of the Special Irish Branch is here, and I think he'll want to interrogate this prisoner."

Both of them stepped outside, and we could hear the inspector going down the hall.

"Quick, lad," Barker said. "We haven't a moment to lose."

20

"TURN AROUND AND SEE IF YOU CAN REACH MY waistcoat," Barker said. "I still have the betty in my pocket."

I did as he said, guiding my hands to his pocket while looking over my shoulder. I'd forgotten about the little skeleton key he'd used to unlock Dunleavy's door. My fingers seemed to belong to someone else, but eventually I dug it out and passed it to him back to back. In almost no time at all, he was swinging the open bracelets around and freeing his other hand. Then he seized my wrist and began unlocking mine.

"I'd say we have about two minutes to get out of here," he said in my ear.

In a moment my hands were free, but I wasn't sure what good had been accomplished, since there was still a guard at the door and bars on the window. Barker put a finger to his lips and moved silently to the door. Then giving me a look that said "prepare yourself," he opened the door, snaked a hand around the guard's mouth, and delivered a kick to his calves, yanking him into the room. I ran to close the door while my employer delivered a blow to the constable's neck, just under the helmet, with the edge of his hand. The officer was knocked cold.

Barker peered out into the corridor and motioned to me with two fingers. We were out of the room, moving down the hallway as casually as we could bear. In a moment, we stepped out the entrance door and melted away into the night.

We were walking along swiftly when I suddenly began to get rubber legged. I couldn't help it. Because I had been incarcerated for eight months, my greatest fear is of imprisonment. I began gulping for air and feeling dizzy. Barker sat me down on the stoop of a shop front and pushed my head between my legs.

"A little too close for you in there, was it, lad?"

"Aye, sir," I gasped.

In a few moments, I was feeling a little better. We'd been inside the lion's mouth, and emerged safely again, but it had been close. My mind knew we were out, but my nerves were still coming to grips with the thought of being behind bars again.

"Feeling better now?" Cyrus Barker asked. He was being patient, but we were still rather close to the station. I jumped up from the stoop.

"Ready, sir," I stated.

Alfred Dunleavy was at the O'Casey house, when we arrived shortly after twelve. Both he and Eamon looked very worried when we came in, and I'd like to think Maire O'Casey had a look of concern, as well. The three of them were amazed when we entered, as casual as you please, as if we'd just had an evening's ramble.

"We'd heard you'd been taken!" Eamon O'Casey said, hurrying up to us. "Fergus is outside, keeping a watch out for the police. They know we are in the area and so far they have not located the address, but it is only a matter of time. So what happened?"

Barker threw himself into a chair and began patting his pockets for his pipe. "Ja, well, we did not care for the accommodations. Thomas and I wished to sleep in our own beds tonight."

"No chance of that, I'm afraid," Dunleavy stated briskly. "We are nearly packed. What were you doing out at night, and how did you escape?"

"We had heard a rumor that a large shipment of glycerin was to be moved from a soap factory to the docks in the morning, on the way to Mr. Nobel's factory near Glasgow, and we didn't want to pass up the chance. We decided to investigate. Unfortunately, it proved to be just a ruse." Either Barker thought fast, or he'd been preparing this story as we walked back to the O'Caseys'. "We were overtaken by constables in the Strand. They marched us to Wapping Station and put us in a room. As I said, we did not care for the accommodations, so we left."

"Did they know whom they had captured?" Dunleavy asked, looking very serious.

"Of course. I told them," Barker answered. "I'm afraid Liverpool is now too hot for us. We have overstayed our welcome and must be smuggled out and sent elsewhere."

Maire O'Casey had brewed tea. Domestic tranquility reigned over us all for a moment or two, and we sat and waited for our cups. As she poured, she looked over at me. Despite her spirit, I could see she was frightened. She said not a word but set the pot on the table and left to let the men discuss strategies.

"I suppose we must go back to the cottage," Barker grumbled, "and live on rabbit until such time as the monies arrive."

"You shall be pleased to hear that the money has arrived, gentlemen," Dunleavy said, helping himself to a biscuit and tea.

"So, it is finally here," Barker said, shooting me a glance. "Is it enough?" Obviously the funds had not come from the Americans, as we had just seen a telegram warning of a delay. Perhaps that was what Maire O'Casey, if it indeed were she, had been doing in the night—collecting the money from some other source. I wondered if Dunleavy had told her what it was or had merely sent her to pick up a package for him. I wished I could find out what she knew.

"It is enough and to spare," Dunleavy assured us. "Perhaps it would be best if you gentlemen began collecting materials for our next venture. I suggest Paris. They will not sell to the Irish there, but a German—"

"Impossible," Barker rumbled. "The British government shall be looking for me here and in Paris, combing the coasts and stopping ships along the way. I must stay out of sight for the time being. There is only one place I can go on this island where they will not be looking for me."

"And where might that be?" Dunleavy asked.

"London," Barker continued. "As your Mr. Poe pointed out, the best place to hide is in plain sight. Mr. Penrith shall have to go and collect the materials in Paris and have them shipped to Victoria Station. He speaks French well enough that he should be able to conduct business quite easily."

"Me?" I asked, astonished. I'd never been out of the country before.

"They shall be looking for him as well," O'Casey pointed out.

"Not if he were part of a couple," Maire O'Casey said, coming in from the kitchen.

"You know I don't like involving you too much in all this," O'Casey protested. "My sister cannot travel to the Continent with him unchaperoned! It isn't right. It's unseemly!"

"But it is the perfect disguise," Dunleavy stated. "A young couple, honeymooning in Paris. Why, they won't look twice at him."

"Honeymoon!" O'Casey cried.

"Not a real one, Eamon," Maire assured him.

"If Mr. Penrith is in need of a temporary wife, why not simply get one of the streetwalkers here in Liverpool to go with him, instead?"

I thought back to the poxy women I had seen in the underground hall and shuddered.

"You trust a common trollop but not me, is that it, Eamon

O'Casey?" his sister demanded. "Do you think I'm not up to the task? I'm a grown woman and certainly able to handle an assignment as simple as this. I'll only be window dressing, I'm sure. Mr. Penrith will behave like a perfect gentleman. If not, I'll box his ears."

O'Casey looked at us. He was quickly running out of reasons to protest. Dunleavy was adamant, Barker silent as a statue, and Maire ready to counter any objections he put forth.

"Maire—" O'Casey began.

"It's fine, Eamon," she responded. "Don't worry about me. I'll be fine." She looked over at me, but I couldn't read her thoughts.

"It is settled, then," Dunleavy stated, clapping his hands together. "When might you be able to leave, Miss O'Casey?"

"Give me a day or two if you can risk it. How long shall we be gone, Mr. Dunleavy?" she asked.

"Just three or four days, I think. Enough time for Mr. Penrith to purchase all his materials and to have them shipped to London."

"Mr. Dunleavy, I wonder if I might purchase a dress while I am there?"

He looked at her blankly. "What? At our expense?" he asked, seeing more of his money draining away.

"I shall be working for the cause, after all," she stated. "We must keep up the pretense of being a married couple, and married women need dresses." The little minx was arguing for a nice dress! *Do it, girl,* I thought. *Bleed the fellow dry.*

"Not one of the expensive dresses, with the seed pearls and marabou," he blustered.

"As if I'd be wearing marabou in Liverpool!" she cried, her temper rising. "Where would I wear it, may I ask? To mass? To market, perhaps? Shall I wear it in the house, while I cook and do laundry and make beds and pour tea and prepare your meals?"

"You had better accede to everything she asks," Barker arbitrated. "She has got you over a barrel."

"Oh, very well, buy the infernal dress! Drain the I.R.B.'s coffers of badly needed funds. I don't care," Dunleavy huffed, crossing his arms. I thought she had outwitted him rather smartly. She left us to our planning and went off to do some of her own.

"So, Miss O'Casey and Mr. Penrith shall be going to Paris, and you want to go to London, Mr. van Rhyn. You shall accompany me to the Crook and Harp in Seven Dials," Dunleavy said when his temper had cooled. "It is our base of operations in the City."

Barker dug out his pipe. "You must prepare the faction to go to London, and Mr. Penrith and I shall need a large room to serve as a laboratory where we can make the explosives."

"How much money will it cost?" Dunleavy asked. With him, everything came down to pounds and pence.

"It shall be worth everything," Barker said, "when London's government falls and the people of Ireland look for strong leadership who are prepared to tell them what to do."

Dunleavy smiled wearily and nodded his head.

"You are right, Mr. van Rhyn. Forgive me. I have lived frugally and worried over money for too long. When England falls, I shall push for a strong alliance between Ireland and the United States. Dublin shall grow into a fine capital city like London. We shall build a strong navy, and the faction boys everywhere shall be heroes."

"Indeed," Barker continued the thought. "All the countries of the Empire shall have Ireland to thank for their freedom and shall wish to form alliances with you. If an intelligent leader uses his acumen, he might help Ireland acquire an empire of its own from the ashes. The entire map could be redrawn. And you, Dunleavy, could be at the helm. I do not think the jubilant citizens of Ireland shall care that you are American."

"Stop!" Dunleavy cried, putting out a hand and flashing those teeth of his. "It is too grandiose. I'm just an old soldier. Ireland must decide its own destiny. I merely want to give it the opportunity to do so."

"It is late. We should go to bed," Barker stated. The clock on the mantel was nearing twelve thirty. "There is much to accomplish and plan for in the morning. Someone should stand watch."

"The watch schedule has already been set."

"Excellent. Good night, then."

Once in our bedroom, Barker was chuckling to himself. "What an amateur Dunleavy is. He is trying to orchestrate a major attack on London on mere pocket change."

"So you agree that Miss O'Casey and I should pose as newlyweds in order to get our supplies in Paris?" I asked.

"I do, as long as you stick to your purpose and aren't influenced by a pretty face. Keep your mind on the case and away from Miss O'Casey as much as possible. If you don't, Eamon O'Casey will come after you. And if he doesn't, I will."

"Yes, sir," I said. "Actually, it wasn't O'Casey I was thinking of. It was Willie Yeats."

Barker refilled his pipe and lit it. "Ah, yes. Yeats. I had almost forgotten about Miss O'Casey's lapdog. Someone will have to explain to him that it is not a real honeymoon."

"'Stop!'" I said, throwing my hands up in mock horror. "'It is too grandiose! I am just an old soldier.'"

Barker's eyebrows disappeared behind his spectacles. "Cheeky beggar."

21

W**E LEFT LIVERPOOL TWO DAYS LATER, MAIRE** and I. Everyone came to see us off, everyone except for Willie Yeats. The O'Casey house had been a beehive of activity with hours of planning and debates over lashings of tea, but that was nothing new. The odd thing was that amid the flurry of last-minute actions and discussions, Maire and I hardly spoke a word to each other. We had shared one kiss at the ruins of the light-house and now we were leaving on a counterfeit honeymoon without even discussing how we would act. I knew she had con-sented to go, but I reasoned that it may have been out of duty. As far as I knew, she had regretted the impulsiveness of that kiss and wanted nothing more to do with me.

Aboard ship, Dunleavy was shaking my hand vigorously for once, but he was giving me instructions as well. "Don't forget to purchase new satchels, as many as we will need. And obtain a receipt for them. For everything, in fact."

"I shall." I paused, waiting. "You have not given me the money yet, sir."

With a sigh, Dunleavy reached into his pocket and reluctantly gave up a packet into my care. I stepped back to where Barker stood on the deck, surrounded by the factionists as if it were a football scrimmage. He had insisted upon seeing me off despite the police, who were patrolling the docks.

"You know what to do?" he asked.

"Keep my wits about me and concentrate on my work," I stated. "Oh, and be a gentleman."

"Exactly."

Barker and I had visited the slop shops, purchasing my evening kit, since I was supposed to be on honeymoon, and there was no way to tell who might be scrutinizing us. My employer insisted I go to a tailor with him, and have the suit fitted, mended, and pressed; he also provided new collars and cuffs, all within just two days—at a cost higher than the price of the suit. After a haircut and shave, I really did look like the new groom, off on a Continental honeymoon, a bowler on my head and my new bride's hand in the crook of my elbow for ornament.

O'Casey kissed his sister, then pumped my hand, giving me a glare to say he still found objections to this whole affair and that I better make sure they remained unfounded. In contrast, after kissing the bride, McKeller tipped me a wink, as if to say take every advantage in life you are given. Whatever remarks he'd made among the lads were enough to make them all give a knowing chuckle.

When the porter gave the call for visitors to depart, the group of men walked down the gangplank as the steamship *Hibernia* sounded its bass note and slowly pulled away from the dock. Still lost in my private thoughts, I watched the coast slip away until there was nothing left to do but to finally turn and look at Maire. To tell the truth, I was as nervous as a groom on his honeymoon, and a glance told me she was nervous as well.

"Would you like to walk about the ship or perhaps have a cup of tea?" I suggested.

"A cup of tea would be nice," she murmured.

I escorted her to the lounge. The *Hibernia* was a trim little steamer running from Liverpool to Calais. The lounge was sumptuous, with gold-rimmed china, starched table linens, and attentive waiters. Maire didn't speak until our tea and biscuits arrived.

"I feel like a complete imposter, Thomas," she confessed. "I'm not used to this. I feel as if I should be in the galley, up to my elbows in soap suds."

"You have as much right to be here as anyone, Maire," I told her. "Or should I call you Brigid?"

Our passports and papers listed us as Charles and Brigid Beaton. I carried business cards listing me as a chemical engineer for a Liverpool mining firm. Beaton, a very serious young man, would take the opportunity to combine work with pleasure, purchasing supplies for his company while on the Continent.

"No, not Brigid," she said. "I'm not accustomed to deception. I'm not a bomber or an anarchist, like you, working with the famous Mr. van Rhyn. I just keep house for my brother."

Despite the words, she looked like anything but an ordinary Irish girl. She wore a beautiful traveling suit of violet linen. Pearl earrings dangled from her ears, and her hair was swept up in an elaborate style with red curls framing her face. The French would have called her *ravissante*.

"Who's going to cook for Eamon and the boys, and Mr. van Rhyn, while I am gone?" she wondered.

"They'll just have to fend for themselves, I suppose. Scavenge off the land."

"I hope you don't think—" she said, then stopped.

"Think what?"

A blush grew on her cheeks. "It was very forward of me to

---

kiss you last week. I wish you to know it was unlike me. I don't really know why I did it."

"I understand," I told her. "And in case you didn't notice, I was kissing you back."

She smiled behind her teacup. We sat in an awkward silence for a moment. I was fidgeting with my silverware, and she was playing with one of her curls. Finally, she spoke again.

"I suppose you shall be going back to London when this is all over or off with Mr. van Rhyn."

"I believe Mr. van Rhyn intends to settle in Dublin now. He hopes to open a factory. As for me, I haven't made any plans."

"Do you have anyone waiting for you in London? Parents or brothers and sisters, or a sweetheart?"

"A sister, living in Cheapside," I invented.

"The cause could use a man like you."

"Just the cause?"

In answer, she cleared her throat daintily, took some more tea, and changed the subject. "I shan't know what to do with myself in Paris," she said.

"Oh, there are worlds of things to do: museums, opera, ballet, and cathedrals. There are gardens and cafés, shops of all descriptions, art galleries, and palaces. It is more than one can do in the four days allotted."

"I've never been on holiday before," she told me. "My life has been all work." She spread her hands on the table. Though small, they were rough and red from hours of daily toil. I reached over and took them both in my own.

"In Paris, they have creams that will make your hands so soft, one would think you had never lifted anything but a hand mirror in your life. And there are silk gloves to cover them, while it works its magic."

"How you do talk, sir," she said.

I squeezed her hands. "Relax, Maire. Really. We have no idea what the future may hold. Enjoy the present, these few days. Forget about the cause. Forget about me, if you wish. Think about yourself. What do *you* want?"

"I hardly know," she answered ingenuously.

"I know exactly what I want," I said, lowering my voice.

She looked up at me sharply. "And what is that, I'd like to know, Thomas Penrith?"

"To buy you the prettiest dress in all Paris."

We whiled away our hours aboard ship promenading on the deck and staring out over the ocean at the English coast. Maire had never seen the sea from aboard ship before. Luckily, neither of us suffered from seasickness. I demonstrated my utter lack of skill at deck games, and she beat me three games in a row. In one of the salons, we wrote cards to everyone back home, which would be posted on arrival in Calais. The real van Rhyn would have called us bourgeois or the idle rich. Rich we were, and none of it ours. I'd had a peep into the envelope. There was enough to show the girl a holiday she would never forget.

After dinner, a band played in the dining room, and I convinced her to dance. There was no impropriety in our dancing, being newlyweds, of course. In fact, the crew and passengers insisted. Everyone was quite sentimental over the handsome young couple, their futures ahead of them. One could have fit Barker into the space between us—or Willie, at least—but I still felt her hand in mine and the whalebone corset around her slender waist. We were both thinking the same thing. There was a key to our cabin in my pocket, and that cabin had but one bed.

When we finally left, there was a cunning look on the faces of everyone turned our way. It was our first night as a married couple. Everyone knew what was expected of us. But there'd been no wedding and I had promised several people, including my employer, that what was expected of us would not come to pass.

Once back in our room, I changed quickly into my nightshirt

and set up a rude pallet on the floor, while Maire changed discreetly behind a screen. While she was going to sleep in a soft bed with Irish lace and linens and a gold-encrusted headboard, I would spend the night on the floor, with nothing but a blanket and pillow to keep me company. It reminded me in no small way of Barker's Persian rug and his heavy volume of Shakespeare.

Maire came out wearing a white, frothy new nightgown, of which no Catholic sister in Dublin could accuse of impropriety. It came up to her throat and down to her wrists and ankles. There were yards and yards of it, in folds, in pleats. It was in two layers, an outer, lacy mantle with a large ribbon and an inner confection made of silk. She was completely covered, so why was my heart racing?

She looked at me as if I were a Bengal tiger, and she a goat which had just been brought out and tethered. I heard her naked little feet pad across to the bed, and she climbed under the sheets, covering herself quickly. There was at least a year's output of Irish linen and lace in this one bed, all as white and virginal as a bride's wedding gown.

"Good night," she murmured.

"Good night," I responded, turning down the gas. With a sigh, I sank down onto that hard floor to spend the night listening to her breathing and idly tracing the pattern on the ceiling with my eyes.

The next morning, I awoke as if the memory of every wound, bruise, scrape, and cut I'd ever incurred had all come back to haunt me. I loosed my limbs from the fetal position and rose to my feet, every bone and tissue protesting. My eyes strayed to the bed. It was empty. Where had she gone?

Maire stepped from behind the screen. She was dressed in an outfit of many shades of green. It set off the russet of her hair. Until yesterday, I had seen her in nothing but black and white, like a maidservant. I couldn't help but pull my blanket up about me and to bow, formally, in my nightclothes.

"I trust you slept well, Mrs. Beaton," I said.

She bobbed a curtsy to me gravely. "Mr. Beaton."

"If you wish, you may go to the dining room. I shall be down directly."

"Indeed, I must not," she said, looking uncomfortable. "I shall wait for you, if I may."

What was that about? I wondered. I needed a cup of coffee before my mind could cogitate. I nodded agreement and went behind the screen myself. Choosing a suit, I dressed rather self-consciously, knowing she was in the room. What had happened? Did I snore or thrash about in my sleep? On further reflection, had she believed it all a mistake? I finished tying my four-in-hand and stepped out from behind the screen. Maire O'Casey was reclining on the edge of the bed, which I noted she had made. A hand was across her brow, and I thought I saw a frown upon her features. Perhaps she had awoken with a headache.

"Shall we go and break our fast?" I asked.

"Thomas, I would prefer to spend the rest of the journey in our cabin."

"Of course. Are you unwell?"

"No, I feel fine. I simply can't face the horrid people in the dining room."

"Horrid?" I asked. "I don't know what you mean. They seemed agreeable enough."

"Yes, but can you not see? Today, if I sat with them, they would know."

It took me a few moments to puzzle it out. Presumably, she had left their company the evening before an innocent maiden but was now numbered the newest of married women. She would not sit at table, knowing that all the passengers' thoughts would be on the night before, noticing and interpreting her every word and expression.

"Oh, I see," I said solemnly, though I was inclined to laugh at her sensitivity. "Shall I go down, then, and see that something is brought up for us both?"

"Good heavens, no!" she cried. "They will think us the worst of libertines. No, you must go and eat and offer my apologies. Have a servant send food to the cabin. Just anything will do."

I did as she requested, and found she was correct. After I sat down, all asked after my new bride. My statement that she was under the weather elicited smiles from most of the table, and a few women offered to see to her, which, of course, I declined. I saw that food was taken up to her and tried to enjoy my meal in peace. Some even commented on my haggard appearance. Honestly, I had no idea the fun others had at a new couple's expense.

We arrived safely in port at Calais around noon and transferred to the Paris train. Finding no empty compartments, we deliberately joined one full of people we hadn't met on the *Hibernia*. Secure in our anonymity, we made our way into the heart of France.

Late that afternoon, our train arrived in the Gare du Nord. On the cabman's recommendation, we stayed at the Hotel Beaurivage in the rue Mozart. The staff treated us well, recognizing by our awkwardness that we were newlyweds. In the dining room, after we were settled in, we were presented with a complimentary bottle of Dom Pérignon with our meal. It was Maire's first taste of champagne. She liked it but would only permit herself a few sips.

Aside from the bed, our room boasted a fine chaise longue. Thankful to have it instead of the floor, I turned it into a temporary bed. We performed our necessary ablutions with less nervousness than the night before. Exhausted by travel, we fell into our respective beds and slumbered heavily.

The next day, I was awakened by the sounds of Paris, as if it were right in my room. Swallows twittered, vehicles bowled by, people cried out greetings in their Gallic way. I put up my head. Maire was already dressed and was on the balcony. She was looking at the sights before her with an air of suppressed excitement. It was her first morning in Paris and she didn't wish to waste a minute of it.

I made a show of reluctance getting out of bed, but I wanted to indulge her. We had coffee and fresh rolls in the dining room, then I hired a fiacre to give us a tour. Over the next hour or so we made a wide circle around the city, getting our first glimpses of places I'd only read about in novels: the Palais Royal, the cathedral of Notre-Dame, and the Champs Elysées. Afterward, we went to the Louvre, where we spent several hours admiring paintings and statuary from ancient Greek times and the latest French masterpieces. So absorbed were we that for the afternoon, I forgot we were there to do anything but sightsee. It was difficult for me to stop indulging the girl, but I finally pushed her into a dress shop on the boulevard de le Madeleine and retrieved my list. Barker, whom I believe knew Paris almost as well as London, had given me the names of several manufacturers and merchants of explosive materials.

I went to the first establishment in the area telling myself that it would be best to test the waters. After all, I probably wouldn't like French prisons any more than English ones, possibly even less. I went in, purchased a handful of blasting caps, presented my papers, and that was it. There were no recriminations or problems.

Having completed my duty of the day, I took Maire back to the hotel, where we changed for the evening. Forgoing the dining room, I took her to the Café Le Procope, the oldest restaurant in Paris, if not the world. After dinner I tried a mixture of coffee and chocolate, which the waiter assured me was the favorite of Voltaire, and Maire indulged herself for once, since the café was justly famous for the invention of vanilla and chocolate ice cream.

I wanted to pinch myself. Nothing like this had happened in my first case working for Barker. I had been nearly murdered several times over. If half, or even a quarter, of the work involved squiring beautiful women about Paris, I could see why so many applicants for the position had been there the day I first came to Barker's door.

We couldn't decide what to do next. We'd had too much coffee and ice cream to sit through a long opera or ballet. Neither of us was the sort to desire a visit to the notorious Chat Noir to see its cancan dancers, yet it seemed too early to return to the hotel. We ended up simply walking along the boulevards, arm in arm, eventually making our way along the Seine, that gentle queen of rivers.

"What are those people doing over there?" Maire asked, looking at some people in the shadows.

"I believe they are kissing."

She stared harder. "You are right. There are several couples kissing."

"That does not surprise me." And leaning in, I kissed her for the second time. And the third.

She heaved a great sigh. "I still can't believe I'm here."

Arm in arm, we continued along the Seine, enjoying the warm night, the pale quarter moon, and the beauty that is Paris. It was one of the most wonderful nights of my life. Had I known how this adventure would turn out, I would have treasured it all the more.

22

THE NEXT DAY WAS A BUSY ONE FOR ME. WHILE
Maire was out shopping, I had primers to buy, glycerin to obtain,
and satchels to purchase. My first stop was an industrial supply
company where I obtained thirty fuse caps, a large spool of
wire, and numerous other articles necessary for the infernal
device–building process. Their purchase required identification,
and I was glad of the false papers and business cards they had
provided me in Liverpool. Afterward, I had everything sent to
the Gare du Nord.

There was a chemical supply store in the rue de la Grande
Armée, where I explained that I needed supplies for my company,
and there was no better place to get them than Paris. I flashed my
business cards and talked explosives with the clerk, whose entire
life, both waking and sleeping, seemed devoted to the art of
destruction. I was able to procure gallons of glycerin, some fulmi-
nate of mercury for the detonation process, and all the other
chemicals necessary for the making of infernal devices.

So now I was to build bombs for the Irish Republican
Brotherhood, though they were not to be functioning ones.

Barker and I had discussed it. Since Niall Garrity was the only one who knew how to build bombs and he would be in Dublin, we could build inert devices, though all the parts would be there.

"*Transportez le paquet à la Gare du Nord, s'il vous plaît,*" I told the clerk.

"*Oui, Monsieur Beaton.*"

I stepped out into the street. All I needed now was thirty satchels and a like number of timepieces. Oh, and the pistols, of course. Thirty of them, to be used to detonate the bombs. That was going to be tricky.

I met Maire back at the hotel. The room showed evidence that I had not been the only one shopping. There were close to a dozen packages on a table by the window. My pretty companion was trying hard not to smile, which resulted in a dimple in each cheek.

"What have you been up to?"

"Why, nothing," she said, all innocence. "Whatever do you mean?"

"That money was earmarked for the poor," I said, wagging a finger at her in imitation of Dunleavy.

"If you'd taken a look in my wardrobe lately, you'd have seen who was poor. All these nice traveling dresses I've been wearing I've borrowed from friends. I promised I'd bring them back some French lace and gloves. You wouldn't have me be ungrateful, would you? Besides, if I know Mr. Dunleavy, the money would have gone to his tailor or a drink."

"Did you buy your dress?" I asked.

She couldn't help herself. She hopped up and down a time or two and clapped her hands. "I did."

"Excellent. And I suppose you bought some nice shoes and some perfume and powders and such."

"Well, if you can go to a chemist, I don't see why I cannot," she maintained.

"Of course," I said. "Are you hungry?"

"Famished. Shopping gives me an appetite."

After lunch, we took in more sights. We visited the cathedral of Notre-Dame, where Maire went in and prayed. Then we shook our heads in wonder at the beauty of the Jardin des Tuileries and strolled about the gardens.

"I know this is all pretend and we're not really on our honeymoon, Thomas, but I want you to know I'm having the best time of my life."

"I am, as well," I told her.

"I haven't always had an easy life," she continued. "It hasn't turned out the way I could have wished, so far. Certainly, I never expected to be strolling in a French garden with a handsome fellow my own age. It would be too much to hope for. Oh, I've made you blush again! You'd make a poor spy, Thomas. All your emotions are on your sleeve!"

"What do you mean by that?" I asked. Had I betrayed myself? As far as I knew, there had been nothing in my conduct that had revealed who I really was.

"I mean you're as open as a book. You need to spend more time in Paris, among all these suave boulevardiers."

"Oh, I like that," I protested. "Thank you very much. And to think I bought you lunch. I wonder how you dare be seen in Paris with an oaf like me."

She laughed and took my hand. "You're not an oaf, Thomas. You are a dear. And I shall always cherish this time in Paris with you."

She kissed me then. For a moment, I felt as if all subterfuge was gone. Names and affiliations did not matter. It was just the two of us.

"Shall we go to the opera tonight?" I queried.

"Oh, yes, let's!"

I wasn't prepared for the sight of Maire in her new evening

dress. It was a masterpiece of gold and silver with a bustle, but it showed far more of her neck and bosom than I was comfortable with. She was brave to put it on, but balked at the last minute.

"Is it too much?" she asked, closing a matching mantle over it. "Or rather, too little? The seamstress assured me it was *la mode* this year. Everyone shall be dressing this way."

"Very well," I said. "But you must hide that dress from your brother, or he will kill me."

"Oh, don't mind Eamon. I've got the boy wrapped around my finger."

"Really? And which finger have you got reserved for me?" I wondered aloud.

I found out after the opera. The performance was *Manon,* a very tragic story. Our eyes were glued to the stage throughout the entire production. She wept openly at the end, and even I had a lump in my throat. We were rather subdued in the carriage ride back to the hotel.

I began preparing the chaise longue for the night while she changed.

"I feel dreadful, your sleeping on this chaise here," she said.

"I'm used to it."

She came out from behind the screen, wearing only her night-dress. It was unbuttoned. I saw the gap, the long, thin gap of ivory-colored flesh, all the way to the floor.

"It is very cold in a marriage bed, all alone," she murmured, her hand stroking my cheek. She pulled me over onto the bed. She was wearing a new French perfume that made my head spin. Her soft lips pressed urgently against my own. I was intoxicated. I could feel my own passion begin to ignite. However, I had been training for months in the production of explosives, and I knew what kind of chemical reaction would happen if things went too far.

"No!" I said, pulling myself away, off the bed.

"What is wrong?" she asked in a low voice. "Have I displeased you? I only wished to show you how I feel about you." The latter came out almost petulantly. She pulled the corner of a blanket over her bare limbs.

I sat down on the edge of the bed. My shirt was suddenly damp; my heart was pounding. "I care for you, as well," I said. "More than you know. But I cannot accept what you . . . offer. It is not mine to take. It belongs to your future husband."

"But what if you are my future husband?" she countered, looking me in the eyes.

"Then I should have it after we are married. Not now."

She slowly pulled the blanket up over her head. I heard her sniff back a tear.

"I've been a fool," she said from inside her makeshift cave. "You must think me terribly wanton. I've never done anything like this before in my life."

"I believe you," I said. "And I'd never think you a fool."

"I don't know what it is about you, Thomas Penrith," she continued. "You've got me thinking the maddest thoughts and doing the wildest things. I'm not like this, you know. I'm a sensible girl."

"I know. I've been thinking the same thoughts about you, Maire." I brought her hand to my lips and kissed it. She came out from beneath the blanket, which had disheveled her beautiful auburn hair.

"I've been seduced by Paris and the pretty clothes and the opera," she said. "And by you, or at least the thought of you. You aren't like anyone I've ever met."

"I was worried that Willie might have had a prior claim on you," I told her.

"Willie," she said with a sad smile. "Willie is wonderful and handsome and a man of great talent, but he is not a—a lover. You are a lover, Thomas. You smolder."

Smolder, eh? She said I smoldered. I had the absurd desire to go down to the street and inform passersby that I smoldered. Me,

Thomas Llewelyn. Or was it Thomas Penrith? Or Charles Beaton? No matter. No woman had ever told me that before.

"I'm sorry," I muttered. "I care for you too much to allow this to happen. Part of me is mad for it, but another part will not allow it. I cannot stay here. I need some fresh air."

I threw on a jacket and was about to quit the room.

"Stay," she demanded, seizing my wrist.

"I cannot. I must clear my head."

"No, I mean come to stay in Dublin when this is all over. Stay with me."

"I don't know," I said. "I don't know what I'll be doing."

"Stay, or take me with you."

My head was suddenly swollen with millions of thoughts. They were far too heavy for my weary shoulders.

"Perhaps," I said, as I dashed out into the hall. Having escaped the scene, I leaned my shoulders on the other side of the door and breathed in cooler, less electrically charged air. I heard a sob, almost a wail in the room behind me. My hand reached toward the knob, but I mastered myself. I ran through the hallway and down the stairs.

In the street, a sound escaped my throat, a more masculine version of Maire's wail. I could feel my heart thumping, shooting blood too quickly through my limbs and head. I lurched like a drunkard until I found a bench, where I collapsed and buried my head in my arms. When I'd taken this case, I hadn't meant to fall in love.

Was it love? Barker told me once that women were my weakness, and I tended to agree with him. I had not known Maire for more than a few weeks, but how long did a man need to know a woman before falling in love? There is such a thing as love at first sight. Certainly, Maire was a woman any man could fall for. I could picture going home to her after a day's work, her fussing over me, looking at her by the fire. What had Thomas Hardy said, in *Far from the Madding Crowd*? "Whenever you look up, there I shall be—and whenever I look up, there will be you."

I madly combed my fingers through my hair. Who was I trying to fool? Did I really expect to go home from our offices in Craig's Court to an I.R.B. princess? Would Barker allow it? Would she? Would I contemplate leaving my position as assistant to go build bombs for the Irish and become a traitor to England? Of course not. As Barker had told me, the minute she found out I was a spy, Maire would hate me with as much passion as she had almost just loved me.

I got up, pulled my jacket collar up over my open shirt, and stuffed my hands in my pockets. I had hurt her. I hadn't meant to, but I had done it, anyway. It was not her fault that she had been caught up in this. Damn her brother for involving an innocent girl in this dangerous business. And damn me for breaking her heart, because it was inevitable that I would. I was not going to leave Barker's employ, and I would never build another bomb after this case, not if I had anything to say about it. So I found myself desiring Maire, yet not allowing myself to have her, wanting to go with her but forcing myself to follow the path I had promised Mr. Anderson and Sir Watkin—aye, and my own employer—that I would follow. In the end, if all went according to plan, the English would triumph, the Irish would be imprisoned, and poor Maire would be left behind to bear the brunt of my handiwork. By doing that which I believed to be right, I would make myself the lowest of bounders. There was no satisfactory solution.

Mercifully, she was asleep when I got back. I crawled into my makeshift bed on the chaise longue, and soon was asleep myself.

I awoke the next morning as she moved past my bed. A polar wind came with her. It was no less than I deserved, I thought, and I bore it stoically. I got up and threw on my clothes, leaving her to her toilette.

"Why don't you try the little café on the corner this morning?" she suggested. "I shall be down in a while."

Had she suggested a café in the middle of the Gobi, I would have found a way to get there. Anything to please her. I couldn't bear her glacial coldness, and I felt I had behaved like a cad the night before, though I would have been a worse cad had I allowed myself . . . It was simply a matter of choosing the lesser evil.

So it was that I was seated at a picturesque café in the middle of Paris, sipping a strong cup of coffee and spreading preserves over a warm croissant when Maire O'Casey came over to my table. She was wearing another new dress, an aniline-dyed cobalt blue that fit her like a glove. From somewhere in the city, she had purchased a rouge pot, and her lips were the color of cherries. With her hair pulled back loosely, she looked fresh out of one of the paintings by the fellow Renoir, who obviously had a passion for redheads. No man watching her—and, believe me, every man in the street was watching her—would have taken her for an Irishwoman. She looked like a Parisian society woman.

I dropped my knife on the table. This was the vision from my dream, down to the last detail: the coffee, the preserves, the woman in the blue dress. She moved slowly through the crowd, leaned over me, and whispered in my ear. "I forgive you."

A jolt of electricity ran down my spine as if I were a tree trunk split in half. I don't know if it was her breath on my ear or the memory of my dream.

"Good," I said, when I could finally breathe again.

"But you are cold as a mackerel to have turned down the offer I made you last night."

I seized her hand. "Do you think it was easy? I would sooner cut my throat than do it again."

"Do not worry. The offer shall not be given again." She ordered coffee and fussed over the menu, flustering the slavish waiter who groveled beside her. It was as if a knife were twisting in the area of my heart. She had worn the dress and painted herself so on purpose.

———

"You are still angry with me," I stated. "I deserve it. I beg your forgiveness, Maire, for hurting you in any way."

"I said I forgive you. You are a man, after all. What else were you made for but to break my heart?"

"Oh, please, Maire!"

This went on for some time. She was good at it, torturing me. Perhaps all women are. I was reminded how Barker could take hold of my collar and elbow and flip me in a way I hadn't anticipated, and then get me in some hold where I would be writhing in pain if I didn't give up. Maire did the same thing, only with words. At the end of fifteen minutes, I felt as if I'd been grappling for several hours and had come out the loser every time.

"What shall we do today?" I begged.

"Oh, I don't know. I'm not much in a mood for seeing sights. Have you collected all you need?"

"Everything but the satchels. I believe they have a good selection at the Paris Market in the Eighteenth arrondissement. It is a street market. You are a little overdressed, but you might enjoy yourself. If you're feeling better, we could then see the Bois de Boulogne."

"I didn't say I was feeling poorly," she bristled.

"Of course not! As you say."

There is something engrossing about a street market. It is like treasure hunting. Somewhere amid these piles of civilization's refuse are treasures, one keeps telling oneself. It is as addictive as gambling. One keeps moving from one booth to another, convinced Marie-Antoinette's hand mirror or Napoleon's walking stick are in the next bin.

As I purchased three dozen used satchels of all sizes and descriptions, I kept an eye on Maire. She was inclined to be aloof, but slowly the booths drew her in. She played with a small parasol that matched her dress, looking every inch a princess, and picked among the items in the booths with a listless air.

"Madame is out of sorts this morning," a voice said in French behind me. It was a woman of some fifty years, who ran a booth. She had a sharp nose in the middle of a round face.

"Oui," I responded. *"Madame* is very *much* out of sorts this morning."

"Naturellement," the woman responded. "Now you must buy your way out of it. Get her something extravagant. Reassure her that you still care."

"What would you suggest?"

"A necklace, perhaps, or a pair of earrings. I have a nice cross set with sapphires that might go with that dress."

"Show me."

I looked at the cross. It was small but elegant, very French. It consisted of four sapphires in a row, with one more on each side. Maire's throat was bare, I noticed. The necklace would sparkle like the dress.

"How much?"

She named a price. It always sounded like a fortune when one said it in francs, but when I converted it in my head, it was merely expensive. I gave in with a shrug.

"Avez-vous une boîte?"

I couldn't resist giving her the box in the carriage on the way to the Tuileries. The gamble worked. She was delighted. She kissed me, forgave everything, and was the perfect companion the rest of the day. The icicle she had thrust between my ribs up into my heart melted away in the warm Parisian afternoon sun.

23

WE CAME BACK TO LIVERPOOL TWO DAYS LATER, our mission completed. Some sort of understanding had been reached between Maire and me, save that generally, when both parties in a disagreement reach an understanding, they both understand the terms. All I know for certain was that she didn't seem angry with me anymore and we had been inseparable since she had forgiven me. Her gentle hand seemed permanently set into the crook of my arm as we strolled the deck of the steamer home. I knew better than to think that would bode well with everyone in the faction in Liverpool. Personally, I wondered how Barker would react. I had fended off a more permanent relationship, but somehow one seemed to have developed anyway.

O'Casey and McKeller met us at the dock. I wondered if it was a show of genuine affection when Maire squeezed my left arm as we came down the gangway, or whether she was merely tweaking her brother's nose. The way he screwed up his mouth, he certainly looked as if there were something that bothered him. As for McKeller, he was all grins and wiggling eyebrows in my direction.

"It's good to see you two," her brother said, gripping my hand as hard as McKeller had. My other arm was still otherwise engaged, so my only defense was to squeeze back. "Did you have a safe journey back?"

"It was uneventful," I said, as our palms grew red and hot and my fingers began to ache. "The sea was calm."

"That's good," O'Casey continued, as if wholly unconcerned with the struggle going on. "And was the hon—Oww!"

Maire had given his hand a sharp rap with her parasol. She was wearing her blue dress, and though she'd put away her paint pot for prim Liverpool's sake, she wore her hair in the French mode. She had left the city an innocent girl and returned a Continental beauty. It was a wonder her brother was not wringing my neck instead of my hand.

"Maire, you're looking well," O'Casey said with more than a trace of irony. He kissed her on the cheek. "Penrith, did you manage to get all of your work done while you were in Paris?"

"You know it is always work first with me," I told him. "By the end of the day there shall be several large parcels arriving at Victoria Station, to be left until called for. I was able to buy everything. Now I know why you Irish are so fond of going to Paris. If you know where to look, Paris is like a sweet-shop for anarchists."

"Mr. Dunleavy has asked that you return any monies you have left, along with your receipts, of course."

"Here they are," I said, handing the depleted envelope to him. "And just where is your leader this morning?"

"He is in London with your mentor. They are seeing how things stand down there."

"Bar—er, van Rhyn is in London already?" That was close. I had forgotten Barker was going to London and I had nearly blurted out his real name in shock.

"Yes, and not a moment too soon. For a man with limited

205

vision, he's got eyes in the back of his head. He predicted we'd be raided, and sure enough, we were."

"Raided!" I cried. "Was anyone arrested?"

"No. All they found was me studying Maire's Gaelic in the kitchen. One of the constables was all for dragging me down to the station, but the inspector, a fellow named Johanson, knew there was not a shred of evidence to hold me on. That's one I owe Mr. van Rhyn. When this mission is successful, we'll be glad to offer him a permanent home in Dublin, if I have any say in the matter."

"Did they leave the place in a shambles, Eamon Patrick?" Maire demanded. Gone instantly was the Parisian coquette, and in her place was the Irish girl who kept house for her brother.

"Aye, they did, I'm afraid. Fergus and I tried to put things back in order the way they were as best we could, but they were pretty thorough."

"Get my bags, gentlemen," she ordered imperiously. "I've got a house to straighten."

McKeller and I collected the luggage and boxes she'd brought back from Paris.

" 'Tis a good thing we was raided, Penrith, old man," the big Irishman said in my ear. "It covered up what terrible housekeepers we was."

"You stayed at their house while we were gone?"

"Aye, we had a lot of planning to do. We're on, Penrith! We're going to London as soon as Dunleavy sends word!"

"That is excellent news," I said. Apparently a lot had happened since we left.

"Maybe I can finally do something with this waste of a life o' mine. Saints, but Maire did a lot of shopping in Paris. I think she bought half the bleedin' town."

We were coming down the gangplank when McKeller managed to crack me in the ribs.

"So, how was the honeymoon, 'Mr. Beaton'? Is married life all they say it is?"

I had some quick thinking to do. "These Catholic girls are strong. I stormed the battlements for days with every weapon in my arsenal, but all I got for my pains were a few chaste kisses."

"Aye, Maire's a tough nut to crack, but keep trying. To tell you the truth, I'd prefer you to Willie as a husband for her. As far as I'm concerned, he's too much of a dreamer."

"Is there anything else I should know about?" I said, as we began walking away from the docks.

"There is. The house is being watched. They're about as subtle as a herd of dairy cows. We'll have to go into the next street and come in through the back door."

"Marvelous," I said. It was not welcome news about the raid, or that the local constabulary were still surveying the house. I didn't have Barker and his skeleton key to get me out if I were arrested.

"Oh, and Willie would very much like to punch your nose, I'm thinking. He danced quite a merry jig when he found out you and Maire were on your way to Paris. Most entertaining, it was."

"I see. So, tell me, McKeller, is there anyone else in this town that's waiting to tear me to pieces, besides O'Casey, Yeats, and the police?"

McKeller counted slowly on his fingers. "No. That's the lot."

Taking a circuitous route to avoid the police, we eventually found ourselves near the O'Casey home. Slipping down the alley, we came up to the back of the house, where I could hear Maire before I saw her.

I braced myself and went in.

"Just look at this place!" she cried in the kitchen. There were dishes stacked in the sink and piles of laundry everywhere. "Did you let the pigs in here while I was gone?"

I rather thought he had, but didn't dare say anything. O'Casey sat in a chair at the table holding his head. He'd met his match or, rather, his superior.

She wheeled on me. "And I suppose you brought a parcel of laundry home from Paris."

I almost said I had brought no more than she, but stopped myself. It was more than my life was worth. I nodded distractedly and went into the parlor. Everything was out of order. The Liverpool constabulary had gone through drawers, lifted cushions, and looked behind pictures on the wall. McKeller and O'Casey had not tried very hard to put things back as they had been before. Reasoning that I might be in less trouble if I were actually doing something, I brought my luggage in and carried it upstairs. Then, I began to carry her parcels and bags into the house.

It didn't fully register in my mind that Barker was in London until I set down my bags in our room. His bed was empty and had been stripped. He had decamped with Dunleavy and was now more than a hundred miles away. I'm sure his first order of business once there would be to give the colonel the slip and check in with our office. Perhaps he would communicate with Anderson and Inspector Poole. He might even find time for a reunion with Mac and Harm. Meanwhile, I was left in Liverpool alone, still relatively untrained and surrounded by a dangerous and desperate group of men.

Were I to blunder and reveal my identity somehow, would they really kill me? These were men about my own age, and they were not without feelings. I could remember McKeller dancing at the ceilidh, the grin on O'Casey's face as he scored a goal in hurling, and the Bannon brothers scrambling to fill their plates with peas. They seemed just like lads, fellows I would pass on the street without noticing, not hardened killers.

Then, I thought of them in the moonlight, wild figures

painted blue, as lean and hungry as a pack of wolves. I remembered the unwelcome pressure of McKeller's hand crushing mine, the way they had branded me as if I were cattle, and the poor bloodied victims the night of the bombing. *Thomas*, I said to myself, *of course they'd kill you. They'd beat you to death with those heavy sticks and lash you to a post as an example for those who dared oppose the faction.* Suddenly, London and safety seemed half a world away.

When I came out of my reverie, I felt the desire to talk to Maire. She, at least, was not involved in this. I had to admit I was glad O'Casey had allowed his sister to go to Paris, but he had no right to keep her here, with the faction involved in such dangerous doings. Surely, there was some aunt she could be sent to live with. Though they had left the house a mess, O'Casey and McKeller had shown they could get along without her to pour tea and do the cooking.

Perhaps if she stayed with an aunt in Ireland, she would be safe until this entire affair was over, for good or ill. Maybe there was some way I could visit her and explain why it was necessary for me to act as I had—presenting myself as someone I was not.

I became aware of voices downstairs. I couldn't make out who was speaking, but I could tell something was occurring. I went downstairs to find out what it was and blundered right into the inevitable crisis between Maire and Willie Yeats.

"So that's the way it is to be, then," Willie stated.

"I fear so," Maire responded, her chin high. I noticed her eyes were glittering.

Yeats pointedly crumpled a piece of paper in his hand and let it fall to the floor. I had just enough time to throw myself into a chair before he came into the kitchen.

"I'm afraid I shall not be accompanying you to London, gentlemen," he said. "I am quitting the group."

"You can't quit," McKeller growled. "It ain't allowed."

Yeats went up to him and they stood toe to toe. They were both tall, but Yeats was half McKeller's weight. One swing from the big Irishman would shatter him, but he stood up to him, cool and unafraid.

"Are you going to stop me?" he asked.

McKeller seemed about to say something, but looking at O'Casey out of the corner of his eye, he backed off. "You wouldn't peach on us, would you?"

"Of course not," O'Casey stated. "Willie is no traitor."

"May my tongue be torn out by its roots and my breast opened if I repeat a word of this faction during my lifetime. I swear as an Irishman," he said with a raised hand, echoing part of what he had made me swear in the initiation ceremony by the sea.

"I'm sorry things didn't work out for you, Willie," O'Casey continued.

Yeats turned his head and gave a long, final look into the eyes of Maire O'Casey. He flicked his eyes in my direction, and I saw the anger and resentment there in that brief glance. In the silence of the room, I heard him slowly exhale. "Some things cannot be helped, gentlemen. I wish you luck, and I hope to celebrate your victory. But for now, I must bid you all good day."

We parted, and he passed between us and out the back door, the very picture of wounded pride.

After a moment, Eamon spoke to his sister. "Maire . . ."

"Not another word!" she snapped. "Not one. Will you look at this place? Do you think I'm stupid enough to believe the police did all this? I'm nothing but a drab to you boys. Just a washer-woman and cook. And you, Thomas Penrith. You're as bad as the rest! Maybe worse! I'm going to get changed."

I couldn't help noticing the piece of paper Yeats had dropped. So far, there had been several papers in this case: the letter in Dunleavy's room, the letters in Maire's box. As casually as possible, I scooped up the ball of paper. Smoothing it out, I read.

TO KINGDOM COME

How many loved your moments of glad grace,
And loved your beauty with love false or true,
But one man loved the pilgrim soul in you,
And loved the sorrows of your changing face.

I shook my head in wonder at the beauty of it, and my heart fell when I read "with love false or true." It was all my fault, I realized. I had little chance of a relationship with Maire, yet I had insinuated myself between this poet and his muse. Perhaps I had ruined both their lives. Barker was right about my weakness for the fair sex. I'd blundered in and made a hash of everything.

I retreated to my room for the rest of the afternoon, occasionally rereading the verse of the poet I'd wronged. His leave-taking had been a model of decorum in the face of wounded pride. He was more of a man than I had taken him for, to stand up to Fergus McKeller. I regretted every depreciating thought I'd had about him. William Yeats was a better man than I.

24

"**W**HAT IS WRONG, THOMAS?"

"Nothing," I answered, but I was still upset after the scene with Yeats the day before.

We were standing at the platform at Lime Street Station, waiting for the London train. Maire was seeing us off.

"You seem so distant. Have I done anything to anger you? I'm sorry you had to come in on my parting with Willie yesterday. There was never much between us . . . on my side, I mean."

"You owe me no explanation, I assure you," I said.

"Make me a promise, Thomas!" she said.

I have not the makings of a Le Caron, I'm afraid. There are elements of the spying life I could never ascribe to, such as making promises I had no intention of keeping. I looked warily at the girl.

"What kind of promise?"

"That you'll come back when your mission is over. I'm not saying come back for good. I have no right to ask that. But at least, come back and say good-bye."

"I can make no such promise. I could be arrested or even blown up."

"Don't say that!" she said, looking terrified. "You're more important to me than this mission. If you ask me, it's a mere fool's errand. Promise me this, then. Come back to me if it is within your power."

"Very well. I shall come back, if it is within my power."

She kissed me then, one final time, and she put all of herself into that kiss. It was a kiss of virgin chastity and the promise of passionate nights, a kiss of graceful youth, middle years spent side by side, and of old age together, with grandchildren around us. It was everything a kiss could be, pure and powerful. I could not help but fear it might be our last.

We parted. I watched her walk away through the crowd until she was gone. The whistle gave a plaintive cry that matched my mood exactly, and I was alone with a crushing weight I couldn't describe. I made my way to the carriage and sat down beside O'Casey and the faction members, who were making jokes among themselves at getting another chance at London. I must have been dull company for the entire journey.

It was the most welcome sight in the world when I saw Barker's stern, impassive figure on the platform at Euston Station. I hadn't expected to see him awaiting us.

"Welcome to London again, lad," he murmured, shaking my hand. I felt as if all my emotional burdens were falling off me. I'd give them all to Barker and let him sort them out. We collected my luggage and soon were in a hansom bound for the Crook and Harp. The rest of the faction would split up and arrive singly in a roundabout fashion, so as not to attract the attention of the Special Irish Branch.

"So, how was Paris?" my employer asked, as we watched O'Casey and his men separate and slip through the crowd.

"I got everything we needed for the work, sir. We got in a little sightseeing at the Louvre and the Tuileries. Oh, and we visited the opera one evening."

"I don't care about the itinerary, Thomas. Did you discover anything of interest?"

"Willie Yeats quit the faction, after a break with Maire."

"Did he, by Jove?" Barker asked, taking the pipe out of his mouth.

"McKeller was inclined to be belligerent, but O'Casey let him go."

"Faction members have been murdered for trying to resign. O'Casey must have exhibited great control and been very sure that Mr. Yeats wouldn't inform on the cell. It's good he got out when he could. I don't believe these rascals shall come to a good end."

"So, how are things progressing in London?" I asked.

"Famously. Harm is fine, though I believe he has pined a bit from missing us. He seems to have lost some weight. The garden is coming along well, but I discovered some blight on the Japanese maple."

We were about to blow up half London, and the Guv was going on about his dog and his garden. I listened patiently while he went over his garden in detail, rattling off Latin names as if I knew a bluebell from a buttercup. Finally, he got around to the part I was interested in, the part about Inspector Poole and Scotland Yard.

"Poole assures me the Special Irish Branch can be in position all around the Crook and Harp at a moment's notice. He paid an informant to tell him where the various tunnels under the area led. Dunleavy is ensconced at Claridge's in high style, on a floor higher than Parnell. The hotel now boasts two pretenders to the Irish throne. He has had a setback, however. Apparently, the Pope has answered Parnell's enquiries and is moderately favorable to a bid for Irish independence. In a way, he has cemented Parnell's position of authority. It has dampened the colonel's enthusiasm and resulted in another bout of drinking."

"So, what are our plans, exactly?"

"We have rooms reserved at the Crook and Harp. It is a shambles of a place, with walls knocked out, steps going up and down, and odd turnings, not to mention the tunnels and bolt-holes. We shall collect the materials from Victoria Station and set them up in a makeshift laboratory on the premises. You and I shall prepare the bombs."

"You do mean inert bombs, don't you, sir?" I asked.

"We don't want to cause an actual explosion, but I suspect they shall want a demonstration that our dynamite works. We might set off a single stick in one of the tunnels. I suggest connecting one stick to a cap and fuse. The difficult part will be bundling each of the inert bombs into the satchels, under the very eyes of the faction. Luckily, the one who really knows explosives is Garrity, who is in Paris."

It felt very good to be back in London again, but I must state that I didn't care for the Seven Dials, the area which, along with St. Giles, formed that part of town facetiously called the "Holy Land." "Unholy" would have been more appropriate. Prostitutes and thieves had staked out their territories along the streets, idly waiting like spiders for flies to fall into their traps. When I saw the faded and sooty sign for the Crook and Harp, my spirits flagged. This would be where I lived and worked for the next few days. If I wasn't careful, they might be my last.

The cabman charged us extra for having to come into this area, and we had to spring from the moving cab, for he wouldn't stop. As he passed us, we saw a couple of street arabs already clinging to the cab under the driver's very seat. We too kept moving, rather than risk standing in our drawers, though I'd like to see them dare try it if Barker were in his regular clothes.

The Dials were where seven streets all came together. It looked as if a three-layer cake had been cut into slices and separated; but if so, it was a most unwholesome one, reminding me of Mrs. Havisham's wedding cake in *Great Expectations,* and yet the

Dials were within a dozen streets of our respectable offices in Whitehall. It was all one with Barker, who would walk into the vilest warren in Whitechapel the same as into Buckingham Palace.

Barker brushed past a brutish-looking clerk with a splinter of wood stuck in his teeth, and went up some dilapidated stairs. He led me down a hall, and I saw what he meant by the Crooked Harp being made from several buildings. There was a hall going twenty feet, then a step and a floor leaning toward the right, then two steps down and another hall with a leftish slant.

My employer retrieved a key from his pocket and unlocked a door on our left. Inside was an antique cabinet bed, the kind that was all the rage in about 1811. There was a circular table decorated with knife marks and water rings, with a quartet of mismatched and spindly chairs around it, and another bed that had last been aired when Nelson drew breath.

"Couldn't you have gotten a better room?" I asked.

"This is the best room in the house," Barker stated. "Would you prefer a garret in Islington?" The latter was a reference to the room I'd been living in when he'd hired me—or, rather, not living, since I'd stolen out without paying the rent. In his tactful way, Barker was telling me not to be so particular.

"It's fine, sir." I'd seen worse. Or at least just as bad.

There was a knock at the door, and O'Casey and McKeller came strolling in, as if we were still back at the O'Casey house. The fact that we would soon be blowing up whole sections of London seemed to have affected them not at all. Fergus McKeller even had his hands in his pockets, and he sat down and put his feet up on another chair.

"Good day to you, Mr. van Rhyn," O'Casey said. "When did you last hear from Mr. Dunleavy?"

"Yesterday. We shared some schnapps at Claridge's."

I marveled at the way he could slip into a German accent so easily.

"Cart's downstairs, to get the parcels from Victoria," McKeller said, a trifle bored. "We'd better leave soon before everything's stolen but the shadow."

"I'd like to show Mr. Penrith the laboratory first," Barker stated.

"Wouldn't want to mix the wrong chemicals and surprise St. Peter a few decades early," O'Casey said. "Lead the way, Mr. van Rhyn."

The room was in the very highest and farthest corner of the inn, a garret room, empty except for a few tables. It had a large skylight and several west-facing windows which someone had even gone to the trouble of wiping down. It was better than I would have expected.

"This is very satisfactory," Barker said. "A man could definitely build bombs here. Penrith, why don't you go along with these gentlemen to the station and collect the packages. We have a lot of work ahead, and I'm sure you are as anxious to get started as I. Later, we shall all go to the public house below and have a meal and drink, if you gentlemen are agreeable."

"Oh, we're very agreeable," McKeller put in. "You're in luck, Penrith. They have Guinness!"

I'd had enough of trying to keep up with McKeller where drinking is concerned. By then, I was beginning to feel as if my entire circulatory system had been emptied of blood and replaced with the national drink of Ireland. At best, I offered a halfhearted reply.

We rode in the cart to Victoria Station, with McKeller driving. I wondered how my London friends, Ira and Israel, would react if they saw me in the back of a dogcart with a group of Irish ne'er-do-wells. In Liverpool I'd somehow felt I'd be safer once I was in London again. Now, I felt less safe than ever.

The parcels were all waiting to be claimed in the goods shed. I presented my identity papers, all fake from top to bottom, and

signed the stack of forms that formally exchanged the responsibility for the parcels from the railway company to me. I wondered if
a keen fellow in the railway's employ could have looked on the
cumulative list of materials and figured out what we were up to.
If there was such a one, apparently he wasn't working there that
day. The two Irishmen helped me load up the cart and we left
without incident.

"You know what I'm thinking, boys?" McKeller asked as we
were returning.

"You're thinking you've worked too hard, and you'd like a
drink right about now," O'Casey said with an air of disapproval.

"That's the problem with having friends," McKeller said.
"Takes all the mystery out of everything."

"You can have a drink when we get back."

"I'll perish by then," the big Irishman complained. "First pub I
find, I'm stopping."

"But we have a cart full of supplies," I pointed out.

"This is Charing bleedin' Cross. Nobody'll steal nothin' here.
There's one right now, on our right. Whoa!" He pulled the cart up
in front of a pub called the Admiralty Arms.

"We really shouldn't stop, McKeller," I urged.

"Just a pint. I'll drink it fast. Eamon, we're near the Thames if
you're thirsty."

O'Casey gave me a look which said *I can do nothing with him,*
and we reluctantly followed him through the blue-and-gold
doors. It was mid-afternoon, and the owner was setting out a side
of beef on the bar. The smell made me hungry. I supposed it
wouldn't hurt to have a sandwich and a pint of bitters.

"Two pints, publican," McKeller ordered, as we set our feet
on the rail, and our elbows on the polished mahogany. "And bring
my teetotal friend some *whather.*"

The proprietor leaned forward and spoke to us in low tones.
"Here, now, clear off, you lot. I don't want any trouble."

"Trouble?" McKeller asked. "We don't want trouble. We only wanted beer. We have money."

"I don't want your damned money, Paddy. I want you out of here. I don't serve Irish vermin here."

"Perhaps we'd better leave," O'Casey said, being the most coolheaded.

"Let's go, McKeller," I said, taking his arm, but he shook it off and uttered a string of obscenities. The Irish have a natural poetic gift for obscenities, and in a few dozen words, McKeller had insulted the publican, his bar, and most of his ancestors. The heavily mustached proprietor reached under the bar and hefted a large axe.

"You can go out on your own pins," the man said, "or you can be carried out."

Neither McKeller nor O'Casey had brought their bata sticks, and that was probably a good thing or the public house would have been torn apart and the three of us thrown in jail. It didn't seem fair, I'll admit, but tempers were running high in London at the moment, and those two men were the actual cause of it.

We crawled back up into the cart, and with a rough lash of the reins, moved off. McKeller was seething and O'Casey trying to calm him down.

"As you can see, Penrith," O'Casey said drily, "being Irish isn't all shamrocks and singing."

"I'll blow this town to smithereens!" McKeller vowed. He was so angry, he was almost choking on the words. "I'll raze it. I'll tear it down to bricks, then I'll grind them into dust. I'm not leaving London till I've seen that publican's blood spilt! You mark my words!"

"Take it easy, McKeller," O'Casey soothed. "We'll each buy you a pint at the Harp."

McKeller uttered threats and curses all the way back to Seven Dials.

Once there, O'Casey stepped inside the Crook and Harp and found Colin and Padraig Bannon, who came out and unloaded the cart while we went into the pub. Here, we were accepted, but there was more to it than that. Here, we were welcome, even revered. We ordered two pulls of the tap and O'Casey's water, and tried to get McKeller to calm down.

As I was listening to McKeller's litany of complaints against the English, I happened to look over his shoulder, where I spotted a familiar face. At the far end of the room, Soho Vic was seated, leaning against a wall, a pint in front of him. He was engrossed in trimming his nails with a pocketknife and seemed not to notice we were in the room.

My spirits rose. One of Barker's watchers was in residence, and I hoped the police were nearby waiting for a signal. Thanks to the publican at the Arms, the Irish were now demoralized. I almost felt sorry for poor McKeller being tossed out of the public house. Now all we needed to do was build up a few fake explosives, let them get caught by Scotland Yard with them, and that was that. These faction members would be in Wormwood Scrubs and we'd be safe at home.

A hand suddenly came forward and patted my shoulder.

"Hello, Mr. Penrith. Fellows. How are things?"

It was Niall Garrity. I could feel my blood suddenly run cold. It appeared Barker and I would not be making bombs alone after all.

25

GARRITY WAS HERE. MY HEAD BEGAN SPINNING with the implications. Was Dunleavy in charge or was Garrity? Or was Seamus O'Muircheartaigh manipulating us all like puppets? Eamon O'Casey himself seemed capable of running a faction all by himself. More important, Garrity was here and would no doubt insist on helping us make the bombs. How could we be sure they were all inert with him watching? Certainly, his presence here had one effect: it made me nervous, which is not a good thing when about to prepare explosives.

"Fergus," Garrity said, noticing McKeller's red face and angry look. "What's eating you?"

"Me blood's up. One of them nose-in-the-air publicans refused to serve us because we're Irish. By Gor, I'd like to bowl one o' them bombs right in through his front door."

Garrity put a finger to his lips. "Don't be spreading it all over town, or the game'll be up before it starts. Penrith, Colonel Dunleavy is here, conferring with Mr. van Rhyn. I think they want to see us."

The four of us went upstairs to the makeshift laboratory.

Dunleavy was seated at a table talking, and Barker sat across from him, listening, making adjustments in our plans as the information tumbled forth. It was rather like watching a couple of chess masters at play, only the board was the city of London.

Colin and Padraig Bannon came wandering in with the last of the packages from the cart, and we all sat down to a meeting.

"Everything has arrived safely, Colonel Dunleavy," O'Casey told their leader.

"Good!" he said, flashing one of those grins of his. "Mr. van Rhyn, provided you have all the necessary equipment, how long will it take you to create the bombs?"

"Several hours, since Mr. Penrith and I shall be making the nitroglycerin ourselves. Let us say five hours, to be safe, sir."

"Very well. Prepare your infernal devices tonight. Tomorrow evening at six o'clock, we shall set London on its ear. Remember it, gentlemen. Thirtieth June, 1884. It shall be a day of celebration in Ireland forever.

"Niall Garrity has returned from Dublin and is anxious to lend a hand," Dunleavy said. "He hopes to pick up some experience under your tutelage, Mr. van Rhyn."

"I'll help with mixing the nitroglycerin," Garrity put in, "and with setting the timers. You have no objection, I trust, if we test your explosives to make certain they work?"

"None in the least," Barker said. "Blow up the building if you wish, though it might alert the local constabulary. It makes no difference to me."

"We'll leave the Harp intact, thank you," Garrity stated with a dry chuckle. "There is a tunnel below where we can test your explosive. It is of stout stone and there is nothing to damage. Shall we prepare?"

An hour later, Garrity, Barker, and I were dressed in gutta-percha-lined aprons and rubber gloves that reached almost to our elbows. All our supplies were spread out across the tables, and carboys and a large block of ice were on the floor near us, so we could get to them. There was no turning back now. I opened the windows and slowly moved some materials around to cover up what I was really doing, which was praying. I thought it an odd way to spend the Sabbath day, building bombs.

"You may still leave us if you wish, Mr. Garrity," Barker told the Irishman. "It is not necessary for you to be here during this process. Nitroglycerin is unstable, and even an old bomb handler such as I can still blow the roof off a building."

"No, I trust you," Garrity answered. "I would like to work with a master like you. I'll stay."

"Mr. Penrith, will you keep a constant eye on the thermometer once we begin?"

"Yes, sir. I will watch carefully," I stated. "Should it get above freezing, Mr. Garrity, the nitroglycerin will either explode or form a heavy gas that will kill us all."

"I see," Garrity said. "What can I do, Penrith?"

"For now, start chipping ice for all it is worth. Oh, and I'm afraid we shall all have headaches for the next day or so. It is an unfortunate side effect of the process."

Garrity took the ice pick and began chipping away at the block.

"Fill this bucket with ice almost to the top," Barker instructed. "We'll need to get to it quickly."

The Guv removed the lid of the nitric acid bottle and decanted the red liquid slowly into a beaker. He then settled this glass container into the bucket of ice, and as it chilled, carefully opened the carboy of sulfuric acid. With Garrity's help, I filled a larger beaker half full of the deadly chemical. This I pushed down into a second bucket of ice.

"Keep chipping," Barker ordered. "The temperature will rise sharply when I mix these two together."

Slowly, he poured the nitric acid into the beaker of sulfuric acid.

"The temperature is rising," I warned.

"More ice, Mr. Garrity, if you please."

The Irishman quickly packed ice around the large beaker. I noticed he was already perspiring freely and the ice was melting as well. It was the twenty-ninth of June, and the weather was warm. If we ran out of ice during this operation, we'd also run out of time.

Barker opened a container of glycerin and poured it into a new beaker. Picking up a medicine dropper, he squeezed the rubber bulb and drew it full of the pale liquid. I realized I was holding my breath.

"This is it, gentlemen," Barker said. "I fear there is no turning back now."

Drop by drop, he began covering the acid mixture with the glycerin, which floated.

"The temperature is rising again, sir," I said, tensely.

"Yes, it is nitrating and producing heat. More ice, quickly, Garrity, or we shall all perish."

"Twenty-six degrees, twenty-seven, twenty-eight," I said, reading the mercury as it rose.

"If it reaches over thirty, we are done for."

"I'm chipping as quickly as I can, gentlemen!" Garrity cried, stabbing the pick into the block repeatedly.

"Almost done," Barker said. "Mr. Penrith, will you scoop out some of the water? Dash it on the floor, if you wish. We need room for new ice. And time me with this watch of mine, please."

Finally, he had a thick layer of glycerin floating on top of the acid mixture. Gingerly, my employer inserted a glass pipette and stirred. I could see the nitration occurring, the bubbles dancing in the acid. This was the most critical stage of the process. Barker had to stir for ten solid minutes, and if he stirred too quickly or too slowly, we wouldn't live to tell of it.

"Ohhh." My head began to throb. Garrity made a face, and even Barker turned his head uneasily.

"How is the temperature?" he asked.

"Twenty-eight and steady," I answered. "You've been stirring three minutes."

"Keep chipping, Garrity. We'll need yet more ice."

Gamely, he chipped away. Barker stirred, and I scrutinized the thermometer. I watched the glycerin at the top of the beaker slowly becoming nitroglycerin through the chemical process. It was a filmy, yellowish substance that looked rather like liquid wax. One would think we were making candles or soap instead of explosives.

"Five minutes," I intoned.

I could see Barker's arm was getting tired, but I dared not interrupt to take over stirring. At any moment, we could cease to exist, atomized by the chemical reaction. In a detonation, the reaction releases gases that rapidly expand and give off energy as they ignite. The effect is so fast it is nearly instantaneous. There is no time for pain. One second one is there, and the next one is not.

"Two more minutes. The temperature is twenty-nine."

"Ice!" Barker thundered. "We dare not gain another degree."

There was a twitch in his shoulder. I felt as if he'd been stirring for an hour. Perspiration was sticking the shirt to my back, and I could have poured the sweat out of my rubber gloves. Fifteen seconds . . . ten seconds . . . five.

"Time!" I cried, and we all three exhaled at once. "The temperature in the beaker is twenty-eight degrees Fahrenheit."

Barker filled a bowl with water from a pitcher, and slowly poured the nitroglycerin into it. The nitroglycerin, instead of rising again, formed a sediment on the bottom. With my aid, Barker carried the bowl over to an empty carboy, inserted a funnel, and slowly poured the water and acid mixture into it, leaving only the sediment on the bottom. Gently, very gently, I set the bowl on the table.

"Gentlemen," he said, "we have our nitroglycerin. There is enough here to pull down three streets. You can finally stop chopping now, Garrity. Could you mix me some of this bicarbonate of soda in water?"

Garrity did as requested. "What is the soda water for?"

"It neutralizes the acid and stabilizes the mixture."

Garrity poured the soda over it, and we watched the compound fizz until it was done. Then, finally, with a spoon, Barker transferred the nitroglycerin gently to a beaker.

"Shall we test it?" he asked us. Grimly, we nodded.

Barker took the dropper and set a single drop on a bar of iron we had collected for the occasion.

"Mr. Garrity, would you do the honor of igniting it? If I have mixed the compound correctly, it should burn with a blue flame."

I heard the scratch on the Irishman's matchbox and he lit the small drop. A clear flame of the deepest blue danced atop the bar, like a fairy light. A very lethal fairy light, it was, too.

"It is good," Barker pronounced, and we all shook hands, as if we'd done something clever, rather than having just created an engine of destruction.

"What do we do now?" Garrity asked. "How do we add it to the silica?"

"We must pour it slowly into the tubes full of kieselguhr," Barker said. "*Ach,* my poor head! We must fill each tube, add the cap and fuse, then lay them on this oilcloth to set."

"Thank you, gentlemen. It has been an honor to work with you," Garrity said. "After this is finished, I'll stand you both a pint downstairs. If you're going to have a headache, anyway, why waste it?"

"*Danke,* Herr Garrity," Barker responded. "I am certain we could use a pint to steady our nerves. I shall start assembling the devices now, while you gentlemen pour the nitroglycerin into the tubes of kieselguhr."

My hope was to distract Garrity while Barker incorrectly assembled the clocks and primers. Since Garrity had already been unsuccessful with two bombs, I hoped we could pull the wool over his eyes. The last thing we wanted to do was to put live bombs into the hands of these terrorists.

My employer began wiring the first pistol to the clock.

"When shall we set the devices?" Garrity asked.

"Tomorrow, just before they leave. The first batch will be set for six-thirty, the next for seven o'clock, and the last for seven-thirty," Barker said. "We must give the boys time to get to their destinations and back again. It would be easier if they set the timers when they put down their satchel, but unfortunately, that is when they have the least time and the most mistakes are made."

"Let me help you wire the primer to the cap." He looked closely at the device that Barker was working on. "Mr. van Rhyn! You have set up the primer incorrectly!"

Barker looked over his shoulder. "Surely not," he said. "That is how I always set them."

"I have spent my time in Paris studying explosives manuals, trying to learn more about the art. The way you have it, the bullet will miss the primer entirely. This way the bombs shall be inert."

"Surely, it will not miss," Barker said, looking affronted. "I have been building bombs for decades."

"No," the Irishman said. "I insist. The primer must be shifted over against the barrel. Come, take a look at this, Penrith."

Reluctantly, I came forward. We were in a fix, thanks to Garrity's recent studies in Paris. I pretended to look carefully, but I was watching Barker out of the corner of my eye. He lowered his chin just a fraction of an inch, then raised it. He was right. I had to agree with Garrity or raise the bomber's suspicions.

"I'm afraid he is right, sir. You have wired them too far to the right."

"My apologies, *meine Freunde,* my eyesight is not what it was. *Danke,* Garrity, for checking over my work. I would not like to have come all this way, and waste time and your brave countrymen's money, only to build bombs that will not explode."

"We all make mistakes," Garrity said with a shrug. "I'll rewire them. Won't take but a few minutes."

Within ten minutes I was looking down at my first completed infernal device, with enough explosive power to blow up a small building. Garrity set an identical one beside it, and soon there were three rows of them in front of us. My stomach hurt, as well as my head, and I was idly thinking that it might be better if I did something now to make these bombs explode. We'd lose our lives, of course, but even Barker might agree it was better to leave this small section of London as nothing but a large crater, rather than allow this mission to scatter satchels like deadly seeds throughout London. Perhaps Barker could overpower Garrity, and we could find a way to get these bombs out of here without attracting attention. While we were at it, I thought bitterly, perhaps we could grow fairy wings and carry the bombs out the window.

"Nice work, gentlemen," Garrity said, surveying the bombs. "It has been an honor working with you."

"The honor has been ours, Herr Garrity," Barker replied with a Prussian bow. "I can only hope in our small way, we can help your countrymen attain their freedom."

"Shall we test one now?" Garrity asked.

"Let us put the devices into the satchels first, gentlemen, before we test the bombs."

Twenty-nine bombs were gently eased into the unmatching satchels. From the thirtieth, I cut one of the sticks of dynamite away before inserting it into the last bag.

"Here is your test bomb, Garrity," I said. "We have run out of clocks. I hope you do not mind an old-fashioned fuse."

Garrity opened the door for us. "I don't mind at all, provided it is a long one. Shall we go?"

I followed both of them out into the hall. Garrity inserted a key in the lock, while Barker turned to me and held out his hand.

"Stay here, Penrith, and keep an eye on that door. I hope to return shortly," he rumbled, "but nothing is absolute with explosives."

He shook my hand. Being taller than I, his arm was higher. I felt something slide into my sleeve from his.

"Good luck, gentlemen," I told them. Garrity gave me a casual wave and led my employer down the staircase.

Once they were out of sight, I fumbled about with the betty for a few moments before the lock finally clicked open.

I stepped in quickly and closed the door behind me.

I knew I didn't have time to diffuse all thirty bombs, but I could possibly get half. I seized the first one, then thought better of it. Garrity might come back and check it. I moved toward the middle, and tripped a latch on one of the satchels. I took one of the empty cardboard tubes and began ripping it open. I tore a small piece off, eased back the hammer of the pistol, and inserted the piece into the chamber. When the clockwork pulled the trigger, the hammer would land only on the cardboard and the gun would not go off. I closed the satchel and moved on. I did a second, a third, a fourth.

I was at work on the fifth, when the building suddenly shuddered. For a moment, I felt like I was on a ship in the middle of a storm. The walls moved and groaned in protest.

I hurried, knowing I hadn't much time. Finishing four more, I reasoned that my time was up. I closed the satchel and ran to the door, looking back to make certain all was in order. I stepped out into the hall and relocked the door before pocketing the skeleton key. I hurried to the end of the corridor and was leaning and staring out the window when who should I see staring up at me but Soho Vic. He looked up from the alleyway and thumbed his nose at me before walking away. I heard feet on the stair and turned away from the window, just as the two men returned.

"Lovely view you get in London," I stated, "if you like red brick. How did it go?"

"Like a charm," Garrity said. "Wouldn't you agree, Mr. van Rhyn?"

"Indeed. Our handmade dynamite worked perfectly."

Garrity unlocked the door again and led us inside. As soon as he was in, he scooped up the first of the satchels, and flipped it open, peering inside.

"Just checking," he said. "Well, we're ready, then. Since neither Mr. van Rhyn nor I can leave the room now, Penrith, why don't you go down and tell the lads they can come up again, if they're brave enough. Send Colin to fetch Dunleavy, and have Padraig bring a few pints, provided Fergus hasn't drunk the place dry."

I looked at Barker, who had seated himself in a chair. He was as calm as if he were enjoying a Sabbath's rest, not ten feet from rows of explosives. He nodded, and I left the room. I left the planning of how to get the primed bombs out of the terrorists' hands to him.

I hadn't realized how badly my head hurt until I began clattering down the stairs. The movement set off a clamoring in my skull, but I was determined to see this through. I came down the final step and looked at the table of Irish bombers down in the public house, surreptitiously drinking on the off day while waiting for us to finish. They all put down their glasses when they saw me.

"We're on," I said.

26

THE NEXT DAY, A DAY WHICH SHALL REMAIN IN MY memory forever, Colonel Alfred Dunleavy, that old campaigner, came from his stronghold in Claridge's to lead us on a final charge. He surveyed our handiwork—thirty bombs in satchels spread out like so many soldiers in a platoon—and checked his watch. It was five thirty. He cleared his throat as he let the watch slide back into his waistcoat pocket.

"It is time, my good warriors. An hour from now we can be heroes, champions of a new Ireland, standing like gods over the rubble and chaos you've brought upon our enemies. We'll punish them for their countless evictions, the imprisonment of so many good men, and their theft of our land. I've had many a soldier under my command but none such brave and hearty lads as I see before me. It has been a pleasure to lead you."

Garrity and I bent as everyone watched, and began to set the timers. I wondered if he would notice the misplaced gun barrels, but he was too busy setting the clocks. I took the opportunity to push a few more guns out of alignment. Dunleavy reached down and gently lifted two of the bomb-filled satchels. I was relieved to see that the two he chose were disarmed. "I bid you all good fortune."

"I realize it is late, sir," Garrity spoke up. "But I wonder if I may participate in the delivery? Years from now, when people ask me what I did today, I'd like to tell them I did more than just help Mr. van Rhyn make the bombs, with the permission of you all, of course."

There were murmurs of assent from the men in the room. Garrity reached down and took two more satchels. The rest of them in turn took two each. Some of them were inert, but some were live, and in the jumble of movement, I lost track of which were which.

"Half an hour, gentlemen," Barker stated. "You have half an hour to set in place this first delivery of bombs and return before they detonate. I suggest that you do not dawdle, or stop for a dram. *Auf Wiedersehen,* and good luck!"

With silent nods all around, the men marched out in single file, leaving us with our charges. Barker moved to a window that looked onto the street in front of the building and peered out.

"How many were you able to disarm?" he asked.

"Nine, sir. At least half of the ones they walked out with were live."

He winced but said nothing. He knew I'd done my best. I went to work, disarming the remaining bombs while Barker looked down at the street.

"Poole's men are in place," he said tensely, when we were alone. "I can see at least three detectives I recognize in the street, though they're doing their best to blend in among the Irish. I passed Soho Vic a note in the corridor when we tested the bomb. There goes Dunleavy, alone. O'Casey and McKeller are going off to the left, and the Bannon brothers to the right. I don't see Garrity yet."

Everyone went off, and there seemed to be no more than the normal traffic for this time of night. Barker and I looked at each other a moment. Had something gone wrong? Why were the police holding back? Were they not in place yet? Then from somewhere east of us there was the sound of a policeman's whistle. It was followed by a half dozen other whistles all around us. I heard angry cries and oaths, and I crossed the room to look over Barker's shoulder. As I watched, Colin and Padraig Bannon came running back down Monmouth Street, still carrying their bombs. Padraig was cut off by three constables, but Colin got by them, using some of the moves I had seen on the hurling pitch. Just as I feared he might get away, a man stepped out of a doorway in front of him, and his arm caught the Irishman full in the throat. Bannon's legs flew out from under him, and he and the bombs landed on the pavement. Colin tried halfheartedly to get up as the man turned our way and shouted orders to someone. I'd recognize those sandy whiskers anywhere.

"It's Poole!"

"Yes," Barker said. "I taught him that move weeks ago. But look over there!" He pointed to the left. Two men were wrestling on the pavement. One was McKeller and the other a sturdy man who looked familiar. It was one of Munro's bookends. The bookend seemed to be getting the worst of it.

As we watched, the street began to swarm with men locked in battle. Constables, Irish idlers and criminals, and faction members all disputed with whatever weapon came to hand. The Seven Dials had erupted into a riot. I saw a woman attempt to scratch out the eyes of a constable and receive a bloody nose in consequence. I hoped, for London's sake, that Scotland Yard would be able to contain this mess.

"Blast," Barker rumbled. "The Crook and Harp has emptied out, and everyone is trying to protect the bombers. This won't do. I shall have to go down."

From somewhere below we heard a door slam and the sound of feet running swiftly up the stairs. We were across the room from our sticks. Who could be coming, and what would they want?

O'Casey and McKeller burst into the room. They were both missing their caps, and the state of their clothing showed they'd fought their way back. They still had their two satchels, both handles in one hand, while they held their bata sticks in the other.

"The street is full of peelers!" O'Casey informed us. "Someone must have peached."

"Blow it up, then," McKeller growled. "Blow it all up. If you set one of these off, the rest are bound to go off as one. Blow us all to kingdom come. Leave a crater in London so big the English will never forget!"

"I am afraid I cannot allow that to happen, gentlemen," my employer said in his normal Lowland Scots. "You see, we are agents of the English government. It was I who summoned the police here."

McKeller broke into a string of curses, but O'Casey, whether he'd suspected or was merely fatalistic, set down his bombs and raised his stick. We were simply the next obstacle in his path, and he would concentrate on that alone.

"Fergus!" O'Casey barked. "They are unarmed. Take these two down and we still have a room full of bombs to blow up or bargain with as we choose."

I realized we were twenty feet from our sticks, but Barker was ahead of me. He dug into his pockets and threw their contents at the two Irishmen. Not merely his razor coins, but regular ones, keys, a pocketknife, and who knows what else flew at the faces of O'Casey and McKeller. They flinched and stepped back just enough for Barker to get to our sticks. He spun around and tossed one to me.

Sporting a fresh cut on his cheek from one of Barker's sharpened coins, McKeller came toward me, his stick raised. "What's your real name, you blasted Welsh trash? I want to know who it is I'm thrashing."

"Thomas Llewelyn, at your service." I stood up to him. "Are you going to fight or merely talk me to death?"

McKeller came at me with an overhead smash, but I'd fought him enough to know he would begin that way. Instead of my head, he met my stick with the sharp smack of wood upon wood. Behind me, I heard the first clash of my employer and O'Casey. McKeller began a series of blows, swinging the stick about his head—left, right, left, right; high, low—but I blocked each one. Then he feinted, I blocked too cleanly, and his stick got under it, raking across my ribs like a willow wand along a fence. I grunted in pain. He'd scored the first point.

"You can do better than that, Welshman," McKeller taunted me. "Or can you? Best set down your stick and run away."

I came in with my own overhead strike, but it, too, was a feint. While my stick cracked against his, my foot was already up, and I caught him in that ale-heavy paunch of his. It was necessary to show him that I was a better fighter than I had been the last time I faced him. If I lost or was incapacitated, it would be the two of them against Barker, and should the unimaginable happen and the two of them get by him, heaven help London.

McKeller shook it off and lashed out, catching me on the knuckles of my stick hand. I dropped my stick but managed to pick it up with my other hand and roll out of the way with only a thump across my spine for my troubles. I came up and blocked again, and again, and again.

Strategy. Though Barker was in a pitched battle with O'Casey behind me, I could hear his voice in my memory, and the dozens of instructions and axioms he and Vigny had said to me in the garden of our home and in the sparring ring.

Split your thoughts while fighting, lad. Forget your past mistakes. Be in the present, blocking the attack or launching your own, while planning your next.

I blocked a move, ducked away from a second, and lashed out a strike of my own.

Look for weaknesses. Is he left- or right-handed? Does he favor the same moves too often? Does he leave any area exposed?

I ducked as McKeller's stick whistled over my head. I held my left hand out to balance myself and my stick in front of my face.

Keep a rhythm to your movement, Thomas, like a drumbeat in your head. Communicate that movement to your opponent. Get him moving to your cadence. Then, when he's set into it, break the rhythm, and while he's recovering, attack!

Barker's words had kept me alive so far, but I was getting bruised. McKeller clipped my eyebrow, spilling the first claret, and caught me a whack across the right knee which hurt like the deuce. I'd done little beyond the kick, which he'd recovered quickly from, and a blow to his elbow, but he showed no signs of flagging. In fact, he was taunting me.

"You'll have to improve if you're going to beat Fergus McKeller, Welshman!" he said, his face red with bloodlust. "I was born with one of these sticks in my hand. I think we'll tie you up and circle you in your own bombs. Won't that be a nice present for the Queen?"

"I'm not done, yet," I warned him, and launched a flurry of attacks, most of which he parried easily. Secretly, however, I knew he was right. My arms were tired and my energy flagging. If I didn't think quickly, I was going to lose.

I gathered my thoughts and drew back into myself mentally. What would work against this man? He was taller than I, and stronger. He was more experienced and had a longer reach. He seemed to have no weaknesses beyond a slightly injured arm, and, so far, breaking rhythm hadn't worked. For a moment, I wondered if I could just hold my own long enough, perhaps Barker could overcome O'Casey and come to my rescue. *No,* I told myself. I wouldn't allow myself to be rescued. I had to win this match for myself.

Then at last, it came to me, some advice Barker had given me weeks before, but I had almost forgotten.

When all else fails, sacrifice. Offer a target, like a wounded bird. When he commits to it, throw all you have into an attack from a different direction. Shoot your bolt, lad. It's your final option.

McKeller caught me a heavy clout across the head, which set my ears ringing. I'd been too caught up in thinking for a moment. He smacked a second across my shoulder and a third on my left forearm. I blocked the fourth and fifth. It was time to do something or I was going to lose.

I brought my stick up in front of my face horizontally, with most of it to my right, but half a foot or so of ferrule protecting me in front. I tried to pretend I was mostly through, that one final attack would bring me down. Confident that I was near done, McKeller smiled and brought his stick up high. He'd finish the fight as he'd begun it, with an overhead smash through my feeble guard. I saw him commit fully, not realizing that his attack would spin my own stick back in his direction. My stick gave way with the force of his attack and the heavy knob of his bata struck my nose, smashing cartilage and letting loose a torrent of blood, but as he did so the knob of my stick, from the force of his blow, caught McKeller full on the temple with a dull thump, felling him like an ox. I believe the two of us struck the floor together.

"Lad?"

I was sitting. I couldn't tell how long I'd been there. My head was ringing, and my vision blurred. My hands were wet, and my entire shirtfront was thick with my own blood.

"I think he broke my nose."

"It appears so," Barker said, handing me a handkerchief to stanch the blood. "And you'll have a couple of black eyes by tomorrow, but you brought him down, Thomas. We have stopped the faction. That's the important thing."

I looked over to where McKeller lay motionless on the floor.

"Is he dead?" I asked.

"No, but half an inch to the right and he would have been. I'll wager you've cracked his skull."

I focused on O'Casey, who also lay flat on his back on the other side of the room. I wondered if he was alive also, but after a moment, he raised a knee and moaned.

"Get to work, lad," Barker said. "Let us finish disarming these last few bombs."

There was a tramping of feet in the hall, and the doorway was suddenly full, as Inspector Poole and Special Irish Branch Inspector Munro attempted to push in at once.

"Good lord!" Munro cried, when he saw us among the rows of bombs spread out along the room. "Was this it, your wonderful plan, to hand over a few dozen bombs and then fight them for it? It's a wonder the town is still standing!"

"We've got Dunleavy and the faction boys under arrest, Barker," Poole said, "along with half the Harp."

"Are all of the faction members accounted for?" Barker asked.

"Yes. We've got Dunleavy and the Bannons, and here are the last two. That's the lot."

"What about Garrity?" Barker demanded.

"Niall Garrity?" Poole asked. "What about him? He's in Paris."

"He is here!" my employer bellowed. "He took two bombs. I thought you had this building surrounded."

"We did!" Poole leaned back into the hallway and bawled out to a constable. "There's a suspect hiding in the building, blond hair, mustache. His name is Garrity. Find him."

"He is probably long gone," Munro said with glee. "You've blown this one, Barker. You've provided an I.R.B. bomber with special explosives and set him free in London. I'll bet the public would love to hear about this."

"I suggest we stop arguing among ourselves and try to find this fellow," my employer replied. "We'll assign blame later. Come, Llewelyn, let's clean you up a bit."

I washed the blood from my face in the icy water left over from our bomb making, though my shirt was beyond redemption.

"The Queen is not in residence, correct?" my employer asked the inspector.

"She's in Scotland at Balmoral."

"Where is the Prince of Wales?"

Munro thought a moment, then shrugged his shoulders. "He's in town, I believe, but he has no engagements."

"Since they threatened to go after the Royal Family, but the Queen is in Scotland," Barker said, "then, presumably, they might go after the Prince, since he will be king someday."

For once, we all agreed. While Poole shouted orders down the stairs to arrest McKeller and O'Casey, we followed Munro down the stairwell and out into the street. I saw Alfred Dunleavy, looking cool and unruffled despite the darbies on his wrists, talking to a reporter, while the Bannon brothers were being loaded into a Black Maria. Colin Bannon caught sight of me and shot me a look of cold hatred that I shall never forget. His brother, Padraig, was too beaten up to care.

Munro gave a whistle, and a brougham pulled up to the curb beside us. He climbed in, but barred us with his arm.

"Official police business, gentlemen. This is where I cut you loose."

Before we could react, his vehicle rattled off.

I stamped my feet in frustration. How were we to beat the infernal Special Irish Branch inspector and stop Garrity before he assassinated the Prince?

Just then, a man stepped out of the shadows of an alleyway behind us and cleared his throat.

27

I RAISED MY STICK, READY TO STRIKE AGAIN IF
necessary. I must have looked a sight. My nose was swollen, the
skin under my eyes already turning a dusky purple, my hair
wringing wet, and my shirt red with blood. It was appropriate,
therefore, for Jacob Maccabee to step out of the alleyway, immaculate in his crisp suit and bowler, as if he'd just stepped out of a
tailor's shop.

"Good evening, gentlemen," he said, as if we'd just been out
on a perambulation around Hyde Park instead of a month-long
desperate attempt to save London from being destroyed. "Your
vehicle is waiting, sir," he said, turning to our employer, "and I've
brought the items you requested."

"Excellent," Barker said, leading us through the alleyway to
the back, as if it were any other day. When had he alerted Mac? I
wondered. Our private hansom and our mare, Juno, were awaiting us. Mac reached into the vehicle and held something up for
me to don. It was the coat my employer had made for me several
months before, with lead lining in the chest and back and built-in
holsters.

"You've got to be joking. I don't need that," I said. "It is nearly July."

"Wear it," Barker demanded, donning his own. "This business may get more deadly before it is all over." We didn't have time to argue but climbed aboard the conveyance. Our horse, Juno, looked back at us from her traces.

"Where shall I take you gentlemen?" Mac asked, climbing up into the back of the vehicle and opening the trapdoor over our heads.

"I need to find a telephone quickly," Barker answered. "Have you any suggestions?"

"Yes, sir. I believe I can take you to one not three streets from here."

It was closer to four, but I will not quibble. It was in a jeweler's shop in Shaftesbury Avenue. I wondered if Mac knew every Hebrew in town. Though it was after hours, he knocked loudly at the door until it was answered by a small, portly man. There was a short conversation in Yiddish, which Barker, ever the linguist, joined in, and then we were led inside to a telephone.

"Mr. Anderson?" I asked.

"Exactly. It is vital we locate the Prince immediately." He gave the operator an exchange number and waited. In a moment, he was speaking to Anderson, explaining what had just happened.

"You're looking well, Mac," I said.

"Thank you, sir. I only wish I could say the same of you. Allow me to get some ice for that swelling."

"Later, perhaps."

"Let's be off, quickly, gentlemen. The Prince of Wales is in St. James's Street, at White's Club. It is but a few streets from here. We must get there immediately."

The three of us bounded back into the cab. Mac called out his thanks in Yiddish, then cracked his whip in the air. Juno's shoes bit into the cobblestoned roadway and we were off.

We were going as fast as the traffic would allow, but we were all on the edge of our seats going down Piccadilly. If we didn't get there soon, the man next in line to the throne might be dead. Finally, we bowled up to the marble entrance to White's, and alighted.

All seemed well. There were no constables in sight and no commotion. St. James's still had the grand sedateness for which it is justly famous. Barker and I appeared to be the only thing out of place so far, a bearded bomb maker and a bloody anarchist, both glaring anxiously about.

We were moving toward the door when our quarry suddenly appeared from the far corner of the street. Like us, he'd acquired new clothes—a nondescript coat and a bowler, but I couldn't miss those two satchels, having chosen them myself in Paris. Perhaps if I'd been more prepared, I would have shut my mouth until he came closer, but my nerves were at fever pitch. I sang out as soon as I saw him.

"There he is!" I cried.

Garrity was still a couple of hundred feet away. I saw him skid to a stop, pull his hat down, and turn around, running off in the direction of Pall Mall.

"After him, lad!" Barker cried.

We both outraged the public peace by running flat out after the rapidly departing bomber. In doing so, I narrowly avoided colliding with a group of men just coming out of the club. I turned my head in time to see one fellow in the middle—a stocky, bearded chap with hooded eyes—who was removing the cigar from his mouth and staring at us with some interest. I was a block away before I realized that it was the Prince of Wales. It was as close to any royal as I'd ever been in my life. I don't think Barker noticed, and if he had, I doubt he'd have given two straws. His nose was to the scent, and he wasn't going to quit until he'd brought down his quarry.

We ran through Pall Mall after the bomber. When we reached Trafalgar Square, Garrity's arrival had sent dozens of pigeons into the air. Barker had a keen eye, or we would have missed him, amid all the flapping and feathers. Without stopping, he pointed south toward Whitehall, where this had all begun.

I heard a crash of glass ahead of us, as we reached Whitehall, and a minute later, we reached Craig's Court. A new hole stood in the fresh pane of our chambers at Number 7. I saw no sign of our prey anywhere.

"Surely, it hasn't been half an hour since we set the bomb," Barker said, trying to convince himself. It was near time, however, and the last thing he needed was to blow up the chambers he'd just had refitted. Stopping to defuse one bomb would keep us from following Garrity, who still had another. The time had come, I realized, to separate.

"I'll go in and defuse it, sir. You go on after Garrity."

Having no key, I climbed the brick at the front of our building until I reached the bow window. Avoiding the glass, I tripped the latch, opened the window, and crawled inside. It was a matter of only a minute to disarm the bomb. That left only one, but of all the hands it could be in, Garrity's were the worst. He could easily reset the timer and blow up Scotland Yard a second time. I half expected to hear the rocking shudder of an infernal explosion any minute, but it didn't come. I jumped from the windowsill to the pavement and ran along Craig's Court.

I made my way through a narrow alley beside the Telephone Exchange. There was no sign of Garrity or Barker anywhere. I ran around the corner to Scotland Yard, worrying that history might repeat itself. I passed the Sun, which was open and doing a brisk business again. Had I the time, I would have gone in and spoken to Jenkins, who, according to his own orbit, would be reigning over his little corner of the public house. As for the Yard, it was like a beehive, with constables on the alert for the missing bomber. There was no sign of Garrity, and the trail was growing cold.

I was beginning to despair that I'd lost him, and hoping that Barker would arrive any minute, when I heard the sound of feet running. Looking up, I saw movement ahead. Before my mind even had time to react, my body was loping along toward the sound ahead of me. I ran toward the Thames.

On the far side of the railway bridge, right near the water's edge, there was a flurry of movement. Close to a dozen constables were on the ground struggling. I was looking to see if Garrity was among them. Abruptly, my employer stood, but whether he was helped up or they had mistaken him for another bomber, I couldn't say. As I got closer, some of the constables turned toward me, ready to take me down, if I were a threat.

"He's with me," Barker called.

Then I saw Garrity, prone upon the ground, his arms and legs in the tight clutches of Scotland Yard and a look of black anger on his face as he cursed us.

"You've got him, then."

"Yes, but the bomb is gone. We've been tricked. There, lad, up on the bridge!"

I looked behind me and doubted my eyes. The satchel was in the hands of a man wearing a coat and hat identical to Garrity's, and he had just begun to cross the railway bridge. I had no idea who it could be. I was after him, even staying ahead of Barker, for once.

"Stop!" I yelled. It might have come out better had I Barker's low, rough voice, but it had the desired effect. I saw the figure look over his shoulder and then run even faster. Our quarry was on the small railway bridge that my employer and I had crossed on the night of the first bombing. In half a minute I was on the bridge myself.

The bomber was much closer to me than before. I could easily make out his coat and bowler and one of the satchels I had purchased in Paris. He was so close, in fact, that he was within shooting distance.

"Stop, I say, or I'll shoot!" I bellowed, with as much conviction as I could muster. I reached into the leather-lined pocket of my special coat, and my hand grasped the wooden grip of my Webley revolver. I thrust it out, and tried to push down any doubts as to whether I could really kill anyone, or even whether I should.

"Give up!" I cried. "I cannot possibly miss at this range!"

Then, on the wind, a scent came to my nose. Above the noxious fumes of the river, something carried on the breeze, full in my face, something I would recognize anywhere. It was lilac.

"Maire?" I whispered, as I realized who it was.

The figure stopped in its tracks. I did the same. We were no more than fifteen feet apart. Slowly, she turned. She was wearing a man's coat and hat, over a man's suit coat and trousers. It all came together in a flash. Maire O'Casey had been the youth who had set the first bomb, the one the cabman had let out at Scotland Yard.

"Put the gun down," she said to me, as if I were an errant child. "You know you could never shoot me."

"What are you doing here?" I demanded. "You're supposed to be in Liverpool."

It was growing dark, but I could still see the smile on her face. She removed the bowler and threw it over the railing, her auburn hair spilling out around her upturned collar.

"You didn't really think Dunleavy clever enough to think up this little enterprise, did you? If you did, you're even more naive than I thought you were, Thomas."

"If it wasn't Dunleavy, it must have been O'Muircheartaigh," I said bitterly. "I presume he's waiting for you in a carriage across the bridge."

"Is that so? Did you really think he is behind all this?" she asked.

"It was Maire, herself, lad," Barker called out from somewhere behind me. The sun had almost set and he was in silhouette. "She is the leader of the faction."

"That's right, it was me. I thought up this entire plan. I recruited Dunleavy, with Eamon's help. I organized the faction. I planned the entire operation and delivered the bombs that blew up Scotland Yard. And you, Cyrus Barker!" she called out.

"Yes, Miss O'Casey?"

"While you men were at the Crooked Harp, I went to see my old mentor, Seamus O'Muircheartaigh. He had a suspicion that you might be on our trail. You played a very good game, though not quite good enough. I still have this bomb." She looked at me. "Thomas, there is still time. Come with me. Once safely across the bridge, we can blow it up and make our escape. We can begin again together. With my planning and your bomb-making skills, we shall free Ireland yet. What do you say?"

I actually did stop and think a moment of a life with Maire, away from the private enquiry work and my life as it was. It fell like a house of cards.

"I say, I work for Cyrus Barker and Her Majesty's government. Set down the satchel at once, and step away."

She held out her hand. "But, Thomas, forget all that. Come with me," she urged in a low voice. "We can find a cab on the other side of the bridge. We can be in Paris again by tomorrow."

I lowered the gun, staring into the face of the woman I had kissed so recently. My mind couldn't take it in. "Stop it, Maire. You know I can't."

"Of course you can. You can do anything you want to do." She plucked a revolver from her pocket and pointed it over my shoulder. "Not one step closer, Mr. Barker!"

"Miss O'Casey." I heard Barker's deep rumble behind me. "Your game is finished. Put down the bomb."

"Come with me," she said, stepping farther away, ignoring Barker.

"Not another step!" I ordered, but even I could tell it lacked conviction.

"Good-bye, Thomas." She began to turn.

"Stop, blast you!" My finger was squeezing the trigger.

Perhaps it was the sudden anger in my voice that did it. She knew I wouldn't let her leave. She swung the barrel of her pistol toward me and I saw the sudden flash of her gun.

I felt the bullet strike me on the left shoulder. It was caught in the leaden mesh built into my coat. It was as if I'd been prodded roughly with a stout poker. I don't know to this day whether my finger twitched in natural reaction to the shot or whether I deliberately pulled the trigger. All I knew was that my own revolver discharged a second after hers.

Saying there was a boom simply does not describe it. One second, I was on the bridge, my feet braced, and the next, I was blown over the side. I have a memory of Barker's arm reaching toward me, but he was too late. Maire O'Casey was no more to be seen, and I was launched out into the night sky.

28

WHERE WAS I? OH, YES, TWENTY FEET DEEP, JUST
free of that infernal coat, and about to fill my lungs full of vile
Thames water instead of air. It was then that I felt a rough but
familiar hand seize my collar and begin to pull me upward.
Somehow, Barker was beside me. He dragged me up to the surface, and we both took in great lungfuls of air. I had complained
about the dank, fetid reek of the river dozens of times before, but
just then it seemed the sweetest air in the world. I was alive,
soaked like a water rat, and choking for breath, but alive for all
that.

"Hold still," the Guv ordered. "Stop thrashing about."

No longer having the strength to struggle, I stopped moving
while Barker reached over my shoulder and took hold of the
lapels of my waistcoat, pulling me along through the water on
my back. My employer was a strong swimmer and towed me as
easily as if I were made of cork, while I sputtered and coughed,
trying to expel the foul water from my lungs.

As I floated there, my thoughts scudding along like clouds on
a blustering day, I eventually made out the sound of oars.

Someone had alerted the suicide station under Waterloo Bridge, and they had launched a rowboat.

"Over here!" Barker cried. The next I knew, I was being pulled roughly over a gunwale, the hard wood scraping across my stomach, and was left sputtering like a fish in the bottom of the rowboat. A constable threw a blanket over me and rubbed me down with all the gentle tenderness of a turnkey. He made up for it by handing me a steaming mug of tea, leaving me to sort out my erratic thoughts while the others hauled in Barker.

In the boat, to the steady sound of the oars plunking in the water, my mind began to coalesce. Maire O'Casey. The bomb she had carried had exploded, obliterating her on the bridge from which we were slowly drawing away. Maire had taken me in completely, had even taunted my ignorance on the bridge. I'd been a fool. I'd thought her a gentle girl, the kind I would wish to see again if only I could figure out how she could accept my being the spy who turned her brother in. Now there was no need. She'd been leading the faction the entire time, and now she was dead. I felt an emotional mantle settle over me just then, chilling my heart, a mixture of cynicism, world-weariness, and grief. Better I'd been left at the bottom of the river. Had I been able to piece this together then, I might not have struggled so fiercely to be free from the embrace of my lead-lined coat.

When we reached the police pier, I saw the silhouettes of Juno, our cab, and Jacob Maccabee atop his perch against a gas lamp. They must have followed our progress on the water and outdistanced us handily on land. Barker and one of the river constables took me under the arms and helped me onto the dock, where I stood shivering and looking out across the oily surface of the Thames. The constable was tugging at me, and with a start I realized he was merely trying to take the mug of tea. I let go, and Barker bundled me into the cab. I was to go home while Barker worked through the night, giving statements to Scotland Yard and the Home Office, attempting to pacify Inspector Munro and seeing that all our bombs were carted away to be destroyed by Her Majesty's Horse Guards, whose barracks were but a few streets away.

As I sat bundled in the blanket, cradled in the embrace of the hansom, I reflected on the fact that this was the second time my case ended in injury and my being driven home in this very cab. I listened to the steady clip-clopping of Juno's metal shoes upon the cobblestones. My disjointed thoughts were that surely some-where there was a position for a failed scholar, a clerking position, perhaps, or one in a quiet library somewhere, something nice and safe, and free of infernal devices and bridges. Yes, in some nice vil-lage that had no bridges at all.

There is generally a feeling of satisfaction when one returns from a journey of some duration, but I felt numb as I stumbled out of the cab and into our home in the Newington. At the time, I thought there was nothing that could ever make me feel better again. I had not reckoned on Harm.

The dog came charging in from the back library, his black fur rippling. He skidded across the wooden floor and bunched up the rug in front of me with his momentum. He jumped up and tapped me with his paws. He went up on two back legs and danced in a circle, his tongue lolling. He barked and howled his clarion cry, informing the district that the conquering hero had returned.

"Harm, you idiot," I said, scratching him behind the ears. I had to admit, it did feel good to be home. After a hot soak in the bathhouse in Barker's garden, I went upstairs to change into proper clothes. Even I was appalled at how ghastly I looked in the mirror. My eyes were black, my nose as swollen as a prize-fighter's, and my Thames-befouled hair made me look like the worst dregs off the East India docks. After Mac had brought up a ewer of steaming water, I shaved and beat back my hair with a comb, promising myself a good haircut in the morning.

When I went downstairs a half hour later, Mac had set out a supper consisting of cold goose liver pie, salad, and Stilton, finishing off with port and walnuts. It was a far more civilized meal than the colcannon and peas I'd eaten during the case, but I ate like an automaton, despite Dummolard's expertise. Afterward, I went upstairs.

Mac came up to collect my filthy clothing and took pity on me yet again. He lit a fire in the grate and sat me down in front of it before leaving. Harm whined until I let him crawl into my lap.

It was building, I knew it. I've always been one of those who see a man crying as a sign of weakness, but then, I'd just blown up a woman I cared for. One must make allowances. One minute, I was stroking Harm's fur abstractedly and the next, I was sobbing into it. Pekingese are very proud and vain creatures, and normally I would have expected him to object to his coat getting wet; but like Mac, he, too, took pity. He put up with my storm of emotion until it passed as quickly as it had come. I let out a shuddering sigh and finally let the dog go, watching as he scuttled quickly from the room.

Changing into nightclothes, I crawled into bed, though it was just barely nine o'clock. One would think that the events of the past evening would have kept me awake, tossing and turning, reliving them again and again. Instead, I fell into a profound sleep, as if trying to make up for all I'd lost over the past few weeks.

Sometimes when a bad event occurs—the death of someone one cares about, for example—there is a period just when one is waking up before one remembers. One has a general feeling of well-being, a cheery optimism. The day is full of myriad choices. Then the terrible memory returns, and one's entire world comes crashing down about one's ears. At least, that was my experience the next morning. I didn't know which hurt more, that she was dead or that she'd played me for a fool.

Mac was busy opening curtains and greeting my morning. I don't know why he did it, since I was not the master of the house, but a hired employee. Perhaps Barker had asked him to do so. As usual, Mac disguised whatever feelings he might have about me in a professional manner, solicitous but remote.

"I trust you slept well."

"Very well, thank you," I replied automatically. My mind was back on the Charing Cross Railway Bridge.

"Mr. Barker requests your presence in his room at your earliest convenience."

Dressing was not too complicated, and it took only a few moments to run a brush through my thick hair, but during the night my nose and eyes had swollen even more. Barker could not help but comment on it.

"Quite a brace you have, there," he commented over his tea. "You look as if you just went ten rounds with the great Mendoza himself in his prime."

"You wanted to see me, sir?" I asked, helping myself to the contents of the silver coffeepot, which Mac had obviously brought up for me. Dummolard had provided currant scones.

"I thought we might discuss the case," Barker said. "Let me begin by admitting a mistake. I should have gone after Miss O'Casey myself."

"I'm sorry, sir. I didn't mean to shoot her."

Barker poured another thimbleful of tea into his handleless cup. "Oh, that could not be helped, lad. If you hadn't shot her, I would have. She wasn't going to be allowed to get off that bridge with one of our bombs. If your conscience is bothering you, let me state that I have my doubts as to whether you triggered the explosion at all. The actual time of the explosion was very near."

"I'm sure I shot the bag, sir."

"How's your shoulder?"

"It's fine." Actually, there was an ugly purple bruise, with a reddish ring about it.

"I'm sorry you went over the railing, Thomas. I tried to get to you, and my hand was no more than a foot away, but you flew past me too quickly. It was good that you were wearing that coat. It saved your life. I shall have another made for you, and buy a new Webley to go with it."

I sat down and idly began to pick apart one of the scones. Barker was buoyant, and why shouldn't he be? His case was completed successfully, and in the very face of Inspector Munro. I, on the other hand, felt like a complete failure, and a murderer as well.

"Are you feeling sorry for Miss O'Casey and the faction?" he asked. "Don't. Remember, they would have killed us without mercy had they discovered who we were. And if you were swayed by Miss O'Casey's words on the bridge, remember she was still using you, hoping to get you to join their side, but she despised you. When she saw you were of no use to her, she had no qualms about dispatching you. She was a brilliant leader, a strategist, and as ruthless as she needed to be."

I put my hand to my face, then instantly regretted the gesture. "I'm confused," I admitted.

"I thought you might be. Now that the case is finished, I shall go over it with you. Let us start at the beginning."

Had it really been only four weeks ago?

"Very well," I said. "Why did you offer your services in the first place? As everyone has pointed out, you're an enquiry agent, not a spy."

"Scotland Yard is good at what it does—keeping the peace, investigating crimes, and patrolling the city—and I have the greatest respect for the organization, but this operation was beyond their scope. The Special Irish Branch, under Inspector Munro, has made great strides since it was formed last year; but it takes several years to develop the connections I have in this city, and the S.I.B. was not yet ready. As for the Home Office, their members are recruited from the top schools in the country. As good as they are, it was difficult for them to infiltrate the factions. That's why their spies died in the field, all, that is, save Le Caron, whom, you remember, I trained myself. Now, I couldn't make a convincing Irishman, and there are very few people I could impersonate, but Johannes van Rhyn was one of them. It just happened that he was the one man they wanted most of all.

"The last I spoke to him, van Rhyn was complaining because Rossa was attempting to recruit him for his faction. I thought that if Dunleavy knew the other factions were after him, he would jump at a chance to make use of van Rhyn."

"How could you be certain you would discover the faction that blew up the Yard?" I argued.

"The Irish are a loquacious race. We would have had almost no chance of discovering them had they been Chinese, for example. Cathcart deserved his pound a day. As for Soho Vic, I've kept him busy running messages between the Harp and our offices. There was a chance I couldn't discover which faction had blown up Scotland Yard, but I did, so the question is moot."

"Dunleavy was never able to convince you he was the faction leader, was he?"

Barker lit his pipe, in no hurry to answer, running the lit vesta around the bowl before blowing it out. "No," he stated. "Alfred Dunleavy was too weak. He is undisciplined, lazy, melancholy, and a drunkard. He had grandiose schemes and a complaint against the world for not making him a great leader. He could not have thought up or enacted the brilliant scheme of employing a team of five men using timed assaults to bring down London."

"So, whom did you suspect?"

"Everyone, of course. A brilliant leader would be capable

of playacting. Now, confess, lad, even when you found O'Muircheartaigh's letters, I'll wager you didn't once suspect Miss O'Casey of being the leader, did you?"

I had to admit it, but I wasn't going to say it was because she had turned my head. "No, sir, I didn't."

"Yes, well. My second list of suspects, if you considered the faction leaders as the first, were: the O'Caseys, Garrity, McKeller, Yeats, the Bannon brothers, and Mr. O'Muircheartaigh. Oh, and Dunleavy, since there was a small chance he was more clever than I thought he was. That was my list of suspects, and I merely had to winnow it down."

"Yes," I added, "while concealing who you were, making their bombs, and preparing a plan to capture them when they reached London."

Barker gave a cough, his answer to a chuckle. "I've had a little experience doing this, lad. Where was I?"

"The list of suspects."

"Correct. I crossed McKeller off early. It's possible he was more than he claimed, but he seemed so genuine, I believed him. He was a big, violent man, without much of a past or a future. By the way, I must compliment you on defeating him. He was a very dangerous opponent. Did you really intend to put up that weak guard?"

"Yes, sir. I remembered what you said about putting every-thing into a final effort. It was the only way I could win."

"You improve, Thomas."

"Thank you, sir," I murmured. It was rare praise, indeed.

"The Bannons I dismissed because they were twins. I know it was possible for one of them to be the leader, but they were very self-involved, as twins sometimes are. Also, they seemed to be doing mere yeoman service. They had no internal fire."

"O'Casey," I said. "Now, he was the logical choice. Trinity educated and obviously talented. He's good-looking, intelligent, not to mention a trained fighter. What was it about him that didn't make you suspect him as the secret leader?"

"He didn't rise to the bait."

"Bait?" I asked. "What bait?"

"You, lad," he said, taking his pipe from his mouth. "I used you as bait. Surely you must have seen that. A young fellow like Thomas Penrith, armed with all the skills of van Rhyn, with decades to develop more. I thought if O'Casey or Dunleavy was the actual leader, they would have been astute enough to latch onto you early. You'll note that Dunleavy barely spoke a word to you, and young Eamon O'Casey didn't warm up to you until after the bomb demonstration. He was a little closer to you later, but not enough. I would have thought that someone wishing to attach a man of your skills to this cause would have forged a bond with you. He did not, but Maire O'Casey grew very interested in you."

"What of that?" I asked. "She was a beautiful woman."

"I will not say otherwise, but think of it. If she had the world at her feet, if she could have her pick of any man in England or Ireland, why would she choose a little Welsh bomb maker? That is not the decision of a beautiful young woman but the thinking of a leader trying to build a strong faction."

That was a trifle harsh, I thought. I sat there for a moment, trying to look at it all objectively, but it was difficult.

"So you don't think she genuinely cared for me."

Just then, Harm trotted in the room. He came up to me, but when I reached for him, he avoided me, convinced, perhaps, that I was going to blubber in his fur again. He settled into Barker's lap and fell asleep.

"Believe what you like," my employer pronounced, scratching the dog's fur absently. "But it was deucedly convenient. It was that more than anything that made me consider her as a possibility."

"Before we get into that, what about Yeats and Garrity?"

"I'll admit I thought hard about them both. An innocent student would be a good pose to assume, and Yeats did deliver messages to and from Dunleavy, but he was a callow youth. Garrity was not. Ah, I missed that sound."

The sound to which he was referring was Harm's snores. I had to admit, I'd grown accustomed to them. The dog ran to some sort of schedule every night. He began on the ground floor, arrived on my bed around midnight, then vacated it for Barker's nest upstairs sometime in the wee hours. It never happened any other way for one very good reason: the Imperial Dog could climb stairs, but he could not go down them.

"Garrity," I prompted.

"Yes, Garrity," Barker went on. "It would not have been difficult for him to run the faction from Paris, with a puppet like Dunleavy in his hands. But he is already a respected member of the I.R.B. Were he ambitious enough to wish to run his own faction, he could have formed one himself among the Irish in Paris."

"Surely you suspected Seamus O'Muircheartaigh," I said.

"Of course I did," Barker said. "When I get that man behind bars, I'll feel I've accomplished some good for humanity. When I looked over those letters a little more closely, I saw that the final one was written last year, when O'Muircheartaigh was in Dublin. The last was very accusatory. It is possible they had not communicated until the Americans notified Dunleavy that the money would not make it in time. The money that sent you to Paris was likely a loan from him. Yesterday, one of Soho Vic's boys spotted her but couldn't get word to us of it until this morning. A careful reading of O'Muircheartaigh's letters showed that his feelings were not reciprocated, but they parted amicably enough for her to appear at his door and receive aid at a moment's notice."

"Yes, but, hang it all, you make her sound so—so mercenary. This was a girl who cooked for her family, who was sentimental—"

"Sentimental about Ireland, lad."

"I can't believe it," I said with a sigh. "I mean, I do believe it, but it's rather hard. She was so sincere."

"I did not doubt her sincerity," Barker said, "not for the Irish cause, anyway. As for you, who can say? She is gone and cannot tell us either way. Perhaps she genuinely cared for you. For your sake, it would have been better that she didn't, for I would have brought her to justice all the same. Now, come, it is time we left. I believe we need a barber's attention before we visit the Home Office to report."

29

I WINCED AS THE FIRST LEECH BIT INTO THE TEN-
der skin under my eye. It is an eerie sensation, feeling the blood
draining away. One would think in this age of science, with the
latest developments in antiseptics and pharmacology, that there
would be a better remedy for a black eye than the humble *Hirudo
medicinalis*.

"Would you like me to pull any teeth while you are here?" the
barber asked solicitously.

"No, thank you."

He reached into his apothecary jar again and attached another
of the bloodsuckers to the skin under my other eye. The jar was
pink and had the word "leeches" written on it in gold. Perhaps the
beauty of the jar was an attempt to disguise the loathsome contents therein. While he set about doing the more mundane part of
his work, I glanced over at my employer. He was smiling at my
discomfort.

Barker was swathed in a sheet. The gray solution had been
rinsed out of his hair and the stiff length pruned back to its more
austere form, like one of the Guv's Pen-jing trees. His beard was

gone, and he was back to wearing his usual spectacles, round disks with a high bridge connecting them in the Chinese manner, with sidepieces of tortoiseshell.

"Here," he said, reaching into his pocket after we were done. He handed me the spectacles he'd worn while impersonating van Rhyn. "You might wish to wear these."

"You're joking," I said.

"Would you rather go about London looking like an owl?"

He had a point, I had to confess. My face in its present condition would scare governesses and small children. Reluctantly, I put them on. I glanced at myself in the barber's mirror. The spectacles might have been appropriate for Barker, but I looked ridiculous. Having custody of Barker's wallet again, I paid our bill and we left.

We waited a full thirty minutes in the lobby of the Home Office, under the suspicious eye of the porter. I thought it shabby treatment for two fellows who had just saved London. Was Anderson aware we were out here waiting? I wondered. Had he decided the entire affair had been an unmitigated disaster and was dreading speaking to us? I had to admit to being rather nervous, like a prisoner awaiting a verdict.

I need hardly mention how Barker was. He might as well have been waiting for an omnibus. He was sitting in a hard wooden chair, staring abstractedly into nothing, and whistling tunelessly, as he did when thinking. The only good thing I can say about it was that it was bothering the porter even more than me.

"Gentlemen." Robert Anderson appeared and bowed. I immediately tried to gauge his mood. Did he seem satisfied or displeased? Neither or perhaps both. He led us down the hall to the large table with the lion's feet again. There was no Sir Watkin or carpetbag to balance out the ends that morning, only a folder in the middle of the table. Anderson seated himself in front of the folder, and motioned for us to be seated. Then he looked over the items in it and did the one thing I'd been dreading: he cleared his throat.

In between my release from Oxford Prison and my employment with Cyrus Barker, there were several months in which I looked unsuccessfully for employment. I answered advertisements seeking secretaries, clerks, scriveners, librarians, and shop assistants. I offered myself as a domestic. I attempted casual labor and dock work. Everywhere I went, I was met with the throat clearing, which, along with the inevitable widening of the eyes when they saw Oxford Prison among my bona fides, meant I was already late for the pavement. Throat clearing never signals good news. No one does it before telling you that you have just been promoted or are about to inherit five hundred a year. Barker himself is an expert at throat clearing, and the very action of doing it sets the hairs on the back of my neck on end. Understandably, then, my stomach fell when Anderson did it.

The bureaucrat browsed through the file, shuffling this paper to the front, and that one farther back. He ignored us completely, which, if anything, increased my apprehensions still further. Finally, he removed the top sheet of paper and slid it over in front of Barker.

"We've had several complaints about your handling of the case," he informed us. "This is a telegram from Inspector Munro, stating that you hampered his investigation severely. In Liverpool, you injured a guard, and there is reason to believe you were responsible for damage to a piece of property in Wales. According to this, it was a lighthouse."

Barker took the telegram and looked over it as casually as if it were a tailor's bill.

"And this," Anderson said, adding a second yellow sheet on top of the first, "is a telegram from Superintendent Williamson of the Criminal Investigation Department, complaining that we hired a private detective, who is known for advertisements in the newspapers, suggesting that you mismanaged—no, excuse me, you *bungled* the case severely, and had the Yard not come along at the proper time to take control of a desperate situation, London would now be no more than a memory. He says he is consulting with solicitors at Temple Bar about proceedings against you."

Barker took up the second, with no more interest than the first, but I was concerned. Proceedings? What sort of proceedings? My word, was Barker about to be arrested?

"Enquiry agent," Barker said.

"I beg your pardon?"

"I prefer to be called an enquiry agent."

Anderson frowned. "Mmm, yes. I'm not finished. Here, you will be interested to see, is a third telegram, also from the Yard. It is from the office of Commissioner Henderson, superseding the other two and informing me that on advice from counsel, they will let the matter drop, and they hope for better relations with the Home Office in the future. Ha!" Anderson broke into a big smile. "Mr. Barker, can you imagine the reason for the sudden reversal of their decision?"

"I assume that the Prince wrote a letter to the Yard, commending their efforts in saving him from being blown up."

"Exactly."

"And you know that because the Prince is no fool and was able to ferret out the truth of the matter, which is that Scotland Yard had little to do with it. Were I not a Baptist, I would wager that you have a letter from Buckingham Palace in that folder, also."

"Not much gets by you, Mr. Barker, does it?" Anderson asked, extracting the letter. I saw it bore the Royal Crest at the top.

"One almost did, but as the Bard said, 'All's well that ends well.'"

"So," I put in, "Scotland Yard is no longer upset?"

"Mr. Llewelyn, I assure you I couldn't give a tinker's mended pot how the Yard feels. We've trod on each other's feet far too often for that. Here is your check," Anderson said, handing the bank draft over to us. Barker naturally avoided it, so I pocketed it quickly.

"Is there any further business?" my employer asked.

"Just one. The opinions of my superiors are rather mixed. Some believe you showed initiative, while others thought you were reckless. The dossier from the Foreign Office said your methods were irregular, and that has certainly proven to be the case. Most important, you have succeeded in stopping the faction, and that was something the Yard could not have done without your aid. My question to you is whether you might wish to make this a permanent arrangement. There is always more work to be done, and I could use another spy of Le Caron's caliber. Your work was most satisfactory. I would like the opportunity to work with you again."

Barker raised a finger and ran the nail along the skin under his chin, a gesture I'd seen him make when he was considering something. Then he gave a sudden shake of his head, as if coming out of a reverie.

"No, thank you, sir. The idea is intriguing, and there is no one I would rather work with in Her Majesty's government, but I've been captain of my own ship for too long. I've worked hard to make a success of my agency, and I am proud of it. This case was such that I felt it would be churlish of me not to offer my services, but I have people who depend upon me in this city, and I would not wish to disappoint them. I decline your offer, though someday I hope to work for you again."

"May I at least call upon you should something else of extreme importance occur and Mr. Le Caron is otherwise occupied?"

"Certainly, sir," Barker said. "I did not mean that I would not entertain a request for aid, merely that I did not wish to become a government agent."

As if of one accord, the two men stood and shook hands. We left the table, the room, and then the Home Office itself. Barker and I walked down Whitehall to our offices.

In a few moments, we arrived at our refurbished chambers. The change was startling. The outer room had been rather dark when I had first applied for employment here, but now the walls had been wainscoted in white, replastered, and painted, and the yellow doors varnished to a high gloss. There was a kilim rug leading from the door and a new side table for cards and messages.

The clerk's desk was the same, but where once stood a row of wooden chairs, there was a long leather settee and a potted palm almost as tall as I, holding court. There was also a painting after the French fashion which looked like something seen through a rain-streaked window. It was a riverside landscape.

"A Constable," I noted.

"O'Muircheartaigh is not the only one who can collect art," he stated.

"I doubt it will be the last constable we see in these offices," I said drily.

"Thomas, do restrain yourself."

The door opened and Jenkins came out, looking rumpled and half sleepy, but glad to see us.

"Sirs! Welcome back! Come in, I beg you."

We entered our offices. The glazier had obviously returned and replaced the glass a second time. The floors had been sanded and varnished, my desk repaired, the rugs cleaned, and gas lamps had been installed over my desk, as well as a new chandelier. We looked quite the modern professional agency. The only thing that was the worse for wear was the assistant Barker had brought in with him.

"The vase!" I cried, crossing over to the pedestal. Barker and I inspected it together, turning it around in our hands. There was nothing but the faintest gray-white seams where the breaks had been.

"One almost can't tell," I said. "A visitor won't even notice the mend."

"Yes, thank you for your suggestion, lad. I would have hated to lose this."

I was hoping to hear about the history of the vase and how he acquired it, but he was as reticent as ever. He'd spied his smoking cabinet, and in a moment he was reacquainting himself with his meerschaums.

"Had them polished and cleaned and the stems reground while you was gone, sir," Jenkins said proudly. "Tobacconist says they are as good as new."

"They are, indeed," Barker said, stuffing tobacco into the bowl of the pipe, which had been carved into his own image. He lit it, and placed the vesta in the empty ashtray on his desk.

"You'll never guess what they clean them white pipes with, sir," Jenkins said to me. "Raw spirits. The hard stuff."

"Take it from me, Jenkins," I said, remembering all the drinking I had endured over the past month. "It is the only proper use for the stuff. Speaking of spirits, how is the Rising Sun?"

"Never better, Mr. L. I shall stand you a pint at the earliest opportunity."

"Thank you," I said, thinking to myself that it might be a good while before I was thirsty for ale again.

Barker was sitting in his green swivel chair, still examining the vase in front of him. I took up the ledger and retrieved the check from my pocket.

"Good lord."

"Thomas, you know how I feel about swearing."

"Sorry, sir. It is this check. It does not even begin to cover the expenses we've incurred in this case!"

"I expected as much. Normally, Le Caron spends half our time together complaining of how little he gets paid to risk his neck. I did not take this case for remuneration. Sometimes other factors come into consideration, such as duty."

He was silent for a moment, staring at the round vase in front of him as if it were a crystal ball in which he saw a portent. Perhaps, I thought, there was some flaw in the repairs.

"Is something wrong, sir?"

He shook off the mood. "Nothing, lad. You must forgive a Scotsman's brooding. I was just thinking that the world is very like this vase. It seems exactly as it was before, but there are hairline cracks all through it, and I know that it shall never completely be as it was before."

Our thoughts were interrupted by the comforting toll of Big Ben in our ears.

"Peckish?" he asked.

Over the meal, I disappointed the waiter at Ho's by setting down my near empty bowl of shark's head soup before he had the opportunity to rip it out of my hand. Ho's hadn't changed. The room was still as dark and smoky and the clientele still half mad. Ho deigned to leave the kitchen and come to our table.

"You are fatter than ever," he complained to my employer by way of greeting.

"I was on a case," Barker responded, not nettled in the least.

"You ate garbage, I think."

"Yes, but only because I couldn't take you with me."

"What happened to him?" Ho asked, jerking a thumb in my direction. Things were actually improving. Ho rarely acknowledged my existence.

"Stick fight," my employer stated. Ho grunted, possibly in approval, then waddled off into the gloom beyond the reach of the penny candle on our table.

We tucked into an assortment of battered vegetables and meats, accompanied by a ginger sauce and wheat dumplings. I'd like to think my use of chopsticks had improved since I first came here months before. More probably, I'd progressed to the level of the average Chinese four-year-old.

"Try these mushrooms, lad," Barker suggested. "They must have come in aboard ship. England had nothing to do with them."

For once, Barker was caught unaware. We were so engrossed in Ho's bowl of wonders that we hadn't noticed the arrival of a new customer. Seamus O'Muircheartaigh appeared at our table and slid into the seat beside me. He crossed his legs and set his walking stick across them.

"Cyrus," he greeted.

"Seamus," my employer replied. Stiffly he set his bowl down on the table in front of him, the mushroom he'd just put into it untasted.

"Welcome back."

"As you are aware, I've been here a few days, actually," Barker responded.

"Yes, your timing was impeccable, as always."

"I hope we have not inconvenienced you too much, Seamus."

"You haven't. I cannot say the same for your assistant." The Irishman turned his deep-set eyes in my direction. He looked at me as if I were a black beetle he'd found on his plate.

"What is your name, sir?" he asked coolly.

"Thomas Llewelyn."

"You are responsible for the death of someone I cared very deeply for."

"Perhaps not," Barker stated. "It is likely the bomb had simply reached its proper time to detonate."

"Possibly," O'Muircheartaigh acknowledged, "but you will not deny that it was the two of you that chased her onto the bridge."

Barker snorted. "I will not apologize for saving the life of the Prince of Wales."

O'Muircheartaigh shook his head sadly. "A Scotsman and a Welshman helping the English government. Do you think they gave the slightest thought about you?"

"That is our concern, not yours."

The Irishman gave a little tap to his cane, and the small circlet of metal at the tip swung open on a hinge. I was looking into the barrel of a gun, which had been cunningly built into O'Muircheartaigh's stick.

—

Barker had his gun out instantly, but a cleaver bit into the wood of the table in front of us. We all looked up.

"Take it outside, gentlemen," Ho's voice came from the shadows. "You know the rules."

"This is not your concern, Ho," the Irishman warned. The room fell silent.

"Need I remind you that you are in Blue Dragon Triad territory, Mr. O'Muircheartaigh. Mr. K'ing will no like if this boy is killed without his authority."

What, I wondered, *was the Blue Dragon Triad, and who was Mr. K'ing?*

O'Muircheartaigh sighed, as if he were a child caught in some petty naughtiness, and he latched the cover on his walking stick again.

"Rice and tea, Mr. Ho," he said. "Would you gentlemen care to dine with me?"

"I fear we have a prior engagement," Barker said icily. He stood slowly, and I noticed his hand was still in his pocket.

"Good day, gentlemen," O'Muircheartaigh said.

The last I saw, the waiter was setting his rice and tea carefully on the table, as one sets down a plate of meat in the tiger cage at the zoo in Regent's Park.

I was breathing heavily in the musty air of the tunnel, and I stumbled up the stairs twice at the other end. Barker kicked the door open, allowing air and light to flood in, and sat me down roughly on the ledge among the naphtha lamps Ho provides for his visitors.

"You're in bad shape, Thomas," he said. "I think it best if you take off the rest of the day."

30

I WAS PREPARED FOR A NUMBER OF THINGS, BUT
an afternoon off was not one of them. Barker's hansom let me off
in New Kent Road near our home, and I watched him rattle away
to his appointment. My employer had kept me occupied all morning, but now I was alone with thoughts of Maire and what had
happened on the bridge. I began to feel low again.

I went upstairs to read, but it was too hot in the house on a
June afternoon, and so I took a turn in the garden. Harm came
over to sniff my trousers, took a few laps from the miniature pond
under my window, and went back to lie in the bed of thyme. I bent
down and scratched him between his ears. He seemed to like that.

I stood for a moment with my hands in my pockets, listening
to the gurgle of the stream and the swishing of the windmill that
pumped it from underground, if a bit sluggishly. Then the
strangest thing happened, or perhaps it was the most natural.
One of my hands rose to form a beak and the other went out in
the opposite direction as if to ward off a blow. What was the next
move Barker had taught me? Ah, yes, hands together, one atop
the other, with the right foot forward, toe pointed up. I was doing

Barker's internal exercises. I started at the beginning and went through the entire form twice. It calmed my wounded spirit.

"Very impressive," a familiar voice said.

I looked over my shoulder. Israel Zangwill leaned against the frame of the back door. He had never come to the house before, but I remembered he and Jacob Maccabee were acquainted.

"Israel! Good to see you!" I said, pumping his hand.

"I heard you were back in town. That's quite a pair of black eyes you're sporting."

"Yes, well, it's better than the spectacles I was wearing," I said. "I think Barker's trying to turn me into a lesser version of himself. Come into the kitchen. I will make some coffee."

"Thank you. This garden is amazing. I'd hardly imagine such a place existed in London."

His voice suddenly awakened the diminutive dragon that stood guard over our secret garden. I had just enough time to scoop him up before he sank his teeth into Zangwill's trouser leg.

"My word, that's the ugliest dog I've ever seen," my friend said over the animal's frantic barks and howls.

"He's a Chinese imperial dog, and his name is Harm. He belongs to my employer," I explained as the dog screeched in his face.

"Yes, well, your employer is welcome to him. I shall wait in the kitchen, if you don't mind." He backed away slowly and went into the house.

After I brewed coffee on the stove, we sat at the deal table overlooking the garden, while outside Harm attempted to launch an assault upon the window, making quite impressive aerial leaps to see if we were still there.

I wanted to tell Israel everything that had happened, but I knew Barker would have counseled me not to. The most I could reveal was that in the course of our last case, I had managed to fall off Charing Cross Railway Bridge and successfully get my heart broken.

"Your employer certainly doesn't do things by halves, does he?" my friend pronounced. "You may be the only man to have fallen off a London bridge and survived."

"It is not a distinction I covet, thank you. What am I going to do, Israel? I feel as if I may never get over this."

"I am no rabbi, of course, but if I could offer some advice, it would be that time heals all wounds."

"I didn't know that was a Jewish proverb."

Zangwill threw his shaggy head back and laughed. "Yes, it was Rabbi Geoffrey Chaucer, if you must know. Some scholar you are. Oh, and if you're still looking for a reason to live, I can give you hundreds. A fellow doesn't have to travel far to find pretty girls. And allow me to point out that they generally prefer rakish detectives with their exciting tales to humble scholars and teachers, such as me."

"I thank you for the encouragement, but if you must know the truth, I believe I shall avoid women for a while. I'm not very good for them, nor they for me."

Zangwill watched as Harm sailed past the window again. "He really is the maddest creature I've ever seen."

He rose and tossed a coin on the table.

"You needn't pay for your coffee, Israel," I joked.

"That's not my shilling. It is the one you lent Ira before you left. I've been keeping it for him, since money rather melts through his fingers. He told me to tell you he was never so glad to pay a shilling in his life, and that he hopes you realize it was the prayers in the synagogue that allowed you to survive, if just barely."

"Thank him for me the next time you see him," I said.

"Thank him yourself at the Barbados this Sunday, if you can get away. Say, two o'clock?"

"Done," I told him.

Barker came home at dinnertime with a look that said, "Don't ask me where I was or what I've been doing." The Widow was never to be discussed. I suppose we all have our tender spots.

"How was your afternoon?" he rumbled.

"Fine, sir. I got back to the internal exercises."

"Good, good."

"Israel Zangwill came to see me."

"Zangwill," he said. "What did he want?"

"He heard I was feeling low."

"I've always found that work is the best antidote for a sad heart," Barker stated. "What would you say to a new case?"

"Already?" I asked. "We've only just finished one."

"Lad, they can't wait patiently in a queue. We must take them as they come. It's nothing as dangerous as the last one, however. Some securities have gone missing. We should start on Monday."

I thought for a moment. "I'm your man."

Barker nodded. "Very good."

That evening, I finally got around to reading *Midlothian* again. I had hardly begun it when I was interrupted by a jangling of the telephone downstairs. I remarked upon it to myself, but such events are not uncommon in Barker's household, so I went back to my volume and soon forgot it. About fifteen minutes later, I came upon a reference to food and remembered that Dummolard had baked a new apple pie with cognac and caramelized sugar at my request and it was sitting at that very moment in our larder under a glass dome.

"It is the very thing to fix the broken heart," the prickly Frenchman stated. As far as he was concerned, all ills were to be remedied with food.

So far, Barker had prescribed work, Dummolard good food, and Zangwill said that time would heal my malady. I believed them all wrong, like Job's trio of advisors, but certainly a slice of pie would do no harm. I slid off the side of my bed, where I had been lounging, and went downstairs, registering the sound of Barker's footsteps climbing up to what I call his Red Room.

———

Down in the hall, I couldn't help but notice Mac sitting on a bench by the door, with his head down and his hand clutching the top of his yarmulke. Mac seated is not a sight one saw every day. In fact, he is normally so industrious I couldn't recall seeing him seated at all. The fellow was not thirty, and despite a studied manner and a habit of posing as if for a painting of Byron, he is a bundle of energy. So, one can see why I found the sight novel. I thought perhaps he was praying. Just to test the waters, so to speak, I cleared my throat. I thought he would jump up, but he did not.

"Whatever is the matter?" I asked.

Maccabee looked up, as if in a reverie. "What? Oh, the Guv just had a telephone call from Mr. Anderson."

"Anderson? Really? What did he have to say?"

"Quite a lot, actually. Mr. Barker listened for a good five minutes. From what I gather, the Guv was recommended to receive some sort of honor."

I was astounded, but after a moment, I thought that Barker did deserve some sort of recognition. He had saved the life of the Prince of Wales and foiled an attempt to blow up London. Certainly he should have received more than the pittance Her Majesty's government paid him as a spy.

"That's marvelous! Is there any chance of a knighthood?"

"There might have been, but it is out of the question. He turned it down."

Now I really was astounded. "Turned it down? Is he mad?"

"He was rather brusque, I'm afraid. He said he couldn't see how it would benefit him in his profession and might actually close some doors he preferred to remain open."

"Turned it down?" I repeated. "My word!" I sat down on the hall bench in much the same manner I'd found Mac. I knew what my employer's manservant meant when he employed the word "brusque." It meant rude, and unlikely ever to be offered such an honor again.

Barker said nothing to me about it, but spent the rest of the evening exercising in the basement, lifting weights, and beating upon the heavy bag, all in an attempt to return to his normal weight as soon as possible. Eventually he stripped down to his trousers and boots, his broad chest bathed in sweat like a stevedore's. He exercised fanatically and afterward soaked in his bath. Mac heated the water hotter than ever before, far too hellish for my comfort, and had heated some stones in a brazier, which Barker periodically threw water over with the aid of a wooden dipper, until the place resembled a sauna bath. I gave up completely, and left him to his bathhouse in solitude. I had no wish to be boiled like a crustacean.

Barker, of course, is not demonstrative, but he appeared to be glad to be back to his normal routine the next morning. We had missed Sunday services at the Metropolitan Tabernacle, but he spoke of looking forward to the next Sunday and the thrilling and instructive sermons of Reverend Charles Haddon Spurgeon, whom Barker considered the wisest man in London, if not in Christendom. He also was content to be back to our regular schedule, from eight o'clock in the morning to six in the evening, with a half day on Saturdays. This was generally elastic, and many is the time we left at five thirty, or worked late into the night during a case, but for just a week or so after the bombing case, he adhered very strictly to our daily schedule.

I have not always been an enthusiast of employment, and many is the time I've wondered why I was born into a poor Welsh mining family, rather than the eldest son of a lord. I had to admit, however, that Barker was correct about work being an antidote. The new case, dull as it was in comparison to the bombing case, did help me to begin healing after Maire's death. It would be a long process, true, but had I been idle, it would have lasted much longer. Not that I'll ever fully get over her. Even now, I cannot smell lilac without thinking of her.

There is a small postscript to this tale. A week later, Barker received an unexpected box. Normally such a delivery is highly suspect in our profession. I've heard of boxes sent to enquiry agents containing everything from weapons to human body parts. This one was different, luckily. For one thing, it came from Buckingham Palace. It was also quite small. Barker cut it open carefully with his Italian stiletto and lifted the lid.

He grunted and reached inside, lifting out a small case of black leather. Opening it, he pulled out a gold watch and chain. On the lid was an inscription:

> To Cyrus Barker, from HRH the Prince of Wales
> for services rendered to the Crown

I recalled reading somewhere that the Prince was well known for going out of his way to find a perfect gift for some of his personal friends. I thought it a splendid gift and no less than my employer deserved for all he had done.

Barker studied it a moment and then handed it to me. "It is very nice, but I already have a perfectly good repeater, and I have been meaning to purchase a watch for you, lad. Take it."

"Me, sir?" I protested. "But it's from the Prince. It was intended for you."

"It is a matter of simple mathematics. I have two, and you have none."

I took the watch and turned it over in my hand. It was the most beautiful thing I'd ever seen. There were four small diamonds and gold filigree swirls on the cover. I closed the lid and looked at the inscription again. How could he give away such an incredible gift?

"In that case," I asked, "would you mind if I had your name scratched out and mine put in?"

"Cheeky lad," Barker said, with a glint of a smile below his thick mustache. "As if the Prince of Wales would send a present to a rascal like you!"

Acknowledgments

Thank you to Maria Carvainis and Amanda Patten, who have both been most gracious to me and my family. They are more than agent and editor. I consider them friends, as well.

I'd like to thank the coterie of martial artists known as the Bartitsu Society, who have supplied me with information on the stick arts in this book, especially Craig Gemeiner, who aided me in my study of Vigny's *la canne,* and Ken Pfrenger, whose brain I picked concerning Irish bata. They are gentlemen and scholars all.

Lastly, I'd like to thank my wife, Julia, who takes a coffee-stained and pipe-ash-covered handwritten manuscript and turns it into clean, white copy and who listens to my thoughts and ideas with great patience. *Merci, mon ange.*